M000290322

VONNEGUT'S GHOST

(OR "THANKS FOR THE YIP-YIPS")

Max Zero

Meg!
To one
of the best
smiles in Wilton
Hope you like the
book!
Ron (max zero)
wgd
3/12/14

ISBN-13: 9780989843300
ISBN-10: 0989843300
Library of Congress Control Number: 2013915397
CreateSpace Independent Publishing Platform
North Charleston, South Carolina

Acknowledgements

My deepest thanks go to my wife of over 30 years for her steady support through our many adventures (including this book). Thanks also to:

- Mom, for her inspiration; she wrote and sold many stories, articles and poems even while she was raising four kids and partnering with my Dad in a photography business.

- My sister, Gayle, and son Dan for their encouragement.

- My friends, editors and proofreaders who contributed their time and thoughts to make this book better; especially Pat Heston and Susan Steingrubey.

- Matt Wenzel and Ashley Kopp Wenzel; for his very useful recommendations and her incredible cover art.

Finally, my thanks to the authors of the many great books I have read, especially Charles Dickens, Kurt Vonnegut, Jr., Frank Peretti and Steven King. King's book, *On Writing* shares a lot of insight on how to write, and I am in his debt for having read it.

CHAPTER ONE

Demarcus Johnson had just tossed a Mothers' Day card onto the old, rubber conveyer belt. Buck Schneider was bagging Mrs. Sandusky's groceries. He planned to deliver them and then snag a late lunch. Then something *thumped* in the sky. It was a low and ponderous boom that rattled the windows and walls, as well as his internal organs. In this neighborhood, Buck was accustomed to windows rattling due to heavy bass notes as young gangstas cruised by…but this was different. This was a single thump that carried great authority.

There was a burst of light outside, and then a tingling sensation that bordered on pain washed over his entire body. Over in an instant, it left him feeling drained and spacey. His left hand went limp, and the large jar of dill pickles he had been holding fell to the floor with a crash.

Buck turned toward the cash register where his brother, Bud was working. A moment before, Bud's fingers had been flashing across the keys with amazing speed. The Schneider Brothers had resisted adding technology to their neighborhood grocery store; they still used adhesive stickers with the price tags right on the grocery items, and never bought the scanning equipment necessary to read bar codes. They simply had not seen a need to change the way they had been running the store for over 15 years, which was essentially the same way their father had run things for decades before that.

When Buck glanced at Bud, he saw that his brother was standing as still as a statue. The fingers of Bud's right hand were still poised above the cash register keys, and his hand was quivering slightly. Bud's frozen face then twitched and his eyes looked concerned and confused. That was because the pacemaker in his chest had stopped working, which left his heart unmotivated to keep beating. An instant later, Bud joined 27 dill pickles on the linoleum floor of Schneider Brothers Corner Grocery Store.

Buck realized that his own mouth was hanging open, and convinced his jaw to close it. He noticed that the lights had gone out, and the steady hum of freezers and fluorescent lights was gone, no longer the background music of his day. The eerie silence was broken only by the faint sounds of birds chirping outside the store. "Poo-tee-weet?" they seemed to say.

After a few seconds, Buck moved toward his brother's fallen body. Before he even touched Bud, he knew he was dead. Buck sensed correctly that it was the kind of dead that no amount of chest thumping would reverse.

And so it goes.

• • •

Listen:

Back in the days of Jimi Hendrix and black light posters, there was a great American author who often wrote, "And so it goes," whenever someone in the story he was telling died. It still seems like the thing to say, in my book.

• • •

Buck gently closed his brother's eyes and un-crumpled his body; even if Bud was dead, there was no need for him to be uncomfortable. Someone was standing above the two brothers, watching. Buck turned and locked eyes with Demarcus Johnson, a teenager from the neighborhood who worked for the store on occasion. Buck had always liked Demarcus. He was a good kid. At the moment, Demarcus' teen-aged eyes were bulging and he smelled like fear. "What the hell happened?" Demarcus asked Buck.

"Gubb," Buck replied. His grief and confusion had risen up and strangled his vocabulary. Shrugging weakly, Buck shook his head. Just then, he heard a crash at the back of the store, and a voice asking, "Hey, Bud! What happened to the lights? You got a flashlight? I just knocked over a big stack of cans back here."

Buck reached into the drawer underneath the cash register and brought out the khaki-colored Boy Scout flashlight he'd had since he was a boy. It was made of metal, and the light came from the stem at a 90 degree angle. He flicked the switch, but nothing happened. He thought that was strange, as he had put new batteries in it just a few days before.

"Flashlight's dead, Anderson!" Buck heard himself say. So is Bud, he thought to himself.

Buck's attention was drawn outside the door to the sound of loud voices in the parking lot and street. He pushed the heavy deadness of the no-longer-automatic door out of his way and stumbled into sunlight. It was a beautiful spring day, and the flowering trees scattered around his store were in full bloom. A bunch of people were walking around and shouting things to each other. Some were cussing about the fact that their cars had stopped dead in their tracks. Not a single car was moving, in the parking lot or the street. Cars had simply decided to stop working, much like the pacemaker in Bud Schneider's chest.

People were in various stages of assessing the problem. Some were popping hoods, others reaching for cell phones. Strings of profanity burst out as people discovered that their cell phones were not working, either. "My ipod is dead," said a boy in a hoodie. His face sank low, much like the baggy jeans that revealed his *Family Guy* boxers. "I will rule the world!" the toddler on his

3

underwear said. The child on his underwear had greater expectations for him than anyone else that knew him.

As their individual efforts failed, people gravitated toward Buck, forming a klotch near the door of the store. As customers trickled out of the store, the klotch became a small crowd. Among them was Sarah Perkins, a pretty girl who had gone to school with Buck's son, Chad. "Anybody know what time it is?" Sarah asked. Six guys of various ages eagerly responded to her question, and like gunslingers went for their cell phones and watches to give a speedy reply. Two cell phone guys cursed as they were reminded that their phones were totally dark. Three guys with digital watches found them dead as well. Randy Edgar, an off-duty fireman, found the hands of his battery-powered watch frozen at 2:17.

Buck had a self-winding watch. It was an old watch that his father had worn for years. He glanced down at it, and it was still working. "About two thirty," he told Sarah.

"I have an interview on the other side of town at 3:15, and my car is dead. Can someone give me a ride?" Sarah asked. Those who had been in their cars when the sky thumped all reported their cars were dead as well. Customers who had been inside the store moved toward their cars to see if they were working.

It was at this point that Buck remembered that his dead brother was lying on the floor of the grocery store next to a broken jar of pickles.

• • •

Ellie Pence had worn her hair long all the 61 years of her life. It was steel-gray, and hung about halfway down her back. She generally wore khaki and pale green clothes that looked like an Army uniform, though she considered herself a complete pacifist. She was short and wiry and physically fit. She consumed mass quantities of granola, roughage and herbal supplements every day. Ellie drank fair trade coffee and cared much more for the environment than she did for human beings.

Ellie had recently retired after 35 years of being a pain in the butt at a local insurance company. As the company gradually slouched its way toward oblivion, Ellie had managed to survive eight different layoffs because she was a highly productive worker. Her productivity was powerful enough to offset the fact that she was a pain in the butt. One hundred seventy nine people who were nicer than Ellie lost their insurance jobs, but Ellie made it all the way to an early retirement.

One Black Friday, her best friend, Cheryl had come to Ellie's desk and took a Kleenex from the khaki-colored box. (Cheryl selected Ellie as her best friend because she had masochistic tendencies.) "Thirty-five people got laid off today," Cheryl said tearfully.

"I could care less," Ellie replied. Actually, Ellie meant that she *couldn't* care less, which was true. She just said it wrong. She knew she said it wrong but she didn't care about that, either.

On the day the sky thumped, Ellie was working in the garden in a mostly-futile attempt to grow a number of items she hoped to eat. Most of what would actually grow there would be eaten by animals and bugs, except for the squash. Ellie always had more squash than she knew what to do with. The neighborhood animals and bugs were all grateful to Ellie for most of the food in her fine garden, but they could care less about her squash.

When the sky thumped, Ellie lifted her eyes and saw a big puff of dark smoke that had sparks flying around in it. "POOT!" was the sound the sky made, only it was a deep, bass "poot" that rattled everything around her, including her tomato cages. Then Ellie felt a tingling that felt like little knives digging into her bones. It only lasted an instant, and then the world was completely silent, except for the birds, who seemed rather unimpressed by the thump in the sky.

"Humph," Ellie said, and pondered what had just happened. She heard a high-pitched whistling sound, and looked up to see a jet heading toward the airport. Jets flew over her house on a daily basis, so this in itself was not unusual. Ellie noticed, though, as the jet disappeared over the trees that it seemed to be moving too quickly and at an odd angle. She stood in her garden, her fingers absently holding her garden weasel as she stared at the horizon, pondering the odd things happening in the sky. After a moment, she was aware of the birds singing merrily, and she heard a rumble or two of thunder in the distance. She glanced at her watch: it was 2:17. "Better get back to work," Ellie shrugged to herself. Her eyes surveyed her little garden, noting that the squash was looking good again this year.

● ● ●

Schneider Brothers Corner Grocery Store and Ellie's garden were both located in the town of Almost. "Almost" is not the town's real name, but it almost is. I like to call it "Almost" because it is a small town that was *almost important* on a number of occasions. Hence, the name. Almost was almost the state capital. It was almost a railroad hub. It was almost an important port on the Mississippi River. In the twenty-first century, it was a rust belt town where you could almost make a living.

Almost constantly tried to be an important town, but it just could not get itself motivated, much like Bud Schneider's heart without its pacemaker. There was a circle of grass in the center of town that was lassoed by a street. The circle of grass is where the state capital was almost built one hundred and fifty years ago. There was a fountain in the middle of the circle of grass that squirted water high in the air. At night, a bunch of spotlights would make the water change colors.

On hot summer nights in the 1960s, Buck and Bud Schneider would beg their dad to orbit the fountain in their car so they could watch the fountain put on its light show. Their car did not have seat belts and they hung halfway out the windows as they drove around the fountain. One night a lightning bug smacked Bud in the teeth, and when he laughed he swallowed it. The next day, Bud and Buck hovered over the toilet to see if ingesting the lightning bug would make

Bud's poop glow. Tragically, the boys were unable to detect anything different in Bud's poop, even with the lights off. This was a great disappointment to all the kids in the neighborhood except for Ellie Pence. When she heard the news, she tossed her reddish-brown hair over her left shoulder and sniffed, "I could care less."

At 2:17 in the afternoon on the day the sky thumped, the fountain in the circle of grass in the heart of Almost quit working. The fountain was dead, perhaps never to squirt water into the air again.

And so it goes.

CHAPTER TWO

Big Sam Cavanaugh sat on a bar stool in Joe Kelly's Famous Grill and Bar. "Famous" had been in the name from the day Joe opened the doors. It became genuinely famous not long after that because everybody thought it was supposed to be famous, even though nobody knew why. Perhaps it was because Joe had taken the innovative step of calling it a "Grill and Bar" instead of a "Bar and Grill." Big Sam was watching baseball on the TV above the cash register. The Cardinals were beating the Cubs, and the folks in Joe Kelly's Famous Grill and Bar were pretty happy about that. Everyone except Ned Pepper, the local car salesman who was one of a limited number of token Cub fans in the area.

"Looks like your Cubs are losing again, Pepper!" Big Sam called across the bar.

"It ain't over 'til it's over," Ned Pepper replied dutifully. Ned knew that, as a token Cub fan, he served an important function, giving Cardinal fans in Almost someone to spar with. Ned knew that people felt good about themselves when they were around him, because their baseball team was better than his. People pitied Ned and his baseball team, and some of them bought cars from him because they felt sorry for him. "Poor old Ned Pepper" expertly milked their sympathy and sold a lot of cars.

Big Sam watched a lot of baseball at Joe Kelly's. Sam was the mayor of Almost, and in keeping with the spirit of the town, he was almost competent and almost honest. His favorite bartender, Kayla Ellis, was on duty. Kayla was his favorite bartender because she was cute, wore low cut blouses, and had an intriguing little rose tattooed just above her left breast. Also, Kayla treated Big Sam with respect. Sam appreciated that, because he was getting old and had a big basketball belly hanging over his impossibly long, thin legs.

"Whattyahave today, Mr. Mayor?" Kayla said as she used her bar rag to wipe the area between Big Sam's elbows.

"Cheeseburger, fries and ice tea," Big Sam replied, "Got a meeting this afternoon." Big Sam felt it was important to explain why he was not having his usual mid-day beer.

"Comin' right up," Kayla called over her shoulder as she took the order ticket, clipped it to the wooden wheel in the kitchen window and gave it a gentle spin. "Poetry in motion," Big Sam thought to himself.

Big Sam's eyes turned back to the ball game just as *Mr. Impossible* settled onto the bar stool to his right. *Mr. Impossible* was the secret identity of Rick Gage, a guy who apparently made a lot of money doing something. His identity was a secret because Rick Gage did not know he was Mr. Impossible; however, everyone else in Joe Kelly's Famous Grill and Bar knew.

"It's impossible for someone's teeth to be that white and their hair to be that perfect," Joe Kelly had said some time back. "And it's impossible to have suits and ties that perfect. The man has never had a wrinkle in his life; in his skin or in his clothes. It's just impossible."

"Well, I guess that makes him *Mr. Impossible*," Kayla cracked. And from that point forward, that's who Rick Gage was, at least behind his back.

Mr. Impossible took the latest cell phone from his pocket and said something very important to someone even more important than he was, loud enough for everyone in the Grill and Bar to hear. Nobody knew why Mr. Impossible came to

Joe Kelly's Famous Grill and Bar. He frequently tried to order healthy food they did not have and rarely drank anything besides Perrier. He would usually end up with a salad made with ingredients that were a day or two past fresh and his green bottle of fizzy water. Despite the fact that the fare did not meet his obvious high standards, he pretended to eat there a couple of days a week.

Go figure.

It was about the third inning, I guess, when the sky thumped and light blazed through the front window into the oily darkness of the Famous Grill and Bar. People yelped as something shot through them for an instant. The TV winked off and the only light in the place trickled faintly from the front window.

"What the hell was that?!" Ned Pepper yelped. "Felt like I had my finger in a socket for a second there."

"You did this, Pepper!" said Big Sam. "You just couldn't stand to see your Cubs lose again." Everybody laughed as Ned looked down sheepishly.

"Whatever," said Ned Pepper. Everybody else in the room felt better about themselves for a moment, even though the power was off and they couldn't see the game.

Big Sam moved to the window and peered at the sky. "Weird. Not a cloud in sight. No storm caused this. Wonder if someone smacked their car into a telephone pole and took out a transformer?"

"My phone's dead!" Mr. Impossible screeched. "Right in the middle of an important call!" Several people nodded sadly; they knew his calls were always important.

The mayor reached for his own phone. He would call down to the police department and see what was going on. "Mine's dead, too," Big Sam said a moment later. The room buzzed with surprise and profanity as everyone in the

Grill and Bar discovered all their electronic devices were as dark and dead as the Famous Grill and Bar itself.

Big Sam stepped out into the bright sunlight and stood on the sidewalk. Not a single car was moving on the usually hectic street; they were strewn about the streets, with their owners wandering aimlessly among them.

Big Sam felt like his genitals were full of helium and his chest was full of lead. It reminded him of Vietnam, because that was the last place he remembered being scared to the point that he thought he had no excrement remaining in his digestive system.

"Not good," Big Sam said quietly.

"No excrement!" said Ned Pepper. Or something like that.

"Exactly," Big Sam thought to himself.

• • •

It was the bottom of the third at Busch Stadium in St. Louis when the sky thumped. After the flash of light and the painful buzz, the scoreboards were dark and the loudspeakers silent. There was mild panic in the stands as people began to discover all their electronic devices were dead as well. All the players, umpires and a few people in business attire made a small crowd between the mound and home plate. Within a few minutes the officials decided to resume the game.

With the Wurlitzer organ and sound system gone, the sounds that were hiding behind them could be heard; the ball hitting the bat or glove, the bellowing of the umpire, the gentle murmur of the crowd. By the time the game ended, most people remaining in the stands were not exactly sure what the score was, or even who had won. The final score circulated by word of mouth through the small crowd, and then everybody filed out into the relative stillness of the big city streets. There they would discover that driving home was just as impossible as phoning home.

• • •

Listen:

Harry Carey was a guy that looked old even when he was young. Harry was the world's greatest baseball announcer. He was singularly unattractive, wore coke-bottle glasses and drank beer during most of his waking hours. During the 1950s and 1960s, he was the announcer for Cardinal baseball games on the radio; later, he announced Cubs games on TV. For years, Harry Carey sang *Take Me Out to the Ballgame* very, very badly during the seventh inning stretch for games played at Wrigley Field in Chicago. Harry Carey was a *real character*, and people loved him. Real characters are now an endangered species and are no longer allowed to hold important jobs, especially in broadcasting.

If Harry Carey had been at Busch Stadium on the day the sky thumped, he would have shouted, "Cubs win! Cubs win!" at the end of the game.

But Harry Carey was dead. Like St. Louis. Like Chicago.

And so it goes.

• • •

Sister Mary Margaret Marion walked briskly down the hospital hallway. Sister Mary Margaret Marion always walked briskly. Some people called her, "3M", but not to her face.

"3 M" was the name of a big company in Minneapolis, Minnesota that made scotch tape and many other useful items. At least, they did until 2:17 in the afternoon of the day that the sky thumped.

Sister Mary Margaret Marion had grown up in Bosnia, and had seen a lot of horrible things. Frequently, when people see a lot of horrible things, they become pretty horrible, too, or they become very unhappy. Sister Mary Margaret Marion decided to buck the trend and dedicate her life to being very happy while healing and comforting people. Anybody with half a brain liked the nun. People with less than half a brain usually liked her, too.

Sister Mary Margaret Marion was the president of Our Lady of Perpetual Sorrows Hospital. Despite the pessimistic name of the hospital, she remained very optimistic. She thought it curious that a place that was dedicated to making people feel better would have such a depressing name. However, she knew that people who were not religious also gave their hospitals depressing names. For example, the other hospital in town was *Almost Memorial Hospital*. Sister Mary Margaret Marion thought the name of her hospital was sad, but at least it did not have an epitaph for a name.

"Besides", the nun thought to herself, "Our Lady is not sad anymore. She's in heaven with Jesus." She pictured Mary, Jesus' mother, busying herself about heaven, putting a spit-shine, perhaps, on a pearly gate. Or maybe she was walking briskly down a street of gold, on her way to doing something nice for a martyr. In her mind's eye, the Virgin Mary's gentle smile looked a lot like the one that Sister Mary Margaret Marion generally wore.

Sister Mary Margaret Marion was walking briskly down the hall when the sky thumped. The sound reminded her of something that she had heard in her youth. When she was a novice in another city, a boiler had exploded deep in the basement of the hospital, *Our Lady of the Unfortunate Incident*. This new sound was even more ominous than that.

Her mind flashed further back to her days in war-torn Bosnia as the windows rattled around her and she felt something jolt through her body for an instant. The hallway went dark and cries of despair and frustration spilled from the rooms behind her and in front of her. The nun stood frozen in the hallway for a moment, mouthing a silent prayer and waiting for the backup generators to kick in. Nothing happened. There was faint light in the hallway, spilling out from the windows in each of the patients' rooms.

Sister Mary Margaret Marion turned and bolted back to her office. She was still pretty agile and pretty fast; she still played football (or *soccer*, as the Americans called it) every year at the hospital's employee picnic. She and the other sisters presented quite an unusual sight in those games, but make no mistake about it, they played pretty well. By the time she arrived at her office, the power had been off for nearly three minutes, she guessed. A short time that was an eternity when lifesaving machines were not functioning. The nun grabbed the phone on her desk and her fingers dashed out the number for Charlie Mason's cell phone. Charlie was in charge of hospital maintenance and was very good at his job. She wondered how things could possibly have gone so badly. Where was the backup generator?

When Sister Mary Margaret Marion put the receiver to her ear, she found the phone was dead. She ran to the extension in the next room; dead, too. She had left her cell phone on her nightstand at the convent that morning, so it was not an option. She headed for the staircase and opened the door. The stairwell was in complete darkness. She worked her way down eight flights of stairs as quickly as she could, taking care not to injure herself in the process. When she reached the bottom, she groped for the knob on the door that led to the underbelly of the hospital, where the machinery that heated and cooled the buildings lived. She opened the door to more darkness.

"Charlie!" she cried out.

"In here, Sister!" she heard the distant reply.

"What's going on? Why are the generators not kicking in?"

"Beats the heck out of me, Sister!" Charlie replied. "The flashlights aren't even working. I grabbed some Sterno out of the cafeteria and we're using that to see with. We have no idea what's going on. The generators are dead and we can't get them to stir in the least bit. It's the darndest thing I've ever seen."

"Charlie," Sister Mary Margaret Marion said more softly. "We've got to get some power soon or a lot of people are going to die."

There was a brief moment of silence. "I know, Sister. But the phones are dead, my cell phone is dead and we can't hardly see a thing. I have no idea what the hell to do next."

For an instant, Charlie regretted saying "hell" to a nun.

Sister Mary Margaret Marion stood in the darkness, pondering his words. After a moment, she spoke again. "I know you'll do your best, Charlie," the nun called out as she groped again for the stairway door, "I'll be praying for you. I'll be praying for us all! God bless you, Charlie!"

Not waiting for an answer, her fingers found the knob and she plunged back into the darkness of the stairwell. She worked her way back up the stairs toward the intensive care unit as quickly as she dared. There was no time now to wonder about what had happened. People were suffering and dying in the rooms above her.

CHAPTER THREE

Randy Edgar and Demarcus Johnson helped Buck Schneider carry the body of his brother into the walk-in refrigerator. Nobody's car was working, so there was no way to transport the corpse to a hospital or funeral home. No phones were working, so there was no one to call, either. Buck thanked the guys for their help, and quietly closed the store. Gradually, people began leaving the parking lot and began walking to wherever they needed to be when they were scared. Buck stood by the cash register, staring down at the dill pickles and glass that had sprayed across the floor. After a moment, he wept briefly as he thought about his next move. He swept the pickles and glass into a dustpan and walked the mess out to the dumpster. At least the pickles presented a problem that he was capable of solving.

There had been power outages before, of course. Generally they only lasted a few hours and posed only minor inconvenience. About five years before, an ice storm had knocked out the power for three days, which was a huge challenge for a grocery store. The Schneiders had spent a lot of money to upgrade their generators after that debacle. But this was no ordinary power outage; even generators weren't working this time. Whatever had taken out the power had taken out cell phones, cars, flashlights....virtually anything that relied on electricity in any way.

With no radio, TV, internet or even a newspaper, there was virtually no way to find out what had caused the problem, or how long the situation was going to last. Was the thump in the sky some kind of neutron bomb? Was the United States being invaded? Or was this just a local phenomenon? Unanswered questions raced through his mind, generating a rising sense of fear as they careened around his brain. Across North America, millions of other brains were doing the same thing.

Buck fumbled around the store until he located some candles and matches. He solemnly strode back to the walk-in refrigerator, went inside and stood next to his brother, who was carefully laid out on top of cases of Snapple, Dr. Pepper and Mountain Dew. Buck smiled slightly as remembered that Bud started every workday with a 24 ounce bottle of Mountain Dew. Bud would approve of this temporary resting place. If the power did not come on within a few hours, Buck would need to move his brother's body to the freezer. If necessary, he could remain there a day or two before he began to decompose. (Along with the rest of the meat, he thought with a dark chuckle.) Schneider's Brothers Corner Grocery Store was known for its high quality meats, which was why he had not put Bud in the freezer in the first place. If the power came back in short order, he could still sell the meat in the freezer. He wasn't sure how he'd feel about selling that meat once his brother had been packed in there with it.

Buck stood in the cool darkness, holding a candle and looking at the body of his slightly older brother. "Thanks a lot, buddy!" he thought to himself. Buck sensed he was entering the biggest crisis of his life, and he would have to do it without the partner and friend who had stood by him every step of his journey for the last 55 years.

Bud Schneider had cast a very long shadow over Buck's life. And while Buck had often wished he were independent of his brother, he suddenly realized that Bud's leadership had provided a certain security in his very uncertain life. At the moment, he greatly missed the shadow of his brother and wished he could bring it back, at least for a while. Buck sighed deeply. He was not looking forward to it, but he'd best be thinking about what to do next. Bud was not here to do the thinking for the two of them.

Walking through the store, Buck blew out the candle when the light trickling in through the glass bricks was sufficient to find his way. He walked out into the parking lot, pulled his pipe out of his apron pocket, packed it and lit it. As he stood puffing in the sunshine, he stared up the hill at the large old house that loomed over the store. "Mom," he thought to himself. He knew he had to check on her first, and give her the news about Bud. The first of many rotten things he was going to have to do in the near future, Buck suspected.

Buck's mother, Luella Schneider, lived in the old two story house with a crow's nest that was perched high above the Schneider Brothers Corner Grocery Store. It was a historical landmark house that a doctor had built in the 1850s; at one point, it had been used as a mental institution of sorts, and as a clinic during an outbreak of small pox at the end of the 19th century. When Luella moved in, her own traces of insanity and emotional disease felt right at home there. There were times when Buck felt he could physically feel the shadow of that house, and his mother's brooding spirit within it, eclipsing all things bright and beautiful in the store below. Buck's mother had not worked in the store for over 25 years, but she still owned over 50% of it. As such, the brothers Schneider had been at her mercy ever since their father had died fifteen years before. Luella's mercy was a pretty scarce commodity, by the way.

Jack and Luella Schneider had named their sons *Herbert* and *Norbert*, but only called them that when they were in serious trouble. The boys had been *Bud* and *Buck* for as long as Buck could remember. At times, Buck would stop and wonder why you would saddle your kids with names that you had no intention of ever using. Bud had always been his parents' favorite. Bud was like the "inside dog" that you treasured the most; the one that got to sit on your lap and receive steady attention. Buck was the "outside dog," who was kept fed, watered and somewhat sheltered, but rarely got more than a brief rub on the head. Like the outside dog, Buck had always been a bit wilder and tougher than Bud, and as a result had a life that was littered with broken people.

When Luella got stubborn about decisions affecting the store, Bud was usually able to get her to lighten up and be semi-reasonable. Buck added another big entry to his list of reasons why life without his brother was going to stink, big-time. Standing alone before his mother made him feel like the cowardly lion that quaked in the throne room of the great and powerful Oz. In the classic movie, the cowardly lion dove through a huge window to escape the presence of the Wizard of Oz. Buck kept the bay window in his mother's dining room in mind as a similar means of retreat. Even at 55 years of age, he could endure her presence only with great difficulty. Luella Schneider was famous for shooting the messenger, if the messenger had the audacity to tell her something she did not want to hear. This was especially true if Buck brought her bad news. Telling his mother that his brother was dead was a terrifying prospect.

With the resignation of a condemned man about to walk the last mile, Buck tapped his pipe against the retaining wall at the edge of the parking lot, and the fiery tobacco embers showered into the loose gravel behind the parking blocks. "May as well get it over with," he thought to himself as he began the trek up the hill. Perhaps by the time his mother was done keel-hauling him in an ocean of guilt, the phones would be operational. Then he would be able to call his sister-in-law and tell her that her husband of nearly 40 years had died in the line of duty. Bud had gone down with the ship, his fingers flashing over the cash register keys at the Schneider Brothers Corner Grocery Store. Buck thought his brother would have wanted it that way.

• • •

Sister Mary Margaret Marion finally made it back up the stairs to the intensive care unit at Our Lady of Perpetual Sorrows Hospital. She huffed and puffed a little as she headed for the nurses' station to determine the number of patients and their status. Without the computers, there wasn't much information available. She remembered that Bobby Anthony was among the patients in the most distress. The nun moved swiftly down the hallway to his room. Bobby was on life-support; a breathing machine, if she was not mistaken. Bobby Anthony was 77 years old. Up until a week ago, he had looked like a vigorous African-American man in his early 60s. As she entered his room, Sister Mary Margaret

Marion could not help but jump a little at the sight of a man who had withered nearly overnight into a shadow of his former self.

Bobby Anthony's eyes looked at her pleadingly as he struggled for breath. The nun grasped his outstretched hand and cradled it in both her arms to her chest as she leaned over and kissed him on his forehead. His brief, grateful smile was quickly replaced by a look of distress and fear, and he took a ragged breath and asked a silent question with his eyes.

"We don't know what happened to the power, Bobby," Sister Mary Margaret Marion said quietly. "Phones, generators, cell phones are all gone. Nothing works. We have no idea what happened or when it will be fixed." She kept her eyes locked with Bobby's, and they stared deeply into each other for a moment. They silently agreed that, without the assistance of the machines, he did not have long to live.

Bobby Anthony had worked shift work at a local factory for most of his life; he and his wife Sonja had been married over 50 years and had raised five children, all of whom graduated from college and had wonderful families of their own. He had 18 grandchildren and three great-grandchildren. Bobby was a tireless champion for good in the city of Almost. He and his wife fed people, clothed people, and put them up in their home when they needed a place to be. He went to Mass at 6:30 every morning, 7:00 on Sundays, and even though he was a man of meager means, he had been instrumental in raising hundreds of thousands of dollars for Our Lady of Perpetual Sorrows Hospital and other worthwhile causes in town.

Bobby Anthony was one of Sister Mary Margaret Marion's favorite people in the whole world. Bobby's boundless good nature and ministry had blessed hundreds of people during his lifetime. His prognosis had been good; he had been expected to make a full recovery, over time.

Until now.

Sister Mary Margaret Marion did not know what had caused every electronic thing in this huge building to stop functioning. Deep in her heart, though, she highly doubted that whatever it was would be fixed in time to save Bobby Anthony.

Holding Bobby's hand with her left hand, she stretched out her right to grab a chair and pull it to the side of his bed. She prayed that, somehow, Sonja was close by and would make it in time to say goodbye. In any case, Sister Mary Margaret Marion would stay with him until it was over, and hope that the priest arrived in time to give him last rites. If not, she would pray with him as he breathed his last. Either way, Bobby Anthony would be singing with the angels before nightfall. Last rites would be a bonus. Bobby Anthony would be in heaven soon, she knew, with or without the sacrament.

The nun was at Bobby Anthony's side until the end; Bobby's wife arrived in time to tell him goodbye. The priest never made it, but Bobby passed away quietly, with a peaceful smile on his face. Up and down the hallway of the ICU, and elsewhere in the gigantic building, similar dramas were unfolding. Every few minutes throughout the afternoon, someone died. Three, including Bobby, died with Sister Mary Margaret Marion at their side. A fortunate few had family members present. Some were ministered to by the other nuns and the Protestant chaplain. The priest arrived in time to give last rites to some. A few died alone.

And so it goes.

• • •

At about 3:00 in the afternoon, after a futile attempt to start the Crown Victoria that had been provided him by the city of Almost, Big Sam Cavanaugh had extracted his long frame from his car and started the walk toward city hall. Big Sam was in pretty good health, by and large, except for his bum left knee. Hopefully, it would not give out on him during the three-mile journey to his office. Perhaps by the time he got there the phones would be operational and he could find out what in God's green earth was going on around here.

It was a warm spring day, with the temperature near 80 degrees. Big Sam was wearing a light suit with white and blue pinstripes; it was made from something like linen corduroy. He had always loved that suit; he thought it made him look like somebody important from an old movie, *The Long, Hot Summer*. He loosened his tie and unbuttoned the top button of his white shirt after a couple of blocks. At about the half-way point, he had to give his knee a rest, and he sat on a stone retaining wall next door to an antique store that only opened on weekends. It was at times like this that he really missed smoking. A Pall Mall smoldering between his two fingers would be especially appreciated right about now. He thought about Lloyd Bridges' character in the movie, *Airplane*. As things went from bad to worse, Bridges' character had lamented the loss of all of his addictions. In the midst of Sam's worries, the thought made him smile.

As Big Sam sat on the retaining wall, he surveyed the usually-busy *Second Street*. Some folks had pushed their cars to the side of the road; others had left them right in the spot where they had come to a halt. It reminded him of a scene from a 1950s science fiction movie about the end of the world. There were signs of activity within the dark windows of some of the businesses, and pedestrians hurried by, presumably headed for home. Some of them would stop and ask him if he knew what was going on. When Big Sam replied he had no clue about the matter, they would generally sniff or snort, mutter something under their breath, and continue on their way.

"You would think the mayor would know something," he heard one guy say under his breath.

"Yeah, you would think so," Big Sam thought to himself.

Big Sam was about to resume his quest for city hall when Cherokee walked by on the other side of the street. Cherokee was thin and wiry, and dressed in his customary matching grey-green work shirt and pants. His clothes were surprisingly clean and wrinkle-free, but he was a mess from the neck up. His stubbly gray beard covered his sunken cheeks, his eyes were vacant and bloodshot from alcohol and sunken into deep, dark sockets. His mostly gray hair spiked this way and that all over his head, and when he smiled, his mouth looked like a piano keyboard. It was rumored that the seemingly homeless man had a sister who did his laundry and made sure he ate from time to time, but nobody knew for sure if that was true.

Big Sam did not know Cherokee's real name, and did not know anyone who did. Sam did not even know why he was called *Cherokee*, as he showed no evidence of Native American descent. Nobody ever saw the old boy actually *drink*, but if you got close enough to him, the smell of stale alcohol was almost overpowering. The man was in perpetual motion, walking quickly all over town. Nobody knew where he had come from or where he was headed. But Cherokee was always going somewhere at a rapid pace.

"Cherokee!" Big Sam called out, "Geronimo!" He held his right hand high, somewhat like a Nazi salute. Many people called out to Cherokee in similar fashion any time his orbit of the city of Almost intersected with their own.

Cherokee, of course, was the name of a Native American (Indian) tribe. *Geronimo* was the name of a real Indian chief who led a famous uprising. For some reason, it had become a tradition for human beings to yell, "Geronimo!" when they were doing something new and exciting. Like sky-diving. Or, perhaps jumping off the limb of a tall tree into a shallow river. Yelling, "Geronimo!" meant you were doing something thrilling as you entered a new frontier in your experience. Hopefully, you would survive this new and exciting experience. Somehow, yelling, "Geronimo" was an expression of optimism that seemed to improve your odds.

Cherokee stopped and fumbled in his back pants pocket for something gray that had once been a handkerchief. He waved it in the air at Big Sam. "Geronimo!" Cherokee called in reply. "Kiss the girls and feed 'em beans! Feed 'em beans, that's what I say!" That being said, he stuffed the rag back into his pocket and rapidly resumed his journey to wherever the heck he was going. The ritual was complete.

Big Sam stared as the man rapidly faded in the distance. Most of the time, Big Sam felt sorry for the guy. Today, he envied him. Cherokee apparently had no earthly idea that anything was especially wrong with the world…it was business as usual for him.

"Ignorance is bliss," Sam thought to himself. He peeled himself off of the stone wall and started again for city hall.

● ● ●

After several hours in her garden, Ellie Pence's knees popped as she rose to her feet. She tossed her garden tools in the dark green rubber-plastic garden wheelbarrow she had purchased at the giant HomeMart store and pushed it toward the house. It was early evening; she was thinking she would catch the story of the thump in the sky on the six o'clock news. It had been a wonderful day; the most quiet and peaceful afternoon that Ellie could recall in recent memory.

Ellie's big, white house had a grand and wonderful porch that wrapped itself around three-fourths of the building. The gray-painted boards creaked as she walked across it and went in the side door of the house. As she kicked off her shoes on the landing, she reached over and flicked on the light switch. Nothing happened.

"Humph," she said. "Probably a blown fuse," she thought. "ROBERT!!" she called out to her husband indignantly. "Were you running the dryer and the microwave at the same time again?!"

There was no reply. "Humph," Ellie said. Her husband had been home all afternoon; why wasn't he answering? He would pay dearly for his lack of response, she vowed silently.

Ellie went into the kitchen and grabbed the flashlight and a box of fuses. The insurance inspector had wanted her to have the house rewired with circuit breakers, but Ellie did not want to spend the money. Under ordinary circumstances, a company would cancel the insurance policy for such a refusal. In Ellie's case, however, her home was insured by the company she worked for.

No one in the underwriting department had the guts to clock out her policy because they knew that Ellie was an enormous pain in the butt who would make them quickly and sincerely regret their actions. Even though Ellie knew circuit breakers were safer and less troublesome, she was fiercely proud of the fact that no one dared take her fuse box away.

Halfway down the steps toward the basement and the fuse box, Ellie discovered that the flashlight was not operational. Upon her return to the kitchen, she found her two other flashlights were also dead. "Now that's weird," she thought to herself. She grabbed a candle and some matches and headed back to the basement. All the fuses looked fine, but she replaced some of them for good measure. Then she worked her way through the house, trying various lamps and switches, none of which responded.

"Humph," Ellie said. Must be a power outage, she thought to herself. "Robert!" she shrieked again. "Robert, you moron, do you know what's going on with the power?!" She stomped up the stairs toward the bedroom to find her hen-pecked husband and take out her frustrations upon him, as was her custom.

Ellie found Robert sprawled on the bathroom floor, his pants around his ankles. It appeared he had been dead for some time. Like Bud Schneider, Robert Pence had a pacemaker that went on hiatus at 2:17 in the afternoon, at the moment the sky had thumped. Deprived of any shred of dignity during his entire married life, Robert had died in similar fashion.

And so it goes.

CHAPTER THREE

L *isten*:

This chapter is not supposed to be here.

It is really sort of a prologue, containing background information. Prologues are supposed to be located at the beginning of a book. A prologue after three chapters is simply not done. However, there are some important things you need to know at this point. As a narrator, my concern for you (the reader) has won out over my sense of decorum.

Narrators, you see, have great responsibility and great power. (Like Spiderman.) The things they say determine the reality that the reader/listener will experience. For example, before God started talking, things were formless and void. Then He spoke, became the Creator, and the story of humanity has unfolded ever since. What a wild yarn that Guy can tell! He is the Narrator of reality, which looks great on a resume.

Every human being attempts to be the narrator of their own lives, to shape their realities. We are not very good at it. However, Kurt Vonnegut, Jr. said that when we narrate a *story* we are the all-powerful Creator in *that* world. Vonnegut was a hero of mine. A great writer who (unfortunately for the real world) died a few years ago.

And so it goes.

Kurt Vonnegut, Jr. was a *hoosier*. In his case, it means he was born in Indiana. No one in Indiana knows why they are called *hoosiers,* but they are very proud of it. Kurt Vonnegut (famous author), David Letterman (late-night TV star) and Larry Bird (NBA superstar) were all hoosiers because they grew up in Indiana. Though they were famous, talented and intelligent, none of them knew why they were called hoosiers, either.

In the city of Almost, however, if someone called you a *hoosier*, it was not because you were an Indiana native. In Almost, a *hoosier* would be the rough equivalent of Jeff Foxworthy's *redneck*. Someone unemployed who thinks he is as important as Bill Gates. Who believes in wild conspiracy theories. Who has vehicles and/or refrigerators in his yard. Et cetera, et cetera, et cetera.

Buck Schneider had a hoosier in his family. (Most people do.) It was Bud's son-in-law, whose name was *Rod Blackmon*. His extended family and simulated friends called him *Blackie*. Behind his back, folks called him a *hoosier* because he was. (Blackie was *not* from Indiana.)

Buck intensely disliked his family situation. He frequently wanted to strangle Blackie. He had gone through a messy divorce and his children were very angry with him. He was the clear loser in sibling rivalry with his older brother, who was unaware there was even a competitive game in progress between them. But worst of all, Buck Schneider had a heinous mother.

Luella Schneider was a truly horrific mother. That's wrong in the same way that finding a snake in your toilet is just wrong. Toilets are supposed to be safe, a place where you feel comfortable exposing your vulnerabilities. Mothers are supposed to be like that, too

Martin Luther King, Jr. was a great leader who was not a hoosier, in either sense of the word. He once said,

"We who in engage in nonviolent direct action are not the creators of tension. We merely bring to the surface the hidden tension that is already alive."

The thump in the sky did not create the tension in the Schneider family. It had been hidden under the surface. It was already there.

In the beginning, Buck Schneider's life was pretty much formless and void, until the sky thumped. By the end of *that* day, he would think of the formless and void times as, "the good old days."

OK. As your narrator, I feel better now. You are sufficiently equipped with background information to move forward in the story. You are free to move about the cabin.

P.S. If you should happen to see any other loose chapters of this book wandering around, please do not approach them or attempt to apprehend them on your own. They may well be dangerous. This chapter was an exception; it is a benevolent fugitive.

Like Richard Kimble.

CHAPTER FOUR

When Buck looked up the hill at his mother's house, which he did as little as possible, he felt like he was staring at the old house that loomed over the Bates Hotel in the old Alfred Hitchcock movie, "Psycho." Luella Schneider was very nearly as weird and nasty as the mother of Norman Bates had been. But in Buck's world, Luella Schneider was not a fictional character.

Buck knew his mother was home because her car was parked in the driveway.

Everybody in town knew when Luella was around because she still drove her 1961 Cadillac, and she drove it very badly. It was a black car with long fins, a similar model to the one they used to make the first Batmobile on TV. (Many people considered this a very appropriate vehicle for Luella, as they considered her to be an old bat herself.)

A few years ago, Luella had a backing accident in the parking lot of Schneider Brothers Corner Grocery Store. The fin of Luella's car punctured the door of the car behind her, and the lady who was driving had to scoot across the front seat to avoid being impaled by that fin. Despite this, Luella kept backing up until the victim's 7 year-old son got out of their car and pounded on Luella's driver side window. This startled Luella. She got out and looked at the damage, and then screamed at the little kid for scaring her. The lady whose car Luella hit ended up apologizing profusely to Luella out of raw fear. Such was the power of Luella Schneider to strike terror into the hearts of innocent people everywhere and to dole out crippling burdens of guilt to her victims.

Buck walked up the long set of concrete steps toward the house. The higher he rose above the street, the lower his heart sank into his bowels. His key turned in the lock and he stepped into the gloomy hallway.

His mother's voice screeched from above the stairway in front of him. "Herbert?! Norbert?! I don't know who the hell it is down there, but I don't want to see *either* of you until you get my electric back on!"

Buck hesitated to speak. An instant later, Luella's face appeared over the top of the railing. Her hair was in curlers, and she had not yet applied her thick coating of make-up. As such, she was currently without eyebrows. This made her even more terrifying than usual, and Buck felt himself jump slightly. "Well?!" she screamed, "What do you want, Norbert?!"

"I...I've got some bad news, Mom," Buck said quietly.

"Bad news?! Nothing in this whole God-forsaken house is working properly!! What could be worse than that?!" She glared down at Buck, violently daring him to tell her something worse.

Buck felt his mouth go as dry as the bone God had used to make Eve. "It's not just the power, Mom. Cars, generators, batteries of any kind...those things don't work either. Which means..." Buck's throat felt swollen shut and he hesitated for an instant.

"Spit it out, Norbert!!" His mother lashed him.

"The battery in Bud's pacemaker went out, too. He...he's dead." Buck waited for about for his mother's response.

For what seemed like forever to Buck, Luella Schneider stood as still as a statue. Briefly, unimaginable grief and pain played across her weathered face. Then, it was gone. She had regained mastery of her emotions and her situation in less than a minute. Buck was impressed with his mother's terrible strength. Frightened by it, too.

Suddenly, Luella stood straight, throwing her hands into the air. "Great. Just great. Bad enough your father went and left me alone and helpless as a new born babe. At least I had Bud to carry the ball after that. *Now* what do I do?!"

Buck was speechless. His brother was dead, and his mother's primary concern was the inconvenience of it all.

"I asked you a question, Norbert. What do we do now?" the creature without eyebrows glared down at him.

"I can handle things, Mom," Buck said uncertainly.

Luella eyed him contemptuously. "Hmmp!" she said after a moment. "We'll see. Guess we don't have any other options at this point."

Buck's anger gradually replaced a small percentage of his fear. "Thanks, Mom," he replied with as much iciness as he could muster.

"Don't get huffy with me, young man!" Luella scolded, squashing his tiny rebellion. "It's not like we have lots of reason for optimism, here. Look at your track record! You've pretty much botched everything you've touched, haven't you?" Her voice had gone quiet now, which was somehow even worse than her screaming.

"I've gotten by, Mom." Buck said.

"Thanks to your family!" Luella replied. "Well, we'll get by, I suppose. We probably should just sell the store and call it a day."

"I don't want to sell the store!" Buck pleaded.

"Last time I checked, I own over 50% of that store, mister. So what we do with it is not really your call, is it?" Her forehead raised where her eyebrows should have been and she looked down her nose at him.

Buck felt like a fly that was at the mercies of a sadistic 9 year-old boy; he estimated he had maybe two legs left on his *soul* at this point, and his mother was yanking hard on one of them. He swallowed hard and said again, "I can handle this, Mom."

"We'll see soon enough. I hope you don't disappoint me like you usually do, Norbert," Luella said. They stood looking at each other for a moment. As she gazed at him, the bald place where her eyebrows should have been slowly lowered back to its usual position. The worst of the guilt storm had passed, Buck knew. "Where's Bud now?" Luella asked with a relatively calm voice.

"In the cooler at the store," Buck replied. "I'm hoping things will be normal by morning, and we can call the funeral home to come get him."

"And if things aren't normal?" Luella challenged him, "THEN what?"

"I…I don't know yet," Buck admitted.

"If things aren't back to normal," his mother pronounced, "you take that old wheelchair your dad used when he broke his hip. Put your brother in it and wheel him uptown to Hanson's Funeral Home." Hanson's was the funeral home in town of choice for white people who were Protestant, or did not know what they were. The Catholics had their own funeral home.

"Mom, that's about three miles!" Buck replied.

"You got any better ideas, boy? If so, I'm all ears," the subject was closed as tightly as the doors of the Schneider Brothers Corner Grocery

Store. After a moment, Luella issued further instructions. "All right, then. First thing, you better get your tail over to Julie's and tell her about her husband. See if you can get her to come over here. I'm going to need *someone* with a lick of sense to help me figure a few things out around here. God knows I'm not getting any younger. I'm just too fragile any more to handle this kind of thing."

She descended the stairs and held out her arms to her tortured son. "Buck…son…come here." As Luella hugged him, Buck could feel her spiritual leprosy seeping into the parts of his body that were adjacent to hers. "We'll be all right, Buck," she said in icy, simulated gentleness. "We'll be all right, boy. Good thing for you that you still have me."

Buck Schneider choked down the bile in his throat. "Yeah, Mom," he replied meekly. "Sure is."

As Buck stood in the hallway, reluctantly holding his mother, he wondered what was happening with the rest of his family. He had been divorced for nearly ten years, and his wife had remarried and moved across the river to St. Louis. His daughter, April, was married with two small children; she and her husband lived in Cleveland. Buck generally saw her every few months. His son, Chad, was living in Los Angeles, pursuing his dream to be an actor. He was still angry with his father about the divorce, and they rarely communicated. Emotionally and geographically, Chad was even further away. Buck Schneider stood in the darkness of his old family home, holding the only member of his immediate family that he could be certain he would ever see again.

Buck had a sudden thought about the hefty supply of beer in the cooler at the store. It would remain cool for another day or so. "I just might need a considerable amount of it," Buck thought to himself. That was a desperate thought; he had been on the wagon for nearly ten years. Alcohol had cost him just about everything he had, including his marriage. Standing in the gloomy hallway, gingerly holding his mother, losing everything he had seemed like a pretty good idea.

Unfortunately, Buck would find out in the few days that he was wrong, that he still had a lot to lose. Buck was "wrong again," Luella would have said, if she could have heard his thoughts. At present, his mother was not quite able to read minds. However, with Buck's rotten luck, it might just be a matter of time before her evil self developed such a power.

• • •

When Big Sam Cavanaugh arrived at city hall, he found about fifty police and fire department personnel clustered on the front steps. Sam quickly learned what he feared he might; that back-up generators and emergency broadcast systems were just as useless as all the electronic stuff that civilians had. "What about water?" Sam asked nobody in particular.

"Assuming there's no power or working generator at the waterworks, then the pumps will be dead, and once the water that's already in the system flows out, there won't be any more until the power's restored," said Herschel Gonzales, the fire chief. "Just about everybody will be out of water by this time tomorrow. Sooner, if people don't conserve." Herschel was always up on this disaster stuff, Sam thought to himself. And sometimes he could be a real pain in the neck about it. At this moment, though, Big Sam was thankful for Herschel and his expertise. He was glad Herschel was there.

"What happens if there's a fire?" Big Sam asked.

"Not much," Herschel shrugged. "No fire engines, no water pressure. If something burns, it is pretty much burns, along with whatever is too close to it. All we might be able to do is salvage neighboring properties. Maybe not even that. And that's assuming we have some way to even know there *is* a fire!"

"What about guns?" Sam asked.

"We are assuming they are operational, sir, since they don't rely on electric power in any way," replied Dana Crisp, the city of Almost's first female chief of police.

"Since we have no idea what the heck is going on," Sam replied, "I don't think we're in a position to assume anything, chief. Find out if they work, now!"

"Yes, sir," Dana Crisp strode briskly to the side of the building, drew her weapon, and fired it at a lump of earth near the parking lot. At the sound of the report, the heads of the men and women clustered on the steps of city hall nodded grimly.

"Well, folks, we have good news and bad news," Big Sam Cavanaugh said with a sigh. "The good news is that the guns of our police officers are operational. The bad news, of course, is that everybody else's guns will be working, too."

"Including guns bought by all the nutcases who have been afraid of the end of the world," said Herschel Gonzales.

"Nutcases, huh?" said Randy Edgar, the fireman who had helped to carry Bud Schneider into the walk-in refrigerator at the Schneider Brothers Corner Grocery Store. "Are you sure it *ain't* the end of the world?"

Everyone fell silent for a moment.

The mayor spoke again. "As long as we're breathing, we still have jobs to do. Gonzales, what are our priorities in a situation like this?"

After forty minutes of discussion, it was decided that EMTs and other fire personnel would get to both hospitals as quickly as possible, and help keep order there and to assist with emergency medical care. Policemen would be posted at each hospital as well. The rest of the police would make their way to protect key businesses; grocery stores, hardware stores and any business that sold firearms or any substantial amount of food. The fire chief would recruit citizens in the area with engineering background to make their way to the water works to see what could be done to keep the water flowing.

The police chaplain asked if he could say a prayer for their efforts, and everyone mumbled in agreement. They all bowed their heads as he prayed, then they filed off quietly in small groups to begin their long walks to where they would be working through the night.

A number of them had thought to grab bicycles from their homes or neighbors; some had appropriated the bicycles belonging to their children. Chunky cop Phil Mason mounted his daughter's bike and prepared to leave. Darnell Everwood was a young, African-American officer who had gained the respect of even the most hardcore rednecks on the squad. Darnell could not resist giving his older friend a hard time.

"Hey, Mason!" Everwood called. "Love the pink and purple bike! Especially the flowers on the basket! A ride like that should be a big asset when it comes to crowd control!"

Mason rode his daughter's bike straight for Everwood, squeezing the bulb of the horn on the handlebars as he came. The younger cop had to jump out of the way to avoid being struck. As he passed by, Phil Mason shot a mischievous grin over his left shoulder, and extended his left arm in an obscene gesture. His triumph was spoiled when, an instant later, his bike hit a bump and he lost control, spilling him into the decorative shrubbery in front of city hall. The majority of the cops and firemen had been watching this scene unfold, and they burst into laughter as Mason plowed into the bushes. Mason sat up, looking a bit perplexed, discovered he was unhurt, and laughed until tears were streaming down his face. The comedy of the moment was a welcome relief from the heavy burden the public servants were bearing.

"Well, there you have it, Mr. Mayor," Chief Crisp said loudly, "Almost's finest, ready to strike fear into the hearts of the criminal element!" Another brief round of laughter ensued.

After a moment, they again headed for their assignments. As they began their treks, just about all of them wished for the same simple luxury; a phone call home.

● ● ●

As Buck burst from the mothball atmosphere of his mother's den, he breathed deeply of the oxygen and the freedom he found just outside. For a brief moment he wished that his mother, not Bud, had had the pacemaker that fizzled out that afternoon. Then, he caught himself. Buck was not sure if there was a God, but if there was, He would surely strike Buck down for such evil thoughts. Buck decided not to take the chance; things in his life were already dicey enough.

It was late afternoon. Buck walked a few blocks to his little cracker box house. He let his beagle, Bilbo, out into the yard. Beagles are the only real dogs, Buck thought; all other breeds were just cheap imitations. Bilbo was very unique, in Buck's experience with dogs; he actually came when you called him. The dog provided Buck with the unconditional love and respect that he had a great deal of difficulty locating elsewhere. As such, he considered Bilbo to be the greatest dog in the universe. Buck decided to leave the dog out in the fenced back yard while he was gone. He loved to be outside, and had never attempted an escape.

After grabbing a quick sandwich, Buck changed clothes and got on his mountain bike and headed for his sister-in-law's home. Before he left, he slipped his "Convincer" into the makeshift holster he had sewn on to the rear waist band of his black nylon biking pants. The Convincer was half a broomstick he kept handy in case of hostile dogs. A lot of people in Almost let their dogs run loose. As much as Buck loved dogs, he did not like being chewed by them. The Convincer was more than 18 inches long, which made it easy to grab if he needed it to bop the nose of a dog that liked to chase bikes.

Buck loved to bike ride almost as much as he loved dogs; he generally would get in 20-30 miles per week if weather permitted. He had bought himself a very nice mountain bike last fall, so making the trip out to Julie's would not be a strain in any way. Julie lived in a nice two-story house about five miles away, on the edge of town. It was a perfect two story house for what had been a perfect couple...until this afternoon.

As he rode, Buck thought about Julie and Bud. Julie had actually been a classmate of Buck's, and in junior high he had a heavy-duty crush on her. She was not the prettiest girl in his class, but she certainly deserved honorable mention. In addition to being pretty, she was a nice person. Buck had never really had a chance with her, unfortunately. Julie liked him well enough, but her affection always seemed tinged with pity somehow. Eventually, it came as no surprise when she ended up with Bud. Bud was always the favorite destination for peoples' affections, especially if Buck wanted them. Bud always had a ticket to ride; Buck was always the nowhere man.

When he arrived at Julie's house, he found her sitting on the front porch steps, sipping tea while three of her grandsons were running around with other kids in the neighborhood. Buck had not realized that there were so many kids living around there. The lack of television, computers and video games had brought them out of the wood work, he guessed. Julie watched her grandsons after school until her daughters, Megan and Jordan, would arrive home from work. The kids had the day off school for a teacher's institute, so she had had them with her for the entire day.

Julie took the news hard, of course. She and Bud had had a wonderful marriage. They were some of those people that just never seemed to have issues with each other. Now, there were a *lot* of people in the world who *acted* like they never fought. But Bud and Julie Schneider never really did. In the light of his own experience with marriage, Buck had no earthly idea how such a peaceful marriage could be possible.

Julie sat on the porch step and quietly wept. After a moment, Buck sat beside her and clumsily put his arm around her shoulders. She turned and buried her face in his shoulder and began to sob deeply. A few moments later, the grandsons' grand tour of the neighborhood brought them within sight of the scene, and they drifted over to find out what was going on. When they found out what happened, they wept, too. Bud had been a wonderful grandfather and the boys would miss him terribly. Buck was able to control his emotions until the boys started crying. Then he wept right along with them, his chest heaving with deep grief.

After a while, Julie released Buck and scooted a few inches away. She dried her eyes with a Kleenex and gradually pulled herself back together. Minutes later, she spoke with a quiver in her voice, "So what about you, Bucky? What will you do now?" Julie was the only person who called him Bucky. It was a term of endearment, yes, but it was subtly laced with the same kind of pity you might hold for a lost child or an injured pet. Though Buck knew she meant well when she called him that, he felt he was less of a man when she did.

"Well, I will miss Bud, for sure," Buck replied. "But we will find a way to get by. I have a few young people working part-time at the store. I'll probably bring Tim Burrows on full-time, and maybe give the others some additional hours. That's assuming, of course, that they get this power thing fixed sometime soon."

"Buck," Julie looked at him with fear in her eyes, "What is going on with the power? I couldn't even get a flashlight to work…or the generator we bought after the ice storm. Even my watch is dead."

"I don't know, Julie," Buck replied. "I have no idea what happened, or how long it might take to get things back to normal. All I know is, it better be soon, or we're all in big trouble. When people's water and food start running out, there's no telling what might happen."

While they were talking, a few of the neighborhood kids came along and asked what was going on. Some hung around to comfort the boys, a couple of them ran home to tell their moms. A few moments later, a few of Julie's neighbors arrived to offer their sympathies, and to offer their own theories about what had happened to the power. Some of them were worried about their spouses, who had not yet made their way home from where they worked. Some expressed relief that their children had been off school that day; most of the kids had been with parents or grandparents during the uncertain afternoon.

After a while, Julie looked at Buck with concern. "Bucky, you look exhausted. Why don't you go inside and lay on the couch for a while before you head back home?"

Buck nodded in agreement, and left Julie in the care of her friends and neighbors. He went into the house and drank several glasses of water, then lay down on the couch, listening to the buzz of conversation just outside the living room window. He dozed off for a while. When he awoke, it was nearly dark, with the last piece of sunlight streaming through the window. He found his way to the kitchen to get another drink. As he filled the glass from the faucet, he wondered how much longer it would be until the water stopped flowing. Feeling a small panic beginning to rise, Buck dismissed the thought and returned to the front porch.

As Buck emerged from the house into the twilight, he saw that Julie had been joined by her daughter, Jordan, and her husband. His name was Rod Blackmon, but people generally called him *Blackie*. Everybody except Jordan knew that Jordan was too good for Blackie. When he worked, which was not often, Blackie was a security guard. He had tried a number of times to be a policeman, but could never make the grade. He almost always wore cowboy boots and was obsessed with guns.

When Blackie would answer the front door at night, he would grab his .44 magnum (the most powerful handgun ever made, according to "Dirty Harry"), and flatten himself against the living room wall. With his right hand holding his gun up against the wall at a 90 degree angle, his left hand would extend slowly to open the curtain on the front door slightly. Then he would ask in the deepest voice he could muster, "Who is it?" Blackie did not live in a bad neighborhood. He just liked to play with guns.

Buck did not care for Blackie. That was not unique. Besides Jordan and Blackie's mother, the list of people who actually liked Blackie was pretty short. Most of the folks on that short list were not very intelligent or likeable, either.

When Buck joined Julie, Jordan and Blackie on the front porch, Blackie was in the process of telling the women that the power outage was caused by a special weapon deployed by China, which was planning to take over the United States. Buck pointed out that China was in the process of *purchasing* the United States, so why would they want to louse up their investment by sending the country back to the Stone Age? Blackie replied that the Chinese needed to invade the U.S. because they had a tremendous shortage of women and they also wanted the natural resources that the United States had in the ground but were reluctant to drill for or dig up.

Blackie's tiny audience wanted to dismiss his theories as they usually did, but without an explanation of their own, they could not help but give him a fragment of credibility, which Blackie sensed and clearly relished. Jordan looked at her man admiringly. Buck shook his head; in all other aspects of her life, Jordan displayed remarkable intelligence.

"And Buck," Blackie said, "You need to keep a close eye on that store of yours. Right now, it's a friggin' gold mine! If this situation goes on for another couple of days, money is not going to be worth the paper it's printed on. The only things worth *anything* are going to be guns, ammo, food and water. Do you have a gun? If not, I'll give you one. And I'll come and help you guard the store."

Though the light of day was quickly fading, Buck could see the fear and urgency in Julie and Jordan's eyes. He hated to admit it, but Blackie had hit the nail on the head about the store. However, panic was not going to help them at the moment. "Listen, Blackie," Buck finally replied, "We have no idea why the power has gone out. And until we do, we need to keep our heads on straight. We're going to be all right for tonight. Most folks are going to give the situation at least a day before they start getting desperate and doing stupid things." Blackie started to protest but Buck motioned him to silence. "If the power doesn't come on tomorrow, that we will guard the store tomorrow night. So...." Buck could not believe he was hearing himself say this, even as he said it, "if by sunset tomorrow things aren't back to normal, you grab a couple of guns and meet me at the store. And we'll keep an eye on it together."

"That's a good idea, Buck," Blackie replied, "but I'm thinking there's no way I leave my family alone on a night like that." Once again, Buck was stunned to find himself in agreement with his quirky nephew. After some discussion, it was decided that Jordan and her sister Megan would bring their families to Luella's home the following evening. Of all the homes in the extended family, it was the best place to make a stand. It was the huge old house, with room for everyone, and it was close to the store. Megan's husband, Chase, was an outdoorsman and was handy with guns. He could stand guard over the family while Blackie and Buck watched the store.

It took the four of them about twenty minutes to finalize the details of their plan. By the time they were finished, Buck felt an urgency to get back and check on the store, even though he did not anticipate it was in any danger…yet.

● ● ●

Ellie Pence sat on her porch swing, sipping her herbal tea. For the moment, her ancient gas stove was still working; it seemed to be the only thing in the house that was. Ellie was watching the sun set, waiting for the lights to come back on. She had tried starting both of her cars, of course. Neither one of them made so much as a click when she turned the key in the ignition. Gradually, her neighbors returned home, one or two at a time, all on foot. Apparently, no one's car was working… which explained why she had enjoyed such a quiet afternoon in her garden.

Some of her neighbors worked in St. Louis, she knew. They drove 45 minutes or more to work. How long would it take them to get home if everything didn't start working again? It might take a day or two for some commuters to walk from various parts of St. Louis back home to Almost. Some might not be capable of walking such a distance in any amount of time. What would *they* do?

She took another sip of tea. "I could care less," Ellie thought to herself.

• • •

Matt Farmer and his wife Amanda were in their early 30s and lived right across the street from Ellie. They were pretty much the only neighbors that Ellie could bear having a conversation with; the main reason for that was that Matt Farmer was very easy on the eyes. "Cute butt," she thought to herself. Amanda was sitting on the steps of her front porch, watching her three kids play Frisbee in the front yard. Waiting for daddy to come home, she supposed. They would be waiting quite a while, Ellie guessed. Matt worked at a large financial firm in west St. Louis County, about 30 miles away.

As Ellie sipped the last of her tea, she watched an elderly couple cross the street and join Amanda's lonely vigil. The Adams....Ellie didn't know their first names. They kept pretty much to themselves. The old lady was a pretty fair gardener, Ellie thought; almost as good as she was. As Ellie rocked slowly in her porch swing, a handful of others joined them. She could hear pieces of their conversation as it wafted over the brick street between them. (In the still of a machine-less twilight, Ellie could eavesdrop pretty successfully from the comfort of her own front porch.) The neighbors were offering each other their theories for the strange things happening around them.

"Sunspots!" old Mr. Adams kept saying again and again. They wondered out loud about the well-being of their loved ones, and how long it would take for the power to come back on, and for their cars to work again. They were all afraid; some of them tried to act like they weren't, but Ellie could hear the fear in all of their voices.

Ellie detected movement from the corner of her eye. "Oh, boy, here we go," she thought as she watched Pillsbury Franklin and his wife trudging up the hill, holding long poles of some kind. Franklin was a *very* odd duck, and his wife Debbie was so sweet it made Ellie want to vomit. The Franklins walked over to the gathering in the Farmers' front yard and began sticking the poles in the ground. "Hmph! Tiki lights!" Ellie observed. Pillsbury Franklin lit the torches in their bamboo stems and the flames cast an amber glow over the scene. It was comforting, Ellie had to admit, to have light in some form at their command.

Conversation continued as the little crowd brought the Franklins up to speed. After a while, Pillsbury Franklin suggested that the group pray for the situation. Ellie knew that several of her neighbors were not church-going types, and she thought she could see them squirm a bit as the small gathering formed a circle and held hands. She heard Franklin praying for their loved ones, the whole area and the country. She heard someone pray for her and Robert. "Thanks," Ellie thought to herself, "for all the good it will do. He's dead."

It was just after they finished praying that Amanda Farmer finally lost her composure, and broke down in tears, wondering about where her husband was and when and how he would find his way home. A couple of women held her and cried with her.

The rest of the crowd milled around the front yard and had quiet conversations. After a while, two shadowy figures broke off from the rest and walked directly toward Ellie. A moment later, Ellie recognized Pillsbury and Debbie Franklin as they walked up the creaky wooden steps to her porch.

"Ellie," Pillsbury said, "why don't you and Robert join us?"

"Robert's dead," Ellie replied. "His pacemaker gave out, I guess."

"Oh, Ellie, I'm so sorry!" Debbie Franklin moaned. She made a move toward Ellie as if to hug her, and Ellie reflexively stiffened. Sensing this, Debbie settled for resting her warm hand on Ellie's bare shoulder and giving it a gentle squeeze. "Is there anything we can do?"

"Not at the moment," Ellie replied. "Hopefully, in the morning, maybe the car or the phone will be working, and I can get him to the funeral home or something."

"Mmmm," Pillsbury Franklin nodded in agreement,

"Yes, hopefully," Debbie added.

None of them actually thought that the phones and power would return any time soon. However, none of them had eliminated that hope completely. Not yet. They stood in the darkness, saying nothing for a time.

"Would you like to join us over at Farmers'?" Debbie finally asked.

"No, thank you." Ellie replied. "I think I'll just sit here a while, then go to bed. It's been a long day."

"Yes, it has," said Pillsbury. "We'll let you have some peace and quiet now. We just wanted to see how you were doing."

"Thank you," Ellie replied.

"We'll check on you in the morning. See if you need help with…anything," Pillsbury added.

Ellie was about to refuse the offer; then nodded her agreement. "Mmmm," she said softly.

Ellie rocked slowly in her porch swing as the Franklins made their way back to the flickering torch light. She watched them all for quite some time, until they began trickling off toward their own homes. Then she picked up her tea cup and went into the house to catch some sleep. For one final evening, Robert was lying on his usual bed, in the bedroom next to hers. She had banished him there, years before, because of his ungodly snoring. Now, even though he was no longer capable of snoring, Robert was still not welcome in his wife's bed, primarily because he was dead.

And so it goes.

CHAPTER FIVE

At sunset on the day the sky thumped, Matt Farmer was jogging up I-270 in north St. Louis County, headed for Almost. Matt Farmer loved to run. Today, his hobby was very useful. He was weaving in and out among the stalled cars and the drivers who had abandoned them. People were working their way along both sides of the highway at varying rates of speed. Every now and then a bicycle would buzz past him.

Two hours after the thump in the sky, he had tried to get a bike; he went to the bicycle shop a few blocks from his office. The selection of bikes already looked picked-over. Since the owner's credit card machine was down, he would only accept cash. Matt did not have anywhere near enough on him to buy the expensive bikes that remained. He jogged down the street to the bank. The ATM wasn't working of course. He tugged on the front door. Locked. He ran to the drive thru and caught a glimpse of a teller working in the background. He stared at her, silently pleading. She looked at him with pity in her eyes and mouthed an apology through the thick glass as she pulled the shade down in the picture window.

Matt Farmer went back to his car and got out his gym bag. He changed to his running clothes inside the car, stuffed a few things in his gym bag, and put his arms through the handles, turning it into a makeshift backpack. Then he started running at an easy pace toward home.

As he ran, he noticed some columns of black smoke off in the distance, in the general direction of the airport. As he passed the exit to the airport, he saw columns of smoke on both sides of the highway. He was guessing that some of the smoke as from plane crashes. He thought about all that, about everything that had happened, but he moved on. He had to get home as quickly as he could. Every few miles he would slow to a walk. Now and then he would stop for a few moments and take a drink from one of the bottles of water he had stashed in his gym bag.

He was guessing it was about eleven o'clock at night when he finally acknowledged he was going to have to stop for extended rest. According to the mile markers along the interstate, he had covered about 18 miles, and he was exhausted. As he had made his way along the highway, he had seen people wearing out and stopping to rest. When they could go no further, they simply looked for a car that was unlocked and crawled in to lie in the back seat. He knew he would have to do the same. He had another 15 miles or so to go, and he was going to need to rest and recover before he tackled it. He slowed his pace and began looking for a nice car.

Spotting a Cadillac Escalade, Farmer stopped and grabbed the door handle. It was open. He settled into the back seat and sat there a while… his mind was numb. Polishing off a bottle of water, Matt Farmer curled up on the seat and fell asleep almost immediately.

● ● ●

As Buck pedaled his mountain bike back toward home, his mind was racing with thoughts and plans about what to do in the coming days. Although the ride home was only five miles, it was not exactly an easy ride, because Almost was an extremely hilly town. Part of his route took him by a steep embank-ment of woods. One needed to be careful when you rode past it, because of the deer. When he was riding by one early morning, a deer had jumped up from the gully onto the pavement right in front of him, and they had almost collided.

As Buck approached the spot, his mind snapped back to the task at hand; getting home in one piece. Ordinarily when riding his bike at night, he would be concerned about getting hit by a car. Tonight, the problem was just the opposite; he had to keep close watch to make sure he did not hit one of the lifeless cars that were strewn along the streets on his route home.

As he approached the spot where the deer had surprised him some months before, Buck was startled once again; this time by a hooded figure, standing in the road in front of him. "Buddy! Buddy! Hold up a minute!" the figure said as Buck slowed to a stop.

"What's the matter, man?" Buck asked. Under the hoodie, Buck thought he recognized the freckled face of a young man that occasionally came into the store. "Is somebody hurt?" Buck asked the shadowy figure.

"No, buddy," the hooded figure grinned, "but somebody's gonna be if he doesn't hand over his wallet." Moonlight glinted off the long blade of a knife that the tall, thin young man held in his left hand.

Fear and anger rushed into Buck's head and throat. Training provided by his insurance company on how to respond in the event of a robbery at the store quickly came to mind, calming him somewhat. "Listen, dude. I'm wearing my biking clothes. I don't have a cent on me."

The hooded figure looked him up and down. "Yeah, I guess you don't, buddy. So, I guess I'll just have to take that nice bike you're riding." Buck could feel a fresh rush of anger flush his face. His bike was one of his most treasured possessions…and in a world without automobiles, it was practically priceless. Buck knew his bike, valuable as it was, was not worth dying for. On the other hand, Buck was completely fed up with things being taken from him, especially today. He had lost his brother. He had lost a normal world. And he had lost his dignity more than once. And now this had to happen. Yet another humiliation, another situation where poor Bucky couldn't handle things. As his mental debate briefly raged, his aggressor grew impatient.

"Buddy," said the hooded figure menacingly, "Get off the bike. Now!"

Buck knew he was at a complete disadvantage, standing there, straddling his bike. As he swung his right leg off of the bike in order to surrender it, he felt his Convincer broomstick poke him in the back. As he handed the bike over to the guy in the hoodie, a desperate plan sprang into his angry mind.

The guy in the hoodie ordered Buck to step back a few feet while he mounted the bike. As the thief's right leg swung over the bike, Buck sprang forward while whipping the broomstick from behind his back. His right hand brought the sawed-off broomstick down with all his might on the left wrist of his tormentor, smashing it down on the bike's handlebars. The impact sent the kid's knife spinning off into the darkness and it clattered on the street. The kid in the hoodie stumbled away from the bike, wildly off-balance and howling in pain. The bike fell to the ground, adding to the chaos.

As the hoodlum hopped and groped for stable footing, Buck dropped the broomstick and grabbed the kid's sweatshirt with both hands. With all his might, Buck dragged his opponent over the curb and flung him bodily down into the deep darkness of the gully on his left. He heard the would-be thief crash, roll and tumble down the steep embankment and finally come to rest forty or fifty feet below him in the darkness.

Moving quickly, Buck recovered the Convincer and the kid's knife, then stood panting at the top of the gully, his heart racing wildly. After a few seconds, he heard a low moan from his vanquished foe, and a rustle of leaves as the hijacker tried to figure out where he was and what, exactly, had happened to him.

"One...more...thing!" Buck yelled between his gulping pants for breath, "I...am... *not your buddy!*" Buck quivered with rage and residual fear, his fists clenched at his sides. One held his broomstick in a grip of steel; the other clenched the knife of his attacker.

Buck heard the leaves rustle, deep down on the hillside, then there was silence. "Yeah," came a mournful voice from far below in the darkness, "I know."

The leaves in the gully began to rustle again, so Buck quickly grabbed his bike, jumped on board, and pedaled as fast as his adrenaline-charged body could propel him toward home. Buck had no idea whether or not the kid in the hoodie remained a threat to him, but he had no intention of sticking around to find out.

By the time he reached his neighborhood, Buck had calmed down a bit. He had put a quick two miles between himself and his attacker, so he knew he was safe. He coasted a bit on his bike. He decided to take a quick swing by the store before he kept a long-overdue appointment with his bed.

About a block from his house, he passed by the entrance to the alley that ran behind his back yard. He had to apply the brakes as three teenagers in hoodies ran from the alley, laughing as they went. They froze for a moment, staring at him, then resumed running in the opposite direction in silence. "Wonder what they were up to?" Buck thought to himself.

When he arrived at Johnson Brothers Corner Grocery store a few moments later, Buck found Officer Darnell Everwood sitting on the retaining wall above his parking lot, having a cigarette. Buck brought out his pipe from his bike's saddlebag and they smoked together for a little while, reviewing the day's events. Everything was quiet; the pulsing call of tree frogs in the woods was the only sound in the night.

● ● ●

It was well past one in the morning when Sister Mary Margaret Marion finally lay down on an empty bed in a private room. It had taken hours to adjust to the situation. When the air conditioning went out, the air quickly got stuffy and stale. They were only able to open windows in the older portions of the hospital that had not yet been remodeled. As best they could, they moved patients toward the open windows where the air was circulating and they could be more comfortable. With the elevators out of commission, they had done what they could to move the patients to the lower floors of the hospital. The nun was so grateful when a dozen members of the fire department arrived. Their strength and energy had been invaluable in the effort to make all the patients as comfortable as possible.

The emergency room had been busy, of course, but things were not as chaotic as she expected. There had been a number of automobile accidents. Cars that were in motion when their batteries died were difficult to control. Most of the accidents appeared to be minor. She did hear stories, though, of a few fatal accidents out on the highway. The bodies remained where they were because there had been no way to transport them from the scenes of the accidents. With the help of the EMTs, the firemen and a couple of policemen, the nuns and nurses had managed to keep things orderly in the emergency room throughout the evening.

Sister Mary Margaret Marion was not exactly sure how many patients had died that day, but she felt reasonably certain it must have been at least two dozen. She tried to push the thought out of her mind, because she knew she needed some rest if she was to help those who remained alive. The nun lay in the hospital bed, totally exhausted. Down the hall way, she could hear moaning and, occasionally, someone would call out in the night. She wept as she made the decision to force herself to go to sleep. She would be no good to anyone if she did not get some rest.

And in the morning, they were going to have to figure out a way to get all these people fed.

Maybe, just maybe, the power would be back on in the morning, Sister Mary Margaret Marion hoped. And prayed. But deep in her heart, she knew that would probably not be the case. There was a nice spring breeze blowing in through the open window. It helped her relax and drift off to sleep.

• • •

Before he left for home, Buck went into the store for a moment, and grabbed a carton of cigarettes, the kind he had noticed Officer Everwood was smoking. He tossed the smokes to the grateful policeman, got on his bike, and made his way back home. He brought his bicycle inside the house and made sure all the doors were locked. His bike was pretty expensive, yes…but in the coming days, it just might be more valuable than just about anything else he owned.

Arriving home, Buck remembered that he had left his dog out in the yard before he left. As he stepped onto the stoop outside his back door, Buck quickly saw that the gate of his fence was gaping wide open…it was the gate that bordered on the alley. Buck recalled that, about an hour before, he had seen kids in hoodies emerging from that alley, laughing mischievously. Buck cursed beneath his breath. He supposed that he should be thankful that letting his dog loose was all they had apparently done to his property while he was gone. On the other hand, he was not at all happy that the best dog of all time was nowhere to be seen. He walked back to the alley, calling for his dog. He walked up and down the alley, calling for Bilbo to come home. The tree frogs gave the only reply until he heard some guy yell at him to shut the hell up and go to bed. Reluctantly, Buck decided that was exactly what he needed to do.

• • •

Big Sam Cavanaugh arrived home at midnight. It had been a fairly peaceful few hours, as far as he could tell. Throughout the evening, he had heard a few pops of gunfire, coming from the less desirable parts of town, which he had expected. The town just seemed to be holding its breath, waiting to see what happened next. Sam understood that completely; just keeping his own body breathing regularly seemed to require conscious effort on his part at the moment.

Sam sat up with his wife for about an hour, bringing her up to speed on the day's events. She had spent the evening crocheting by candlelight, with her husband's shotgun within easy reach. Prior to entering the world of politics, Sam had been a cop for over twenty years, so Janice Cavanaugh was used to nights full of uncertainty; she took them in stride about as well as anyone could. Sam was proud of the toughness his wife had built in herself over the years. Janice knew that her bravery pleased her husband, and knowing that made her all the more courageous.

When they were done talking, the Cavanaughs moved around the house, filling every available container with water, and filling the two bathtubs and a couple of sinks as well. The real test would come for the city of Almost when the water stopped flowing, Sam thought to himself as he slid his long frame into bed beside his wife. He hoped to God that the power would be on when he woke up in the morning, and he would never have to see what his city looked like when it was steeped in utter chaos. It wasn't easy, but after about an hour of tossing and turning, the mayor of Almost finally drifted off to sleep.

CHAPTER SIX

*L*isten:

    It was a season. I was on my customary early morning walk when I saw my first ghost. It was about ten months before the day that the sky thumped. We were in the middle of the hottest summer I could remember. It was just around sunrise, but already the air was so heavy with humidity I had to run my handkerchief across my forehead every few minutes just to keep the sweat out of my eyes.

    The city of Almost was known for its ghosts, but I had never seen one. From time to time, the ghosts of Almost were featured in books and television shows. Among the most famous phantoms were the woman in the old hotel and the slaves in the tunnel used by the Underground Railroad during the Civil War. There was also a haunted church and a number of haunted houses. Seances were held at a local haunted mansion for a nominal fee, and guided tours of haunted locations were available every October at reasonable rates.

    People said there were many ghosts in Almost because the town was built on lots of limestone. Ghosts, paranormal experts say, are especially fond of limestone. According to these experts, limestone and water are able to hold more of the energy the spirits need to manifest themselves. Almost was built on limestone; and since it was on the Mississippi River, there was lots of water nearby, too.

I was walking briskly through the oldest part of downtown, near the river. As I came up a hill, I squinted into the dawn at the brick courtyard where two bronze statues stood. Lincoln-Douglas Plaza marked one of the spots where Abraham Lincoln had debated Stephen A. Douglas, the incumbent U.S. Senator at the time. Douglas had been re-elected, beating Lincoln. However, not long after that, Lincoln returned the favor, besting Douglas and a couple of other opponents as he rose to his destiny as the 16th president of the United States of America.

Douglas was a short, pudgy guy, and his famous nickname was *The Little Giant*. I always figured him for a guy who suffered from *short man syndrome*, also known as *Napoleon syndrome*. Short man syndrome is a type of inferiority complex that causes short people to overcompensate in other areas of their lives. It is somewhat like *small penis syndrome,* where men feel inferior because they believe their most private part is smaller than it should be when compared to others. According to Wikipedia, the human penis is bigger than that of a gorilla. I don't know about you, but that makes me feel a whole lot better about things.

I once met a very famous science fiction writer whose name I forget. He said that this sort of inferiority complex actually occurred all over the universe. He said small planets are very jealous of the big planets known as *gas giants*. He called this condition *small planet envy*, and said that Pluto had this complex and was going to destroy the earth because of it. So far, the Channel 2 meteorologist tells me he has not caught Pluto making any hostile moves, but he promised me that he would keep a close eye on it. The *Farmer's Almanac* does not mention the problem, which puts me somewhat at ease. Still, you just can't be too careful.

As on most days when I walked past the Lincoln-Douglas Plaza early in the morning, I was the only pedestrian for blocks, and cars passed by only on rare occasion. As the sun began to peak above the horizon, I saw there was a solitary figure, standing thoughtfully in the center of the Plaza. As I approached, I saw that he was wearing an old-fashioned suit, with his hands shoved deep into his pockets. He was a short, stocky man, and he was pacing slowly across the plaza, glancing up and down as if in deep thought.

As I drew closer, he finally took notice of me, and I took better notice of him. He was not in full color, but in various shades of sepia, much like a tin-type photo, the kind I had made of myself at Silver Dollar City when I was a kid. Sepia was a color that you generally did not find in a box of crayons. Most people are at least 30 years old before they find out that sepia even exists.

As I approached the solitary, sepia-toned figure, he withdrew his hands from his pockets and placed them on his hips, smiling broadly. "Well, I'll be doggoned," he said in a booming voice, "You can *see* me, can't you, son??"

My eyes darted back and forth between the ghost and the two statues. I noted that the supernatural figure bore an uncanny likeness to the shorter of the bronze figures. "Yes, Senator Douglas," I replied crisply, "I do indeed see you! And I can hear you, as well!"

"I hope that you are not too disappointed," Stephen Douglas said, "that I am not the ghost of my much more-esteemed colleague, Abraham Lincoln. I have bumped into him here, from time to time, but not in quite a while."

"Oh, no," I assured the ghost, "I feel extremely privileged to make the acquaintance of either of you! It's not often that a man gets to meet such a distinguished figure from American history!"

Douglas hooked his thumbs into the lapels of his suit, obviously pleased with my response. "Why thank you, kind sir! I am most pleased to make your acquaintance as well!" he replied.

"Do people see you here a lot?" I asked the ghost of Stephen A. Douglas.

"No, no they don't, even though I'm here quite frequently. Back in my day, the city of Almost was somewhat like the 'first runner up' in a series of political beauty pageants. As such, I find it to be a welcoming environment for an historical second banana such as myself. Unlike Mr. Lincoln, there are only a few locations that boast a statue of my humble self, and this is among the nicest. I like to stop by from time to time to reflect upon my debates with him. In addition," Douglas leaned toward me and winked, "the limestone here is simply delightful."

"Does it bother you," I asked the Senator, "that in many ways you were more successful than Lincoln, yet he rose to far greater fame?"

Douglas' brow wrinkled in thought. "It used to," he admitted, "but late in the twentieth century I finally overcame my jealousy. One of your television celebrities provided me an example that I shall never forget."

"Really?!" I was stunned. "A man like you learned from a TV star? Who was it?!"

"His name is Leonard Nimoy," Douglas replied. "On your television, he portrayed a being from another planet. He was slightly green and had points on his ears and was called, 'Mr. Spock.' For some years after the final curtain fell upon his program, he deeply resented being identified with the character that made him famous. He even wrote a book protesting his plight, called, *I am not Spock!* Later in life, however, he realized that his curious role had granted him a certain immortality within popular culture, and he finally embraced his fate. It was then I realized that I had received the very same gift. Though faceless when compared to Mr. Lincoln, I was far better known than the vast majority of my contemporaries! Playing second fiddle to a man like Mr. Lincoln, I finally realized, was in fact a great privilege that few men get to enjoy!"

"Interesting," I thought to myself. Douglas had apparently been able to conquer his short man syndrome over time. (The fact that Douglas had conquered his inferiority complex should give a sliver of hope to those of us who are highly concerned with the Pluto crisis.)

"I gather, then, that for over a century you had little use for Lincoln?" I asked.

"Heavens no, good sir! By no means!" Douglas exclaimed, "I have ever been an amiable, good-natured man, and have always taken great pleasure in bearing testimony to the fact that Abraham Lincoln was a kind-hearted and good-natured gentleman with whom no man had a right to pick a quarrel. Lincoln was simply one of those peculiar men who perform with admirable skill each and every task he would undertake."

"I know guys like that," I replied. "Being compared to them can be annoying."

Douglas smiled. "Indeed it can. However, a more dismal fate is being convinced that your own worth is defined by comparing yourself to someone of greater skill than your own, and truly believing yourself to be an inferior creature. Talent alone is not the measure of a man's worth."

I nodded in agreement. "But if you admired Lincoln," I asked Douglas, "then why did you debate him so frequently?"

"I have never been one to shy away from disagreement," Douglas replied, "In point of fact, politics itself is the art of division, of pitting one group of people against another by demonizing the opposition. It is the candidate that folks dislike the least that gains power, and then turns to share it with his invisible friends. Lincoln was different than I. Less cynical, most certainly. He truly believed in something greater than I could see. That's why he died the way he did, I suppose. Men of such noble outlook generally die in great pain, and before their time.

"Only the good die young," I said. "Billy Joel sang that."

"Indeed," Douglas replied. "And the cad is now getting up in years, is he not?" Douglas chuckled at his own joke.

"I'm impressed that you've kept up with popular culture so well," I complimented Douglas. "I was under the impression that ghosts lived exclusively in the past."

"Whether or not one lives in the past depends mostly upon the disposition of the individual," Douglas explained. "Some who are yet alive assuredly waste their time lamenting the past in the same fashion as do many ghosts, I daresay."

"Yes," I agreed, "yes, they certainly do. No doubt about that."

Douglas continued. "Lincoln used to say that there are few things in life that are wholly evil or wholly good. He said that was especially true of government policy. However, I made my living, as do politicians today, by claiming my version of government policy was completely without flaw, while the views of my opponents were the result of ignorance and greed."

"So I guess things have not really changed all that much?" I asked.

Douglas smiled broadly. "Not a whit," he replied. "Not one whit."

After a moment, Douglas added, "'Let the people rule!' has always been my message. And indeed they do. A person's action, or inaction, brings them exactly the sort of government they deserve as a general rule. As the good book says, we reap what we sow."

I had to agree once again. Senator Stephen A. Douglas was a lot sharper than I had previously given him credit for. Even Abraham Lincoln must have had his hands full when they debated.

The ghost glanced at the sky. "Well, I suppose it's about time for me to depart. I have hopes of stopping by all seven Lincoln-Douglas debate locations by nightfall, and if I am to keep to my schedule, I must be moving along," Douglas said. "I must say it has been a distinct pleasure visiting with you, sir! Perhaps the next time I'm in town, the *Railsplitter* himself might stop by, and we both might have the pleasure of his company for a time. He is, you know, quite the storyteller."

Douglas reflexively extended his hand toward me for what would have been a very hearty handshake, if his hand had been composed of solid matter. We both looked at our extended hands and shared a good laugh. "Ever the politician," I thought to myself as he faded from view.

CHAPTER SEVEN

It was very early Saturday morning when Matt Farmer woke with a start to the sound of something breaking. He bolted upright in the back seat of the dead Escalade on I-270 where he had spent the night. Looking through the windshield, he spotted a dark figure reaching into the car ahead of him, opening the door. The man started rooting through the interior of the SUV, tossing an occasional item into one of the two grocery store shopping carts he had with him.

Movement to Matt's left caught his eye; there were two or three more figures in hoodies working their way up the highway, filling their shopping carts as they went. "Looters," Matt Farmer thought to himself. He shuddered as he realized they had probably looked down at him through the window of the Escalade while he was sleeping, and had decided not to mess with a car that had someone inside of it. Matt was glad they felt that way; he had no desire to mess with them, either.

Theft of items from inside cars had been a problem in the area for quite some time. The thieves generally targeted GPS systems, lap tops, smart phones and similar items. At the moment, none of those things were working. It appeared the looters were figuring they would be operational again soon. Matt hoped they were right.

Matt sat in the back of the Escalade munching on a granola bar and watching them work their way up the highway. He wanted to give them some distance before he got out of the car. Glancing out the back window of the Escalade, he did not detect any movement behind him. He was guessing it was somewhere between three and four in the morning. He wanted to get moving soon.

Washing down the last of his granola bar with water, Matt stuffed his things back into his gym bag and quietly slipped out of the Escalade, softly closing the door behind him. He vaulted the median and ran across the highway, weaving among the oncoming traffic that had halted dead in its tracks. He ran down an entrance ramp, and within moments he was on the road on the state highway that led north to the city of Almost. After another mile or two, the rest of his trip would be mostly through rural areas. Matt Farmer was glad of that.

• • •

Sister Mary Margaret Marion also awoke with a start. She had been dreaming; it was a nightmare, or more accurately, a dream replay of her most terrifying memory. She was on the playground of the Catholic School in Bosnia, where she grew up, skipping rope with some friends. A man on a motor scooter rode onto the playground and aimed a handgun at Father Stephan and shot him dead. The school principal, Sister Bernadette, and several children were directly in his path. The man on the scooter pulled up next to the nun and pumped a pair of bullets into her as she shielded two children with her body.

The man on the scooter moved on, and pursued a little girl who was running away from him, her long hair streaming behind her. He rode up beside her and caught her long hair in one hand. He brought the scooter to a stop, lifted the girl up in the air by her hair, and shot her in the face. Then he dropped her and she fell to the ground in a crumpled heap.

The shooter then shoved his pistol in his belt and fled….the sound of his scooter fading into the distance was gradually replaced by the sobbing of the children on the playground. The little girl, the one the man had shot last, was Sister Mary Margaret Marion's younger sister.

As the first rays of sunlight shoved into the room where she had been sleeping, Sister Mary Margaret Marion wiped a tear from her eyes and said a silent prayer. That day on the playground was the worst thing she had ever seen. Her prayer was that, in the coming days and weeks, the day on the playground would *remain* the worst thing she had ever seen.

She knelt next to the bed and thought and prayed for a while about what to do next. After a few moments, she rose to her feet and sprang into action.

● ● ●

Pillsbury Franklin sat in his back yard and tended his little campfire. He was determined that, somehow, he was going to have coffee this early morning. His first attempt had been to put the large coffeepot, the one that made 24 cups, directly over the fire. It had the little strainer inside and he thought that was his best chance at some decent coffee. The fire had turned the plastic base of the coffee pot into molten slag, however, and when he opened the top of the pot, the liquid inside smelled more like airplane glue than coffee. In his second attempt, he had put some coffee in a Mr. Coffee-style filter and tied it off with dental floss. Sort of like a teabag, he reasoned to himself. He sat by his little fire, bobbing his coffee bag up and down in the pot of water that was boiling over the fire. It smelled good.

Debbie Franklin looked out of her kitchen window, and chuckled to herself as she watched her husband's adventures. Pillsbury Franklin, her husband of 26 years, was not quite right in the head, she knew. But he was sweet and he was funny and she loved him with all of her heart. When she looked at him, she often thought of an old song by Harry Chapin, the guy who had sung *Cat's in the Cradle*. The song was called *Shooting Star*, and it began,

> He was crazy, of course
> From the first she must have known it,

But still she went on with him
And never did she show it.
And she took him off the street
And she dried his tears of grieving.
She listened to his visions
She believed in his believing.

Debbie knew that the rapidly balding head of Pillsbury Franklin was filled with wild and fantastical thoughts. But she believed in his believing.

As it so happened, as he sat by the fire, brewing his makeshift coffee, Pillsbury Franklin was toying once again with an idea he had for a novel. He was a writer of science fiction and fantasy, as well as deep philosophy. Pillsbury Franklin had completed, sold and published a book called, *Is There Linoleum on the Ocean Floor? and Other Deep Thoughts* It had debuted to great critical acclaim. Reviewers loved his outrageous musings and warped sense of humor. Unfortunately, Pillsbury Franklin's success unraveled quickly after he hit the talk show circuit. Interviewers and audiences quickly realized that Franklin actually *believed* the crazy stuff he was writing and considered himself a serious philosopher. Once that cat was out of the bag, the talk show invitations stopped and book sales dropped like a stone.

Pillsbury Franklin had also written a series of novels that featured a time-traveling hero named *Idaho Jenkins*. Several of them had been published with mild success. Pillsbury had always been a big fan of the Indiana Jones movies, and thus christened his hero with the name of another underappreciated state. Pillsbury was fascinated with World War II, and frequently found a way to work his favorite war into his stories. He had always wanted to write a story that incorporated the Japanese kamikazes.

Kamikaze pilots were totally committed to winning the war; they flew their missions knowing for certain they would never return. They would hold a big ceremony, put on a special sash and then close the cockpit of their planes forever. They would fly off toward an American battleship, and to try their very best to become living missiles, plunging their Zeros, (their planes), into the deck of the battleship in the hope of sinking it. According to the movies, the kamikaze pilots would scream, "Banzai!" as they plunged their planes into the big battleships. ("Banzai!" is apparently the Japanese equivalent to ""Geronimo!" but a shade more pessimistic.) Kamikazi pilots felt theirs was a glorious way to die.

The premise of Pillsbury's latest novel was that planets are actually living beings. This was not exactly a new thought; Greek mythology had advanced the idea centuries ago. In his novel, the chunk of space ice called Pluto, formerly known as one of the planets of the solar system, had intercepted a transmission from earth and had learned that he was no longer one of the big nine. Pluto, insulted by the demotion, left his orbit and began moving toward the sun on a collision course with earth.

"So I'm not a planet," Pluto thought to itself, "then pretty soon, earth will no longer be a planet either." Pluto had been nursing a real inferiority complex for centuries, as it turned out. On Earth, humans refer to this disorder as *short man syndrome*. On a galactic basis, Pillsbury theorized, most of the heavenly bodies referred to it as *small planet envy*. Pluto had always envied Jupiter for its size and Saturn for its spectacular rings. The loss of planet status had been the last straw. Pluto decided he was going to go out in a blaze of glory.

The other planets had been fine with Pluto being classified as a planet, and did not agree with the demotion, either. After all, Pluto was just a little guy, minding his own business out there in the frigid darkness at the edge of the solar system. If he could be a planet then, well, good for him! That's how Mercury felt about it, anyway. (Being one of the smaller planets itself, Mercury could identify with Pluto, big time.)

When Idaho Jenkins figured out what Pluto was up to, he traveled back in time to Japan during World War II, and kidnapped the guy who was the best motivational speaker for the kamikaze pilots. Idaho Jenkins brought the little guy back to the present in his time machine, and then had him give his best speech into a device that communicated with three wild and crazy comets that were in the neighborhood of earth's solar system. The three brash comets bought what the kamikaze speaker was selling, and plunged themselves into Pluto, which exploded into billions of ice fragments, thus saving the earth.

The three crazy comets were not capable of speech as we know it, but each of them, in his own way, had screamed, "Banzai," as they plowed into poor, pathetic Pluto. Idaho Jenkins picked up their battle cries on his ultra-sophisticated communicator, and re-played it for the kamikaze motivational speaker. The little guy laughed and jumped up and down while clapping his hands in response; he was very pleased that the radical comets had grasped his concepts so quickly. This would look good on his resume.

After Pluto exploded, the ice chunks floated through space until they were swept up in Jupiter's incredible gravitational pull. As a result, Jupiter got a pair of spiffy new rings, courtesy of Pluto's remains. As one might expect, Saturn was really peeved about this, as Jupiter already had the distinction of being the largest planet, and it also had the big swirly dark spot that everyone raved about.

None of the other planets were at all happy with the way things ended up, except for Earth, of course, who was glad that Pluto had not made good on his threat. Since Pluto was dead, the debate was over as to whether or not it was a planet.

And so it goes.

The epilogue: Earth, as it turned out, was none too pleased with her inhabitants at the moment. She had grown paranoid of late, suspecting that her people were trying to destroy her through pollution and/or atomic war. Then this thing with Pluto came up, and he darn near annihilated them all! Idiots. Earth considered throwing a few extra quakes and tsunamis at her inhabitants in order to keep them too busy to insult other planets. (Earth would never consider eliminating her inhabitants entirely. Humans and animals, along with water, were among her most distinctive and attractive features as a planet.)

Pillsbury was pretty pleased with the storyline, as a whole, but was frustrated he had not yet found a way to introduce his trademark philosophical themes into the plot. Blaming the whole thing on large oil companies would be his first choice, of course, but he could not find a way to do it without making the plot seem too contrived.

Debbie stood at the kitchen window, watching her husband in the early morning light. Her thoughts turned to their daughter, Christy. Christy lived in St. Louis. She had rejected the upbringing her parents had provided and was living with her employer, the owner of a bar in the part of St. Louis known as *Dogtown*. Christy smoked a lot of marijuana and was a songwriter and singer. Christy was only twenty, and her boyfriend was a much older man. Debbie had always been concerned that Christy's boyfriend was just using her for a time.

She wondered how Christy was handling the weird power outage. It was a very scary thing, if you stopped and thought about it. Christy did not do well in uncertain situations. Sometimes, even being drunk or high was not enough to keep her calm. Debbie busied herself, preparing a bowl of cereal with brown sugar and blueberries. The milk was still cold, and it tasted especially good this morning. She prayed for her daughter as she ate.

Pillsbury Franklin's interplanetary musings stopped for the moment. His coffee appeared to be done. He poured some into his big gas station mug and sniffed it appreciatively. He looked up and caught a glimpse of his wife in the kitchen window, with a faraway look in her eyes. "She's thinking about Christy," he thought to himself. Mothers' Day was coming fast; the day after tomorrow. He was hoping that, somehow, Christy would find her way home by then. He could not bear to think about his daughter very much; he missed her terribly, and when he thought of her he became sad and worried.

After a moment, his mind returned to cooking up new adventures for Idaho Jenkins over his little camp fire. He would enjoy a cup of coffee by the fire, maybe two….then he and Debbie would go check on Ellie Pence and her dead husband. It was the neighborly thing to do.

• • •

Big Sam Cavanaugh woke up shortly after sunrise. The first thing he did was flip a few light switches and pick up the land line phone. Nothing. Sam wasn't surprised, but in his heart he still had hope that things would be back to normal soon. His head, on the other hand, thought his heart was a moron.

Sam freshened up a bit, using as little water as possible. Then he had a very pleasant and very normal-seeming breakfast. The grapefruit juice was still pretty cold, and Janice fixed him bacon and eggs. Janice had found an old fashioned coffee pot, the kind you heat on the stove, fished out of the large supply of junk they had accumulated in the basement over the last 40-plus years in their home. The gas stove was still working, at least for now. At this moment in time things were still pretty good in Almost. He wondered how long that would last.

Sam pushed away from the kitchen table. After breakfast, it was his custom to collect the morning newspaper from the front sidewalk, move to his favorite chair, and then page through the news while he enjoyed his last cup of coffee for the morning. He opened the front door and scanned his front yard. No sign of a paper, of course. He would have been stunned if there had been one. Sitting in his chair without the paper just felt wrong, and he did not stay there long. He chugged his coffee, took the cup to the kitchen sink, kissed his wife and headed out the door for the walk to city hall.

• • •

By Sister Mary Margaret Marion's best estimation, about half of the hospital's morning shift had shown up for work. Some of the nurses and staff, like her, had found a place to curl up and sleep for a few hours. When they awoke, some elected to stay and fill in the gaps where needed. Others, while apologizing profusely, indicated their need to get home and check on their families. All promised to return to the hospital as soon as they could. Some office staff had also reported for duty. Without computers or electricity, they were unable to perform their usual tasks, but Sister Mary Margaret Marion quickly assigned them other responsibilities.

The police and fire personnel who had spent the night before were moving out the door. Other firemen, along with some retired policemen and fire fighters, trickled in throughout the morning, offering their services.

Sister Mary Margaret Marion directed the cafeteria people to assemble breakfasts that utilized foods that were likely to spoil quickly. This resulted in some rather unusual breakfast offerings. Under the circumstances, hopefully there would be few complaints (but she was certain there would be some.) The elevators were not operating, of course, so they needed to find another way to get breakfast upstairs to the patients. The volunteers, office personnel and firefighters formed a sort of "bucket brigade" to pass the trays of food from one set of hands to another up the stairways to the upper floors.

As Sister Mary Margaret Marion stood in the improvised chain gang, passing tray after tray along the line, she turned her thoughts to what to do next if the power to the hospital was not restored within the next few hours. If the situation persisted for days, she feared that each passing day would likely bring fewer and fewer people to work or volunteer and keep things at the hospital functioning. As people became increasingly concerned about their own survival, those who were in hospitals and nursing homes would probably be far out of mind…even farther than they were on an ordinary day, which for most people was already a pretty good distance.

Sister Mary Margaret Marion decided her next move was to get as many patients as possible to go home. As she passed the breakfast trays up the line, she began to think about just how she would be able to do that, given the circumstances.

• • •

Matt Farmer jogged along the road to Almost, weaving between the stalled cars. He occasionally noticed people sleeping in cars, or relieving themselves by the side of the road. Some, like him, were in motion toward Almost. Once in a great while he spotted someone headed the other way. It was a beautiful spring morning; the sun was coming up on his right as he ran toward home.

Matt Farmer was about a mile from the first of two bridges that he needed to cross on the way home. The first was over the Missouri River, the second over the Mississippi. The bridge over the Mississippi was especially beautiful, and its construction had been the topic of a PBS television program some years before. The bridge was the signature landmark of the city of Almost.

As he jogged down a long hill, Matt saw someone was walking up the hill in front of him. As he drew closer to the walker, he saw her to be a rather large African American woman, wearing a purple dress with a bright yellow sash. Her sturdy legs descended into a set of high heels. As he breezed past her, he could hear the "clop-clop" of her confident stride as her heels struck the pavement with authority.

He had gone just a few strides past her when he heard a strong female voice boom from behind him, "Matthew Farmer! Don't you *dare* just run by me without at *least* wishing me good morning!"

Matt Farmer burst into laughter as he trotted to a stop. He stooped over with his hands on his knees as he alternated his laughter with pants for breath. He could hear the "clop clop" of the woman's footsteps rapidly drawing nearer. As he stood up straight and turned, he looked directly into the eyes of Mrs. Vivian Harrison, his home room and history teacher from Almost Senior High School. "Good morning, Mrs. Harrison," Farmer said, chuckling, "Fancy meeting you here!"

"The end of the world is hardly an excuse for bad manners, young man!" Vivian Harrison shot back, smiling broadly. "I would have thought that I had taught you better than that!"

"Indeed you did, Ma'am!" Farmer replied. "In the heat of the moment, my training simply slipped to the back burner."

"Well slip it back to the front burner, then." Harrison replied. "Let us face Armageddon with the utmost dignity and courtesy." They laughed together in the early morning light. Vivian Harrison had always had a gift for breaking the tension during any given crisis. After a grim night of nursing his fears, Matt Farmer was grateful for the change of pace his former teacher provided.

As the sun rose higher in the sky, they chatted briefly, updating each other on what life had brought their way. Then they exchanged theories on what, exactly, was going on in the world at this strange and frightening point in time. Matt gave his teacher one of his bottles of water, and made sure she was not frightened about completing her trek to Almost on her own. Vivian Harrison assured her former pupil that she could handle herself just fine. She had experienced no problems on her journey thus far, and had a little surprise in her purse for anyone foolish enough to give her difficulty.

"Are you sure, Mrs. Harrison? I must admit I am anxious to get home to my family. I know Amanda probably didn't sleep a wink last night, and I want to get home as quickly as I can. However, I would not be able to forgive myself if something happened to you."

"Don't worry about me, Mr. Farmer," Vivian said warmly, "I'll be just fine. I'll be safe at home long before any bad actors are even up for the morning, looking for ways to get in trouble. You go right ahead and head for home. I'll be right on your heels."

Farmer chuckled again, gave his friend and mentor a long hug, then resumed his jog toward home. He knew that anyone stupid enough to mess with Vivian Harrison would find they had more than a handful of hurt on their hands. Vivian Harrison was a woman that was very well-acquainted with handling adversity. If the end of the world was coming soon, she would be on

Matt's short list of people who might be equipped to take the Apocalypse in stride.

• • •

Rick Gage (aka, Mr. Impossible) woke up because he had to go to the bathroom. As his feet hit the floor, he was reminded of the painful blisters he had picked up on his long walk home. His expensive dress shoes were not designed for a four-mile walk. As he entered the bathroom, he flipped on the light switch. Nothing! After responding to nature's call, he walked into his living room, rubbing his eyes and thinking about what to do next. He would be unable to shave (electric razor) unable to cook (electric stove, microwave). Hell, he could not even open a can of food, since his only can opener was electric as well.

He stood in his boxers and surveyed his spacious apartment. He had the latest of everything; huge, flat-screen TV, laptop computer, pod, pad, phone and who knows what other gadgets. All of it was dark. All of it was useless. If the world did not get back to normal soon, there would be very few items in Rick Gage's apartment that would contribute any value toward his survival.

After pondering this harsh reality for a long moment, Rick Gage went back to bed. He hoped the next time he woke up, reality would be a bit kinder to him.

• • •

When Buck got up that morning, he pulled on some gym shorts and went out into the back yard. No sign of Bilbo; his dog was still missing. He went back inside, tossed on some clothes, and jumped on his bike. He began methodically patrolling the neighborhood in search of his favorite companion.

• • •

As Matt Farmer jogged around the corner, the bridge over the Missouri River came into his line of sight. He saw a figure on the bridge, but something about it was not quite right. As he drew closer, he saw that there was a young woman perched on top of the short concrete wall that formed the side of the bridge. She was staring down at the muddy water below. Matt quickened his pace, then came to a stop twenty feet or so from the woman.

"Miss?" Matt Farmer asked, "Are you all right?"

"Do I look like I'm all right to you?" she replied, still staring down at the water.

Farmer paused. "Guess not. Is there something I can do to help you?"

"Tell me the world's not coming to an end," she replied.

"Miss," he said to the young woman, "I truly don't believe it is. I have no idea what's going on, but I don't think it's the end of the world. Not yet, anyway."

The woman on the bridge glanced over at him. "Maybe not for you," she said quietly, "but it's sure looking like the end of the world for me."

Matt Farmer edged a little closer to the woman as he spoke. "What's wrong? I mean, I know your car isn't working; no one's is. What else is going on that has you standing up there?"

"My boyfriend kicked me out of his house. I lost my place to live, my job and my dreams all on the same day. I decided to come back home, which was not an easy decision to make. My parents are disappointed in me. They're not happy with the choices I was making in life. They told me I would end up getting hurt. I hate it when they are right about stuff like that. Then, I'm driving home, wondering what the heck to do, and something weird happens in the sky. Every car on the road, including mine, stops dead in its tracks. I started walking home, but with every step I took, I could find fewer and fewer reasons for going on. When I got to this bridge, I decided I would not go any further. No point. No point at all."

Farmer listened intently as she spoke. He once again moved forward as he began to speak. "I understand. But you're only about twenty-five…."

"Don't come any closer!" the girl on the bridge shouted. "If you come any closer I'm going to jump right now!"

"Okay, okay," Farmer said, startled. "I'll stay right here. Look, you are way too young to die. You have plenty of time to do whatever you want to do in life."

The girl turned and looked at him with a cocked eyebrow. "You're young, too," she replied. "Not much older than me. But you sound just like my parents."

After a moment, Farmer replied. "I'm sorry. Were they mean to you? Are they harsh and legalistic?"

"No," the woman answered. "Worse than that. They are sincere." They stood there in silence for a moment, and the young woman resumed staring down at the water. She spoke again. "Look, I appreciate what you've been trying to do. Don't take it personally, but I'm gonna do this. I don't want to stick around and see what happens next. I'm just not built for bad news, and I think there is a bunch of it on the way."

"Please don't." Farmer answered. "Not yet, anyway. We don't know what happened. Maybe things will be normal in the next day or so. And then you will have thrown your life away for nothing."

"Trust me, it's not a big loss," she replied. "Only a handful of people will even notice I'm gone."

Farmer stood silent, desperately trying to think of another thing to say. The girl resumed her silent staring match with the muddy waters of the Missouri River. At that moment, Matt Farmer heard someone rapidly approaching the scene from behind him. "Clop clop" was the sound the person was making. "Thank God," Matt Farmer thought to himself.

A few seconds later, the booming voice of Vivian Harrison rang out. "Girl!" Vivian said with authority, "What in the *world* do you think you are doing up there?!"

The younger woman turned and replied with a smirk, "I'm bringing a perfect ending to a very bad day."

"Well, lemme tell you, you are making a tremendous mistake," Vivian replied.

"Yeah, this guy here was just telling me that. Spare me the lecture about how young I am, how much I have to look forward to in life, and all that crap. All I can expect from life is more of the same, and I have had enough," the girl on the bridge replied.

"Well, those things may be true, but I'm talking about something different than all that," Vivian said as she marched right past Matt Farmer to within five feet of the young woman's perch.

"Stay back!" The woman thrust out her right hand as a stop sign and wobbled precariously on her perch.

"Settle down, girl!" Vivian Harrison replied. "I'm way too old to try anything physical with you. But at least listen to what I have to say before you jump."

The young woman stood on the lip of the bridge, breathing rapidly, wide eyes trained on the flashily-dressed woman before her. After a moment, she said, "Okay then. You tell me just why it would be a mistake to jump off this bridge, then."

As Matt Farmer stood and watched, Vivian Harrison folded her arms and turned her head left and right. "All right. Look around, young lady. What do you see?"

The younger woman looked around her. "I see you, and a cute guy, and a bunch of dead cars. That's about it."

"And the bridge?" Vivian Harrison asked, "What about that?"

The young woman considered for a moment. She answered, "Nothing special about this bridge that I can see."

"*Exactly*. This is a very boring bridge over some very disgusting, dirty water." Vivian replied, "And, it is within three, maybe four miles of one of the most beautiful bridges in the country. And that bridge goes over water that is considerably clearer and more beautiful than this river."

"So…?" the woman on the bridge asked, more than a little puzzled.

"So, if I were of a mind to commit suicide," Vivian replied, "There is no way on God's green earth that I would do it on *this* bridge. Especially since a far more beautiful bridge is so readily available. Where is your sense of *style*, girlfriend?! If you're going to commit suicide, it should be as scenic and poetic as possible. It is simply out of the question that any person with any artistic sense at all would end their life by jumping off this generic-looking bridge!"

The young woman standing on the concrete wall stared at her lecturer with incredulity. A second later, she laughed from deep within her. She laughed so hard she wobbled on the bridge, threatening to topple into the water by accident instead of design.

Matt Farmer gasped and leaped forward. Before he had moved an inch, Vivian Harrison's right arm shot out, grabbing the right arm of the girl just below the elbow, restoring her balance. The younger woman had reflexively grabbed Vivian's arm in the same spot in return. To Matt's surprise, Vivian did not pull the young woman down from her precarious position, but simply restored her safely to her to her perch.

Vivian looked up into the younger woman's eyes, still holding her arm, gently but firmly. Vivian said after a moment. "Why don't you come down from there and let me walk you as far as the next bridge?"

The young woman stared deeply into the dark brown eyes of the stylish older woman. The warmth and smoothness of the older woman's arm was remarkable, the young woman thought to herself. "Okay," she smiled faintly and said at last. "I think I'll do that." Matt Farmer moved up and lifted the young woman down to safety. Vivian took her by the hand and resumed her journey toward Almost.

"Now, then, young lady," Vivian said softly. "It will take us at least 45 minutes to get to the next bridge…and that's assuming these tortured high heels don't give out before then." The girl chuckled softly. "So tell me, what's your name? We may as well get acquainted along the way."

"It's Christy," the young woman replied. "Just Christy."

"Well, just Christy," Vivian said, "Why don't you just tell me a little bit about yourself. You have the look of an artist about you. Do you paint, or are you a musician?"

Matt Farmer was a few paces behind the women, still in wonder about what he had just witnessed. Some times the most amazing things in life come in the most unique packages, he thought to himself. He knew he would be walking with the women the rest of the way back to Almost, on the off-chance that the young woman would actually attempt to fling herself off of the bridge over the Mississippi.

However, in Matt Farmer's opinion, the odds of that happening after a one-hour walk with Vivian Harrison were somewhere between "slim" and "none." Probably a whole lot closer to "none" than "slim."

CHAPTER EIGHT

Buck Schneider returned from patrolling the neighborhood on his bike, searching for his lost dog. He had passed by a few early morning walkers, including Cherokee, the town drunk. No one had seen his dog. As much as he loved Bilbo, though, Buck Schneider knew it was time to think about other things. He had a lot of other, bigger fish to fry at the moment.

As he brought his bike into the living room, his hand flicked the light switch up and down. Still nothing. He parked the bike and picked up the land line phone. More nothing. He then went to the water faucet. The water was still there, though the pressure seemed a bit weak.

Buck thought back to the big millennium scare, when 1999 was about to click over to the year 2000. Many people thought the world was coming to an end because vital utilities were all operated by computers, and the older ones would crash on New Year's Day. They would be unable to process a year that began with "2000" instead of 1990-something. Newspapers and TV programs advocated stashing food and water. Gun sales went through the roof. Buck had a couple of friends who had actually purchased large barrels of grain and had hidden them in the woods.

Before New Year's Day, such preparations were considered reasonable, perhaps even wise. When the ball dropped at midnight and everything was still working correctly, everybody had a good chuckle about how frightened "other" people had been. Few people had been willing to admit that they, too, had stashed some extra food and water as a precaution against the unknown.

To Buck, putting aside some extra water sure did not seem to be a silly idea at this moment in time. Something weird had happened to the world, and Buck was frightened about when...or if... things might get fixed. He grabbed a few milk jugs he had been saving for sun tea and filled them with water. Then he rooted through the kitchen cabinets and filled pitchers, pots and large bowls with water, lining them up on the counter as he went. When he had filled every reasonable container he could find, he went to the bathroom and filled the tub as well.

When he had finished, Buck turned his thoughts to getting his brother's body to the funeral home. He had not come up with a better plan for transporting his dead brother than putting him in the old wheelchair his dad had used. While a shopping cart was a viable option, and would have been poetic in a way, he felt there was more dignity in utilizing the wheelchair. Buck got on his bike and headed for his mother's house to collect the chair and begin the long trek to Hanson's Funeral Home. Buck had taken many a walk and many a ride with his brother Bud over the years. This walk would be, without question, the saddest and strangest of all.

● ● ●

Listen:

Public schools in the city of Almost were completely integrated, and had been for decades. The city's funeral homes, however, were completely segregated... and regardless of their race, color, creed or national origin, *everybody* liked it that way.

Hanson's Funeral Home was the last destination of choice for white Baptists, Methodists, Presbyterians and semi-religious people who did not know what the heck they were, but wanted a minister to chant a few words over their corpse just to cover their bets.

The Matheson-Drury Funeral Home was for Catholics; no self-respecting Catholic would ever dream of being caught dead anywhere else. The sight of an African-American inside of Hanson's or Matheson-Drury was a fairly unusual one.

Haysbert Funeral Home was located in the heart of one of the city's more troubled neighborhoods; if you were African-American, it was *the* place where you would be laid out. White people rarely went there; most did not even know the place existed. Cemeteries in the city of Almost were somewhat more integrated, though there were a couple that were exclusively Catholic and others that were strongly preferred by people with certain demographics.

While people (of any color or faith) are living, many of them like to keep up the pretense that they are really open-minded and that they freely mingle with people that are different than themselves. However, in the city of Almost, when you died it was *game over*. All those pretenses fell away, and the cold meat that used to be you was displayed and buried among the smoothly homogenous group of people you had actually hung out with all along.

And so it goes.

• • •

Big Sam Cavanaugh arrived at city hall to find fire chief Herschel Gonzales and police chief Dana Crisp sitting on a concrete pylon in front of the building while sharing information. About a dozen cops and firemen were clustered along the sidewalk, most of them nursing a cigarette, a coffee, or both. Sam smiled to himself; the world was going to hell in a hand-basket, but folks were still finding ways to feed their addictions.

Virtually all the cops and firemen now had bicycles at their disposal; they were parked in a cluster on the city hall lawn. As Sam mingled with the crowd on the sidewalk, he heard various tales about the events of the previous night. It was a calmer night than expected, as if the city were holding its breath, waiting for the next shoe to drop. There were reports of gunfire in some of the city's more troubled areas, but without radios, phones or vehicles being operational, there was no way to ascertain the extent of any violent activity. A fireman reported that six shooting victims had appeared at Our Lady of Perpetual Sorrows Hospital. Four of them were young, African-American men. None of the victims were willing to provide details of how they had come to be shot. One of them had died from his wounds.

And so it goes.

A couple of cops had thwarted an attempted break-in at a major supermarket out on the Belt Line Bypass. Three or four guys were banging on the metal back door of the grocery store with a sledgehammer, making so much racket you could hear them for blocks. A couple of shouts and a warning shot were more than enough to send the shadowy amateurs scampering off into the darkness. There was great concern among the men and women on the sidewalk about this incident, however. If looters were already appearing on the first night that the city had been without power, it was certain that many more would be coming out of the woodwork each passing night that this crisis went on. And they would be progressively more organized and more dangerous as time went by.

Dana Crisp had discussed the situation with a number of business-owners in the area, who were debating if and when they should attempt to re-open their businesses if the power outage was not resolved soon. If power was not restored, then the water would run out when the towers' supply was exhausted, which would not take long. Health department regulations prevented most businesses from remaining open if restroom facilities were not operational.

No power meant no cash registers or computers. Many businesses were completely helpless without those things. Checks, credit cards, and debit cards were all rendered useless…in fact, banking of any kind was simply not possible. How could people do business? If employees even showed up for work, which was also in question, how would they be paid? And even if they had money, how would you *spend* it? Under these strange circumstances, the consequences of the country's complete dependence on computers and other electronic devices were simply beyond imagination.

"Well, we're not going to let health department regulations prevent businesses from opening up if they are willing to try it," Sam told Dana Crisp. "You let those business people know that we will not enforce any regulation that prevents them from opening. In fact, if there is any way we can *assist* them in getting their doors open, we will do it. We fully support any *scrap* of normalcy we can get in this town as quickly as we can get our hands on it."

Herschel Gonzales reported that there had been a number of emergency situations on the river as a result of the disappearance of all electric power. All boats and barges had lost power when the sky thumped, just as automobiles had done. Most of the barges had managed to beach themselves in shallow water near the river banks, but one had drifted out of control. It was turned sideways by the Mississippi current, and was slammed into the base of the bridge. It was still there, pinned against the concrete supports of the bridge by the powerful current. Fire and river emergency personnel had lowered a rope from the bridge to draw the barge workers up to safety, one at a time.

Eight pleasure boats had drifted all the way down to the dam, where the current crashed them into the locks, capsizing all but a couple of them. Some people had jumped out of the boats before they hit. Some managed to struggle their way to shore; others had most certainly drowned. Emergency personnel had managed to save a few folks at the dam.

It was uncertain how many people had died in the river that day. At the moment, the emergency crews doubted that they would ever really know.

After bringing the mayor up to speed on these developments, Herschel Gonzales said, "Sam, there's one more thing. I hesitate to tell you about it, because it's more than a little off-beat. But under the circumstances…"

"Let's have it, Herschel! Under the circumstances, I'm willing to entertain just about anything!" Sam replied.

"Well, I told you yesterday that I was going to contact as many engineer-types in the area as I could to brainstorm ideas of how we could keep the water flowing. Ted Atchley, one of the civil engineers down at Lincecum and Associates suggested we get in touch with an elderly dentist that has a practice in his home on the north side of town," Herschel said.

"A dentist?!" Big Sam laughed. "What's a dentist going to do? "

"I know, right?" Gonzales replied sheepishly. "But it seems this dentist has been an inventor all his life. Atchley saw a big exhibit out at the community college last year that had photos, descriptions and models of all this guy's inventions. A lot of his stuff was steam-powered. Steam-powered tractors, lawn mowers, stuff like that. He even built a steam-powered car. Atchley said that steam engines may not be affected the way other engines are, because they are powered by burning fuel, not by electricity. So he was theorizing that maybe this dentist, Dr. Seymour, might be able to hook up a steam engine of some kind at the water works to keep some of the pumps going."

"That's wild. Did the engineers you talked to have any other ideas?" Sam asked.

"No. Not really."

"Then weird as it is, this dentist may be our best hope. See if Atchley will help you track down Dr. Seymour and see if there is any daylight in this wacky idea," Sam replied. "Let's chase it full speed, at least until something better comes along. Who the hell knows? Stranger things have already happened. Two days ago I never would have guessed that the whole blasted area would come grinding to a halt."

"Yeah, that's kind of what I thought," Herschel replied. "Atchley and I plan to head for Seymour's house right after we're done here."

"Maybe we won't have to worry about it," Sam said wistfully. "Maybe the power will kick back on this afternoon and this whole thing will be over like waking up from a bad dream."

"Yeah, maybe," Herschel replied. "I wish."

• • •

The night the power went out Ellie Pence had managed to drag the body of her dead husband into his bedroom, and to hoist it up on his bed. She was now in the middle of an attempt to move it down the stairs to the first floor of her home. A moment before, both she and the body had nearly tumbled out of control down the staircase. Robert's head had banged solidly against the top step. Even though he was not in any condition to feel pain, Ellie felt bad about that. Now Ellie was standing in the middle of the stairway, considering how she might get her husband's body the rest of the way down the stairs without bouncing his head off of each step along the way. Ellie was stubborn, and preferred to do things for herself. She was insensitive by nature, but even she winced at the thought of doing further harm to the corpse of her husband of over 30 years.

As she pondered, she heard a knock at the front door. Through the sheer curtain over the leaded glass, she could make out the distinctive, dumpy outline of Pillsbury Franklin. Ellie reluctantly admitted to herself that she was actually glad to see him.

Within a few minutes, Ellie and the Franklins had loaded Robert's body into the dark green rubber-plastic garden wheelbarrow she had purchased at the giant HomeMart store. Robert's body was *on* the cart more than *in* it, because his body had stiffened almost completely. It was not a dignified way to transport a person's remains, but under the circumstances it was the only means available. Hanson's Funeral Home was three miles away, and there was at least one huge hill along the way. Ellie accepted the Franklins' offer to help push the cart to the funeral home. Before they left, Ellie went into the kitchen and grabbed a six-pack of bottled water. She gently placed it in Robert's lap, and the four of them began the journey across town.

• • •

Buck Schneider glided his bike into the parking lot of Schneider Brothers' Corner Grocery Store. Officer Darnell Everwood came from behind the building, zipping up his fly as he walked. The night had passed uneventfully and Everwood had even managed to catch a few hours of sleep in one of the stalled cars in the parking lot. Now the policeman was going to head home to check on his family before returning to city hall for new instructions. Buck took the cop inside the store and fed him some Hostess Honey Buns and a nice cold Dr. Pepper for breakfast.

"Get 'em while they last," Buck thought to himself.

• • •

Listen:

A thousand years from now, a team of archaeologists will discover the ruins of the Schneider Brothers Corner Grocery Store. While sifting through the rubble, one of them, Z-bop45, will find a Hostess Honey Bun, still in the wrapper. Z-bop45 will rip open the plastic, sniff the Bun, and take a quick bite. "Still soft," Z-bop45 will say to his buddy, RyanSeacrest789.

• • •

Matt Farmer and the two ladies had reached the second bridge. They threaded their way in and out among the stalled cars. Matt paused for a moment to peer over the side of the bridge. There was a huge barge down there, parallel to the bridge, held fast by the power of the river's current. He wondered what had become of its crew. He also wondered what other forms of disaster might have struck the city of Almost. He stood on the bridge, looking at the downtown area; the flour mill, the bars and antique stores. Everything was unearthly quiet. The only movement in the normally busy downtown was a lone figure walking quickly toward the bridge. Matt hoped and prayed that his wife and children were all safe, and as he stared at the quiet town, he became all the more anxious to get home as soon as possible.

As expected, by the time they had arrived at the second bridge, Vivian Harrison had driven all thoughts of suicide completely from the mind of her new friend. Christy was laughing and smiling and engaged in a lively conversation with the older woman. "Well," Matt Farmer thought to himself, "at least something good happened on the way home from work last night."

When they had completed crossing the bridge, the three companions stopped to discuss their logistics. Vivian lived a couple of miles away from Matt Farmer's house. Christy's parents, as it so happened, lived down the block from him. Vivian and Christy hugged and said goodbye, promising to meet up again at some time in the near future. Vivian planted a big kiss on Christy's cheek, and then swatted her behind as she started on her way.

Matt and Christy stood and watched for a moment as the clop-clop of Vivian's heels faded into the distance. Fortunately, Christy was wearing good walking shoes, so she and Matt agreed they could jog the mile or so left on their journey. As they prepared to go, the figure Matt had seen from the bridge was within a block of their position. Matt recognized Cherokee, who was walking around town, as usual. "Geronimo, Cherokee!" Matt Farmer said as the unshaven older man approached.

"Geronimo!" Cherokee replied, waving his hanky in the air. "I see you have a young lady with you," the grizzled man said, winking as he tucked his hanky back into the back pocket of his pants. His forty-proof breath nearly knocked the young people over as he spoke. "Kiss 'er, young man. Kiss 'er and feed 'er beans."

"No, no Cherokee. We're just friends," Matt replied. "And I don't think my wife would appreciate that much!" Matt and Christy laughed as they started in a trot toward home. Matt waved at Cherokee over his shoulder. "See you later, Cherokee! We need to get home!"

"Well, kiss 'er anyway!" Cherokee yelled as they jogged away.

• • •

About every two weeks, Rod "Blackie" Blackmon liked to take his guns out of the locked cabinets and spread them out where he could view them all at once. Usually, he did this in the privacy of his basement, but with no electric light available, this morning he was setting things up in his garage. With the door open, he would have sufficient light to fully appreciate his private arsenal. Blackie made large, makeshift tables out of two sheets of plywood and two sets of sawhorses, then began to lay guns on them, one at a time.

Blackie had collected a lot of different things during his 33 years of life; comic books, autographs from sports figures, matchbook covers, and beer cans, among other things. But his favorite thing to collect, by far, had been guns. Blackie loved to look at his guns, to heft them in his hands, and he loved to shoot them. Once or twice a month he would choose a couple of weapons and go out into the woods to do target practice. He would usually shoot at soda cans, bottles and dead trees, but his favorite things to shoot at were the zombie targets he would buy at the gun shows in St. Louis.

He laid out his Desert Eagle .50 caliber pistol on the plywood; it was plated with titanium gold and had tiger stripes. It was a bold piece of work; the bulk of it sat on top of your hand like a big, gold brick. Next came his Taurus revolver, a huge pistol that had *Raging Judge Magnum* etched on its side. On the other end of the scale, his Hedy Jane Doubletap weighed less than a pound, and strongly resembled an iphone, white plastic and all. He also had an AR-15 rifle, which was guaranteed to stop a zombie dead… (twice-dead, perhaps) …in its tracks. He had over two dozen guns of various shapes, colors and size.

Laying out his gun collection always gave Blackie a thrill, but today...today was different. It was better. He had a feeling in his gut; exhilaration, certainly, but with a tinge of dark, fearful anticipation. It reminded him of how he felt late at night when he was on the computer, long after his wife and children had gone to bed. Tonight, Blackie would be guarding the grocery store with Buck. His guns would be serving a great purpose, not merely providing amusement. Tonight, he would not be shooting at soda cans. Or zombie targets. If he fired his gun tonight, it would be a whole new ballgame.

As he continued to handle and arrange his weapons, Blackie hoped with great intensity that the electricity would not come back on any time soon.

When Rod Blackmon was a kid, he used to travel to all kinds of flea markets with his mom. Flea markets reminded him of carnivals; the people who worked both venues seemed to be from the same extended family. Instead of neon and light-bulb covered rides lighting up the outdoors, flea markets were generally dark and dingy affairs held in steel buildings. The attractions were not rides, but table after table of strange and cool stuff. Old things, off-beat things, hand made things...some things you couldn't even tell what they were or what purpose they served. On one of these excursions, when he was 12, he ran across his first issue of *Real Crime Adventures*.

The covers of *Real Crime Adventures* looked somewhat like comic books, but the figures seemed painted rather than drawn. They always depicted guys with guns and women with torn clothing. Splashes of words on the cover would promise plenty of hard-hitting action was waiting inside. After he found his first issue, Blackie prowled the flea markets relentlessly in pursuit of all the *Real Crime Adventures* he could get his sweaty teenaged hands on, and he built quite a collection. Blackie's favorite stories in *Real Crime Adventures* were about a private detective named Mike "Brick" Walz. Brick Walz was a disillusioned Green Beret who decided to fight crime upon his return from Vietnam. He wandered America in his lime-green 1969 Ford Mustang fastback looking for danger, which he conveniently found wherever he went.

Brick Walz' exploits always involved smoking, hard drinking, bad guys who spouted long monologues, and gorgeous women who found him irresistible. His stories were illustrated with dark, shadowy pen-and-ink drawings. The stories all ended pretty much the same way; Brick shoots the bad guy just as he is tearing the clothes off a helpless and beautiful girl, usually blonde. The closing illustration usually showed Brick Walz standing triumphantly over the fallen bad guy, clutching the terrified blonde to his side, his free hand holding a still-smoking gun. A cigarette dangled carelessly from one corner of his mouth.

Every Brick Walz story had the same closing line. He would raise his just-fired snub-nose .38 to his lips and blow the smoke away. "Case closed, Toots!" he would say to the blonde.

● ● ●

Demarcus Johnson woke up because it was hot; he had been tossing and turning for over an hour when he finally gave up on sleep. He was guessing it was maybe eight or nine in the morning. It was unseasonably warm for early May. Every window in the small house was open, but the air was just not moving. Still sleepy, Demarcus had forgotten about the power outage until he flicked a light switch to no effect. The memories of the day before came flooding back. After helping Buck Schneider move the dead body of his brother into the grocery store refrigerator, he came home to find his mother and his baby sister, Jaylin, (she was 3) very ill. His two little brothers, oblivious to the strangeness of events, were running around the yard because the TV didn't work.

Demarcus could tell that his mama was scared, but she was trying not to show it. Lamiqua Johnson was a courageous woman. She was working two jobs and trying to make ends meet, despite having been abandoned by two deadbeat husbands. Demarcus had pulled together last night's supper for the family from what was available. They ate canned stew at room temperature, and then Demarcus and his brothers finished off a couple of bags of Doritos.

His mom and baby sister not eaten. They both were feverish, and just wanted to sleep. Lamiqua Johnson had some medical background, she was a licensed CNA, but she was not certain what was wrong with them. She was hoping that a lot of rest would heal them quickly.

By around 9:00 that night, the younger brothers finally ran out of gas, and fell asleep on the living room floor. Demarcus sat on the front porch of the house, watching it grow dark. He sat out there for a couple of hours, smoking Swisher Sweets cigarillos and listening to the sounds of the night. At first it was just crickets and tree frogs; later on, he could hear the sound of distant voices, some of them shouting. Once in a while, he heard a gun go off.

Now it was morning, and Demarcus Johnson stood in the living room in his boxers and wondered what to do next. As he stood in deep thought, he heard his mother's voice, coming faintly from her room. He went in to her, and found her lying on her bed; she had kicked all the covers onto the floor during the night and was drenched with sweat. Her thick, dark body was a striking contrast against the white linen sheets and the yellow nightgown she wore. She looked like she was burning up, but not from the spring heat. Lamiqua Johnson was burning up from the inside.

The young man watched as his mother pried her eyes open with great effort. "Demarcus, honey," she said softly, "how are the children?"

"Everybody's fine, Mama," Demarcus replied. "Everybody's still asleep."

"That's good, that's good," Lamiqua said. "Honey, I am simply burnin' *up*! Would you get me a big glass of water, please?"

"Sure, Mama." On his way to the kitchen, Demarcus popped into his little sister's room. She, too, looked hot, but was still asleep. He stood in the half-light of her room, watching her breathe. He was no expert, but he knew the little girl's breathing was irregular and slightly jagged somehow. The teenager went to the kitchen and got out a large plastic tumbler. The freezer had a few slightly-softened ice cubes. He put them in the cup and went to the sink. When he turned the faucet, it coughed and spat out a few spurts of water, then slowed to a tiny trickle.

Demarcus was not quite able to fill the big tumbler before the water stopped completely.

CHAPTER NINE

Moving his brother's body was even more difficult than Buck thought it would be.

Having never had to move a dead body before, he had not thought about the effects of rigor mortis. "There's a reason they call a dead body a *stiff*," he remembered Ed Hanson saying once. (Hanson was the owner/director of the Schneider family's funeral home of choice.) "There is also a reason behind the expression, *dead weight*." Ed added.

It was all Buck could do to get Bud's body off of the cases of soda without dropping the body or causing an avalanche. Once Buck had wrestled him to the floor, the only way he could move the corpse was to grab it under the arms and drag it a few feet at a time until he managed to get it out of the cooler. Buck estimated that his brother weighed a little over 200 pounds while he was living…but now, he seemed to way half a ton!

Maneuvering the body into the wheelchair was no piece of cake, either. His brother's body was stiff as a board. Had Bud's body not been bent at the waist and knees a bit when they set it down in the cooler, the wheelchair option would not have worked at all. Even with that, his brother was nearly standing up in the chair and it was going to be extremely difficult to keep him from spilling out of it as Buck pushed it across town.

Buck grabbed some clothesline off one of the shelves in the grocery store and lashed his brother's body in place as best he could. Even with that precaution, he was going to have to be extremely careful…and extremely lucky…to get the body all the way to Hanson Funeral Home without spilling him out onto the sidewalk.

Finally, Buck had the body secured into the wheelchair as well as he thought he could. As he stood outside the store, looking at his brother's awkward position, he choked a bit as he thought about how undignified this whole situation was for his brother's remains. He spent a few moments wracking his brains for a better way to transport his brother's body to the funeral home, but again came up with no better ideas.

"Better get started," Buck thought to himself. As he moved the wheelchair forward, he realized that pushing this strange and morbid conveyance across town was going to give him quite a cardio-vascular workout. He was glad his bicycling habit had him in pretty good shape. A few years ago, he probably would not have been able to manage this strange, final journey with his brother on his own.

• • •

Amanda Farmer woke after a few hours of restless sleep. She went first to the light switch in her bedroom, and found it was still unresponsive. Then she peeked into her children's rooms; they were still asleep, and their bedroom curtains were blowing gently in the spring breeze that wafted in through their open windows. The peaceful expressions on their sleeping faces quieted her anxiety somewhat.

It was Saturday, so she didn't have to make a decision about whether or not to send the kids to school. She wondered how school could even function if the current conditions did not change. The textbooks in their local schools had recently been replaced with tablet computers. Without electricity or computers, how would school even be possible?

Life for her children, for all children in Almost, would be very different today. No angry birds or other video games. No itunes or ipods. No cell phones, no texting. A lot of kids simply would not know what to do with themselves. Her children would be less impacted than many, as she and Matt had always limited the amount of time their kids spent with electronic things. They had always insisted that their kids spend a considerable amount of their time playing outside. Right now, she was especially glad of that, as life for her children would feel fairly normal. At least for a while.

As long as Daddy came home.

Amanda Farmer's worries had been constantly simmering on the back burner of her mind under a thin layer of sleep. And now, standing in the dim hallway light outside her children's bedrooms, it came welling up to the surface again. She wept quietly and wondered if and when she would ever see her husband again. And even if he did come home, she wondered what kind of life lay in the future for her children.

• • •

After Big Sam Cavanaugh wrapped up his conversations with police and fire personnel, he decided to take a walk down to the riverfront. Just a few moments before, he had been informed that water was no longer flowing into the homes and businesses of the city of Almost. Though this news was not unexpected, when he heard the report his sense of dread deepened. He decided he needed to get away from the office, from everything, and take some time to think about the situation and about what he should do next.

Last night, the city had been fairly peaceful, considering the strange and unsettling circumstances. Tonight, however, would be different. Yesterday was a day of extreme uncertainty with no power, cars, phones or computers; businesses and schools closed; and no one knew why power had been lost or if and when it would be restored. Most folks probably did not sleep well; perhaps they did not sleep at all. Today, they would roll out of bed and flip the light switch and find that everything was more disturbing than it was the night before. Then, they would turn a water faucet and nothing would come out, adding a new crisis to the mix.

For most, this would likely be followed by a frantic inventory of the food they had on hand and the discovery that they only had enough to last a week, perhaps two. By then, the aching sense of fear they felt when they went to bed the night before would be replaced with panic. And when people panic, that's when things get really ugly.

Those with little or nothing to eat or drink will start thinking about where and how they can get the stuff they need to live. Many will begin weighing out just how far they will be willing to go to get that stuff. Those who have stuff will begin thinking about exactly how to protect what they have salted away… and how far they will be willing to go to keep their stuff. And then people without stuff and people with stuff would all start loading their guns.

Sam walked up to the chain link fence that separated Riverside Park from the banks of the Mississippi River. It was another beautiful day in early May, and the view of the river at this point was beautiful. To his left, the spectacular bridge to Missouri reigned over the river. The barges were still pinned against the bridge's footings by the powerful current. He wondered if they would be a permanent part of the riverscape.

To his right was the River's Edge Restaurant, which was built inside of an old, red-brick railroad station. Just beyond it was the towering flour mill. Painted on its whitewashed silos were the words, *Welcome to Almost*. Just below that was a huge painting of an American flag. Big Sam stood at the edge of the Mississippi River and listened to the sound of the water slapping against the large stones that lined this portion of the river bank. For a brief moment, he lost all his cares, and enjoyed the simplicity of it all; the smell of the river, the spring breeze blowing through what was left of his thinning, mostly white hair.

His right hand fished in his pocket and he found his lucky half-dollar. It was a 1964 Kennedy half-dollar. As he ran his thumb back and forth over its smooth surface, he thought about the way the coin sang when you flipped it in the air, and the distinctive pinging sound it made when dropped on concrete or as it clinked against other coins when he dropped them into the tray on his nightstand. It was almost pure silver, a beautiful coin, one of the last of its kind.

Sam considered the Kennedy half-dollar to be his lucky coin because he found it in Vietnam. Sam and his patrol had been working their way through the dense jungle not far from Pnom Penh. As he was trudging along, Sam noticed the sun was glinting off of something in the thick foliage at his feet. When he bent over to check it out, the first thing he saw was his lucky coin, just sitting there on the ground. The second thing he noticed, about a yard in front of him, was a thin strand of wire that was almost completely concealed by the foliage.

"Trip wire!" Sam yelled out, and everyone froze. Had it not been for Sam's lucky half-dollar, he and several of his fellow-soldiers would have been killed or crippled by the deadly booby trap. Sam had carried the silver likeness of President Kennedy in his pocket ever since.

Sam thought it was a shame that he had been unable to return the favor to the murdered president. Wouldn't it have been great if, as his Cadillac limousine rounded the corner into Dealey Plaza, John Kennedy noticed something shiny on the carpet at his feet? Bending over, he would have found a solid silver Sam Cavanaugh half-dollar coin, and the two assassin's bullets would have whizzed harmlessly over his head, thudding harmlessly into the dashboard. The limousine would have sped away with everyone safe and sound, and perhaps the entire decade of the 1960s would have been less chaotic.

But there had been no lucky coin for John Kennedy that day in Dallas. Instead, one of those bullets blew a large piece of his head off, and sprayed his brains around the limo and across the front of his pretty wife's pink skirt.

And so it goes.

Sam drew his lucky coin from his pocket. On the large silver coin at least, President Kennedy's head was still intact. His hair was still perfect. It was a profile in courage, frozen perfectly in time.

As he stroked his lucky coin, the mayor turned around and looked at his city in the morning sunlight. Old and majestic buildings spilled over the hills. It was quiet. It was peaceful. He wished he could freeze the city at this moment in time, while it was still perfect, just like his lucky coin froze the image of Kennedy. He wished he could stop time right here and now, in the moments before all hell was almost certainly about to break loose.

At the moment, the city of Almost was one city, a community. But in the coming hours, it would break into hundreds of pieces, into gangs and clans. Unless things were returned to normal soon, it would be every man for himself. Tribes would form, alliances would be struck, and battles fought for scarce resources. Black vs. white, Protestant vs. Catholic, Nascar motorheads vs. white collar types. Family clans would form.

In short, people would drift into the same sorts of cliques they were part of in high school. But this social experiment would be a much deadlier game. And a house divided could not stand; Abraham Lincoln said so.

Sam thought about when he came back from Vietnam, after watching many of his friends die. He thought about how it was to walk through the airport, relieved to be home, yet scorned by angry crowds for doing his duty in the armed forces. Walking through the airport while people screamed at him, they called him a baby killer, even spit on him. His friends had died to protect these people, and for the honor of the United States. But the state of the union he returned to was far from united. In that moment in the airport, he had felt a quiet desperation unlike anything he had ever felt. Until now.

Big Sam glanced down at the coin in his hand. "Tails," he thought, as he glanced at the eagle. Above the eagle, a banner said, "E pluribus unum." It was

Latin, and he knew the translation was, "out of the many, one." It was a slogan testifying that 13 diverse colonies could be united as states, followed by dozens of others.

Sam turned and looked again at the city he loved. Right now, it was still one city. But soon, it would be more like, "E unum pluribus." His translation: "Out of the one, many." He didn't know whether his Latin was correct or not.

• • •

Christy Franklin watched quietly as Matt Farmer embraced his wife. A few moments before, they had jogged over the top of the last hill that stood between them and home; they were at the far end of the wide brick street with several triangular islands of grass in the middle. As they jogged down the street, one of the Farmer children spotted them, and ran up the front porch into the house, screen door banging behind him.

An instant later, Amanda Farmer burst from the house, shouting, "Matt!!" The young mother and her three kids ran toward them. They all met on one of the grassy islands, forming a crying and laughing jumble of hugging bodies.

Christy watched it all with a mixture of hope and regret. She was glad for the Farmers. They seemed to be genuinely nice people. As she rejoiced with them, her self-pity welled back to the forefront of her mind. What little she had treasured in her relationship, in her life beyond Almost, was gone. Now she was back where she started. Back in Almost. With Mom and Dad.

She felt awkward until Matt Farmer suddenly remembered her. He introduced her to his wife, Amanda, who politely invited her to join them for a late breakfast. Christy smiled and declined. She would just be in the way, she thought to herself. She exchanged some light hugs with her new-found friends and headed down the hill toward home. She stepped up on the front porch of her parents' home, knocked quickly and grabbed the knob. Locked. A few more knocks convinced her that no one was at home. She stood on her tip toes, found the emergency key above the door jamb, and let herself into the large, two-story home.

She stood in the hallway at the foot of the stairs with the door hanging open. Her parents were most certainly not at home; if they had been, her mother would have been yelling by now, "Christy, close the door! Were you raised in a barn?!"

The young woman reached a sudden decision, and then moved swiftly through the home. She had a quick breakfast, then shoved some food items and bottled water into a plastic grocery bag. She ran upstairs to her old room and tossed a spare set of clothes in another plastic bag and headed for the door. She re-locked the front door and put the emergency key back where she found it.

• • •

Ed Hanson's family had been in the funeral home business for about 120 years. Ed sat quietly in his second-floor office, which was dimly lit by the sunlight streaming through the window. He sat quietly, cradling his face in his hands, and wondered if any of his ancestors had dealt with a crisis like this one. Five minutes ago, a fireman had left his office after informing him that there were 27 bodies at Almost Memorial Hospital awaiting pickup by Hanson Funeral Home. Hospital officials estimated there could be ten or 15 more by the same time tomorrow if essential life-support machinery was not restored. As an added bonus, there were three bodies waiting for him at Our Lady of Perpetual Sorrows Hospital as well.

Most non-Catholics in town went to Almost Memorial for their hospital stays. If that stay ended badly, and they joined the choir eternal while there, then what was left of them was shipped to Hanson Funeral Home a high percentage of the time.

Thirty bodies to embalm and inter, and that was just from the two area hospitals. He had not yet received any word from the nursing homes and assisted living facilities in the area. It could well be that thirty more corpses were designated for Hanson's within those troubled walls. Maybe more. Ed Hanson felt overwhelmed. He only had about twenty caskets on hand, with no hope (at least currently) that he could get more any time soon. No hearses or ambulances were available to collect the bodies or get them to the graveyards. He had room to store fifty, perhaps sixty dead bodies, but the refrigeration for this storage was not operating. Nor was the generator that backed up the system. The crematory could not operate without its ventilation system; it would fill the whole area with the stench of burning bodies.

His embalming equipment would not function without power. He had an alternative system that used gravity instead of electricity, but this method was slow and far less reliable. Plus, he had never even attempted to embalm bodies in this fashion, and his father was not around to show him how to do it.

Even if bodies were able to be transported to the graveyard, there was no equipment operational to dig the graves; they would have to be dug with shovels.

What the hell was he going to do?

"Ed?" The sound of his sister's voice came drifting up the stairs. "Ed, I think someone is here to see you…" Something in Elaine's tone indicated that whatever awaited him downstairs was not very likely going to lighten his mood.

Ed Hanson grabbed a clipboard, jogged down the stairs to the back door and stepped into the bright sunlight. He was greeted by the sight of Carl Hornung, a friend from the Rotary Club, pulling a lawn cart across the parking lot. It was a big one, the kind you use to catch grass behind a large garden tractor. Carl was a vigorous man of 70, trim and in good shape. His t-shirt was soaked with sweat and his face was a preview of the unspoken tragedy that was in tow behind him.

As his eyes adjusted to the bright sunlight, Ed Hanson saw what was in the trailer. Carefully nestled amid blankets and pillows was the small, still body of Jane Hornung, Carl's wife of nearly 50 years. Her face was peaceful, and her hands were carefully folded across her tummy. Her body had been carefully and lovingly arranged by her dedicated husband.

"Ed," Carl Hornung choked out, his eyes welled with tears, "Ed, what do I do??"

Ed Hanson dropped his clipboard to the sidewalk and embraced the older man. He cried quietly as he held his friend, who was sobbing from the depths of his soul. Ed Hanson cried for his friend, but he also cried for himself. And for all the families who were counting on him to make sure their loved ones were buried decently. Ed wondered how in the world he was going to be able to do the now-impossible things for his clients and friends that had been a matter of simple routine only hours before.

● ● ●

Vivian Harrison went into her silent house. A glance around the place gave her strong assurance that nothing had been disturbed, that all was as it should be. She sat on the couch in her living room, and slowly removed her pretty shoes from her screaming feet. The low heels were not designed for walking, of course, and she had been forced to hike over seven miles to return home from St. Louis County. She rubbed her sore feet and took inventory of the many blisters she found there. She rose from the couch and drew some water into a shallow, plastic pan, and sprinkled in some Epsom salts. Sitting back down on the couch, she winced as she placed her feet into the water. After a moment, the stinging subsided, and she began to relax.

As she gradually unwound on the couch, Vivian Harrison thought about Bobby Anthony. Bobby was one of the most prominent leaders in Almost's African-American community. As a young woman, Vivian had looked to him as a role model. Bobby had worked tirelessly to make the city a better place. Among his many achievements was the *Almost Hope Center*, located in the heart of the city. Over the years, the Center had provided food, job training and other emergency assistance to hundreds of people in need.

In her middle age, Vivian had become a trusted ally of this dedicated man. Bobby had been admitted to the hospital a few days ago; the last she heard, he was expected to recover fully from whatever it was that was troubling him. Vivian wondered, in view of the current circumstances, if that was still the case. As she drifted off to sleep on the couch, Vivian Harrison decided that, when she awoke, she would wrap her tortured feet in Ace bandages, slip on some sneakers, and make her way to the hospital to check on her friend.

• • •

As Buck Schneider pushed the wheelchair containing the body of his brother toward the funeral home, he encountered a number of other wheelchairs, filled with living people, headed in various directions. The local hospitals were discharging every possible person they could, sending them home because their families were better equipped to care for them than the hospitals were at the moment. It was a strange sight; the streets were filled with cars, but none of them moving. Then there would be the occasional wheel chair or bicycle, or people making their way across town on foot or on roller blades. The whole situation seemed surreal to Buck, and he was sure that the rest of the people on the street felt the same way.

When he was a little over a mile from the funeral home, he saw a small group of people approaching from a side street. He paused for a rest and waited for them to draw closer. As they did, he recognized Pillsbury and Debbie Franklin and Ellie Pence. Ellie had been a few years ahead of him at school, but Buck and Pillsbury had been smoking and drinking buddies throughout high school and college, until the Franklins found religion. While they remained close, as slightly estranged brothers do, they had stopped hanging out together in their mid-twenties.

• • •

Listen:

There's just something about the close friends you make in your late high school and college years (whether you went to college or not). These are the friends you got drunk with, perhaps got high with. They sat up late nights with you, sharing the heartaches of break-ups and exploring the questions that had no easy answers. They were the people who helped you figure out life. You had bottle rocket fights in the woods with them, jumped off cliffs into rivers with them, and cruised town square with them. You stood up in their weddings and they stood up in yours. These are the people that, like you, were very lucky to have survived past their early twenties. These are the people who, though just as immature as you were, helped you grow up.

• • •

Buck Schneider and Pillsbury Franklin were those kinds of friends. And though life and the passage of time had lain a thin veneer of civilization over their late-teen stupidity, they were the kind of friends who knew that, just beneath the surface, they were still essentially the same insecure idiots they had been two or three decades before. And they loved each other all the more for the longevity and magnitude of their imperfections.

"Dough!" Buck Schneider called out to Pillsbury Franklin. (This nickname was short for "Pillsbury Dough-boy," of course.)

"The Buckmeister, Buck-man, Buckeramadingdong, Buckerino!" Franklin called in reply. This brought a chuckle from his wife Debbie, and a roll of the eyes and low groan from Ellie Pence. As they drew closer, Buck became self-conscious about the absurd spectacle the body of his brother presented; it was practically standing up in the wheelchair, and lashed into place with clothesline. He felt bad that anybody he knew saw the body of his brother in such a state.

Then Buck got a look at what Franklin was pushing; a large garden cart with a body draped over it, limbs splayed awkwardly apart. They had stretched a tarp of some kind over the top of the body, secured by bungee cords, but hands and feet had worked their way from underneath the covering. Buck realized that there were probably a lot of people in town doing just what they had to do, and dignity for the dearly departed was a fairly rare commodity at the moment.

"Who?" Buck inquired, gesturing at the tarp.

"Ellie's husband, Robert," Debbie Franklin replied.

"Oh, Ellie, I'm so sorry," Buck said. Ellie Pence smiled slightly and nodded in reply. She was putting up a good front, but Buck could tell the loss of her husband bothered her more than she would ever admit. Debbie rested her soft hand on Ellie's forearm; Ellie flinched slightly, but let it remain.

Discovering they had the same destination, they merged their groups and became a strange little parade, headed for Hanson's Funeral Home. As they walked, a song by *The Doors* called, "The Soft Parade" started playing in Pillsbury Franklin's head. He and Buck had both loved *The Doors* when they were young. Pillsbury Franklin still loved The Doors, despite the somewhat dark and desperate tone of their music, and he suspected Buck Schneider still loved them as well. The song went like this:

Successful hills are here to stay
Everything must be this way
Gentle streets where people play
Welcome to the Soft Parade

All our lives we sweat and save
Building for a shallow grave
Must be something else we say
Somehow to defend this place
Everything must be this way
Everything must be this way, yeah
The Soft Parade has now begun
Listen to the engines hum

For much of the trip to the funeral home, Franklin pondered what attributes a hill must possess in order to declare that it had become "successful." Strange brains tend to focus on things like that. It makes the owners of those brains both endearing and slightly frightening.

CHAPTER TEN

Funny how some things just stick with you.

Chick Baxter has a recurring dream where he is the grave-digger in the classic Lon Chaney, Jr. horror film, *The Wolf Man*. He sees himself standing by a grave, shovel in hand, smoking a pipe. He looks up and sees the Wolf Man coming at him; the pipe falls out of his mouth and he drops the shovel just as the monster springs at him. Then he wakes up.

Chick Baxter did not smoke a pipe, but he did dig graves, though not much of that work was done by hand these days. He had seen the werewolf movie when he was a kid, and it had scared the bejeebers out of him. Now he owned the DVD of *The Wolf Man* and he watched it every Halloween. He still loved the way the movie scared him more than any other, despite the fact that the special effects were primitive by today's standards.

Even now, as an adult (of sorts) he would not venture outside when the moon was full, not even to take out the garbage to the burning barrel behind his house. In his head, he knew there was no such thing as werewolves. Probably. But he tended to see one behind every tree that cast its shadows in his yard when the moon was full. Instead of the fear disappearing as he grew older, his dread of the full moon had actually grown more intense with the passing years. Go figure.

When the dream woke him up, he dragged himself out of bed. He was groggy, and he had a headache. He went into the bathroom, flipped on the light switch. Nothing. He relieved himself, and then went to the sink to splash some water on his face. He turned the faucet, but nothing came out. No big deal. Personal hygiene was something he bothered with only on occasion, anyhow.

He had been the caretaker for the Cemetery of St. Benedict of Reluctant for 17 years. It was a crummy job, but it paid the bills. And he didn't have to wear a stupid tie or worry about what he smelled like every morning.

Shuffling into the kitchen in his well-worn boxers and coffee-stained wife-beater t-shirt, he grabbed three aspirin tablets and washed them down with a little "hair of the dog," a swig of Southern Comfort. He took a second drag for good measure, and snagged a fairly clean bowl out of the dirty dishes piled in the sink.

He grabbed his box of Corn Pops and filled the bowl to the rim; he was thankful that the milk was still pretty cold. Chick Baxter was hooked on *Sugar Pops* (that's what they called them back then) when he was a kid. On TV in the 1960s, a little prairie dog would lasso the cereal and sing about how good it was, and Chick believed him. Now they were called, *Corn Pops* so people would think they were better for you than they were years ago. They weren't. Chick knew that and didn't care. He ate Sugar Pops every morning. Or Corn Pops. Whatever.

Chick Baxter did not feel bad about eating a kids' cereal every day. Lots of macho guys ate kids' cereal. He had read a newspaper article a while back which said that Joe Girardi, who managed the New York Yankees, still ate Captain Crunch every day. Girardi had gotten totally hooked on the stuff when a train had derailed next to a field on his grandfather's farm, dumping cases of Captain Crunch that the workers simply left behind. This manna from the gods of sugary cereal had supplied breakfast for Girardi and his siblings for over a year. Being a Cardinal fan, Baxter had no use for the

Yankees. However, he would be quite pleased if a freight car of Sugar Pops tipped over in his back yard.

The last kernel of cereal was eluding the spoon that was quivering erratically in his hand, so he just picked up the bowl and swept it into his mouth with the cereal-flavored milk. (The milk at the end was the best part of the Sugar Pops experience, in Chick's opinion.) He put down the bowl and lit a Camel (no filter) and took a couple of heavy drags. Then, cigarette dangling from his mouth, he shuffled back into the bedroom and put on yesterday's shirt and this month's overalls, along with this week's socks and his work boots. Shuffling back to the kitchen, he stuck a fresh pint of Southern Comfort in a deep pocket of his overalls and headed out the door.

The caretaker's house came with the job; it was right next door to the cemetery for which he was responsible. Baxter walked down the gravel drive to the guard shack near the entrance to the graveyard. He went inside and opened all the windows. Reflexively, he flicked the switch on the radio, and then cursed under his breath when he was reminded by the lack of response that there was still no electricity available. On the other hand, no phone and no computer meant a low probability of his being annoyed during the day, and that was fine by him. He didn't like the computer anyway and only used it when forced to do so.

Chick grabbed his straw hat and a chair and set up camp in the shade cast by the guard shack. He tipped his hat over his eyes, leaned the chair back against the wall, and began his customary late-morning siesta.

Some time later, he awoke to the sound of footsteps…a lot of them… crunching down the gravel driveway. He lifted his straw hat to see a small flock of nuns, five of them, with about a dozen old people and 3 or 4 teenagers. Three of the nuns were carrying shovels.

Just what in Sam Hill did they think they were doing??

● ● ●

Listen:

In the general vicinity of Our Lady of Perpetual Sorrows Hospital, it was a common sight to see nuns, usually in groups of two or three, walking around the neighborhood. If it was daylight and not raining, you would usually spot a nun or two while you drove through the area. This was a special treat in the 21st century, as nuns were fast-becoming an endangered species.

This particular morning, Dana Crisp, the chief of the Almost Police Department, was pedaling her bicycle toward the hospital, to check in with the cops who were on duty there. Along the way, she had passed eight or nine nuns. It was unusual to see that many out at one time; also, some of them were standing on the front porches of neighboring houses, knocking on doors or chatting with the residents. Dana Crisp wondered what they were up to.

As the police chief rode past the Cemetery of St. Benedict of Reluctant, which was across the street from the hospital, she noticed a small crowd near the caretaker's shack, and she could hear voices being raised, though she could not make out what was being said. She wheeled her bike in a quick u-turn and quickly rode back toward the entrance to the graveyard.

● ● ●

Sister Mary Margaret Marion walked down the gravel drive toward the graveyard with four of her sisters and a number of family members of those who had died in the hospital in the prior 24 hours or so. This small crowd was hoping to give their loved ones a fairly decent burial before their bodies began to generate an overwhelming stench. Sister Mary Margaret Marion had sent a number of the more elderly nuns into the neighborhood; they were going door-to-door to borrow additional shovels and to hopefully recruit volunteers to assist in digging the graves. As they approached the guard shack, she saw that Chick Baxter had just awoken with a start.

"Good morning, Mr. Baxter!" Sister Mary Margaret Marion said cheerfully. Chick's face scrunched up; he was obviously perplexed and most certainly hung over. She answered his unspoken question. "We have come to bury some friends and family."

"You…what?!" Baxter replied. "Sister, you can't just come in here and bury people!"

Sister Mary Margaret Marion paused briefly, smiling broadly. "This *is* a graveyard, isn't it, Mr. Baxter?"

Now he was ticked. "Yeah, but there are *rules*, you know that. You have to own your burial plot. All burials require the approval of two trustees. And there are county ordinances about the manner of burial. You can't just slap a dead body in the ground here."

Sister Mary Margaret Marion adopted a more business-like tone to her voice. "Mr. Baxter, we have no choice. There are twenty-three bodies at the hospital that need to be buried quickly. Under current conditions, these families have no reasonable means for seeing that their loved ones can be buried properly."

"And that's a shame, Sister, it really is," Baxter replied. "But I still can't let you do this. I'm sorry, but if I let you do this, I will lose my job." (Suddenly the job which Chick Baxter held in great disdain just moments before had become the most important thing in the world to him.)

Sister Mary Margaret Marion's voice grew harsh. "These bodies represent a considerable threat to the public health. They are a hazard to the patients we are caring for in the hospital even as we speak. We must bury the bodies here, and we must do it today, and that's all there is to it."

"Listen, lady," Baxter was practically yelling now, as the situation had him thoroughly frightened and angry on several levels. "Maybe you're the Queen of Sheba over at the hospital, but last time I checked, you don't call the shots on this side of the street!" The caretaker's face was red now, and veins were bulging in his forehead. He took a threatening step forward toward the nun. A couple of the older men moved from out of the crowd toward the center of the conflict. Though they were in their 70s, they were not about to let any harm come to the nun who was trying to get their loved ones a decent burial.

• • •

Listen:

Napoleon Bonaparte was considered the founding father of short man syndrome. He was also a military genius who liked to stick his hand in his shirt, especially for portraits. Despite these oddities, he was considered a brilliant politician and motivator of human beings. Go figure! Among the intelligent things he said was this: "Men are moved by two levers only: fear and self-interest."

At the moment, Chick Baxter was motivated by self-interest. The job he had been loathing just a few moments before was suddenly more valuable than a whole train full of Corn Pops and Southern Comfort. He felt like he was being attacked by a little werewolf in a black and gray dress. (Not that Sister Mary Margaret Marion was hairy, by any means. While she may well have sported a uni-brow of sorts in her youth, and may well battle dark facial hair on her upper lip when she gets older, she was a pretty woman who did not resemble a werewolf in any way.) However, at the moment, Chick Baxter was terrified by her assertiveness, she was the werewolf, and he was the victim, frozen with fear.

In fact, both the nun and the caretaker were at the mercy of their innermost fears, and both were frightened and angry enough to do stupid things. Large numbers of dead bodies represented the chaos and carnage of Sister Mary Margaret Marion's youth. In the desperate corner of her mind, these bodies must be buried quickly; order must be maintained. She did not want the living hell she experienced in Bosnia to resurface in America, where she had come to know great peace. She was not going to let a drunken caretaker stand between her and keeping the situation as orderly as possible. Her fears simply would not permit it.

There were a couple of other ingredients you could add to this potential recipe for a small and quirky disaster. A lovely cocktail of Chick Baxter's self-loathing, in-bred disrespect for authority, and Southern Comfort was washing over what remained of his brain cells. Thus, to Chick Baxter, a fist fight with a pack of nuns and a couple of gnarly old men seemed like a perfectly reasonable way to spend a lovely spring afternoon.

As it so happened, the two old guys who were moving toward confrontation with Chick Baxter were veterans of the Korean War. It was a shame that their war was not very sexy or marketable, and got little air time on the History Channel. These men were just as brave and capable as the generation before them, but had not received the acclamation of their elders. Had they been eight or ten years older, they could have been part of the *Greatest Generation* that had conquered evil Nazi Germany. Tom Brokaw would have written a book about them.

The leaders of the opposing forces in Korea were not memorable maniacs, and the enemy troops did not have cool uniforms or collectible flags and hand-guns. The Korean conflict generated shrugs of indifference from most people, if they even knew it existed at all. M*A*S*H was the only thing that most folks knew about Korea (and many people thought M*A*S*H was about Vietnam, which it sort-of was), and the TV show lasted three times as long as the conflict itself. Even the negative spotlight of Vietnam might have been preferable to the obscurity of being a Korean War vet.

If he had been present (and non-fictional), Idaho Jenkins would say that, like the planet Pluto, those two Korean War vets would be entitled to a nasty inferiority complex about the defining events of their lives. Thus, an improbable victory over a drunken caretaker could offer them a shot at one last gasp of glory! It was nowhere near as cool as a German luger or a Nazi helmet displayed on a book shelf in your study, but in this life, you take what you can get.

To an outside observer, it would have appeared to be a pretty ridiculous conflict, but to the nuns, the drunk and the old people it was serious business. The strange circumstances of the power outage had planted an icy fear deep in their hearts, and when people (even nice people) are afraid, they get mean. Things were still in the shouting and shoving stage when the shriek of Dana Crisp's police whistle pierced the chaos.

"Stand down, all of you!!!" She shouted with authority. "Calm down and back off *now*, unless you want a face-full of Mace!"

Dana Crisp could not imagine using Mace on nuns and old people, but it seemed like the thing to say at the time. No one wanted the Mace. The police chief decided to give the key players the chance to tell their sides of the story. She drew Chick Baxter and Sister Mary Margaret Marion slightly away from the crowd and gave them the opportunity to vent a bit. Most of the crowd could hear the conversation that followed.

"Officer, I'm glad you're here," Baxter said. "Explain to this....*lady*...that there are ordinances to be followed here!" Baxter gave the chief a long list of reasons why the nun should be turned away from the graveyard, and perhaps even arrested for her activities.

After a few moments, having had his say, Baxter had calmed down. Sister Mary Margaret Marion had listened attentively and respectfully, and waited for Chief Crisp to tell her when it was time for her to speak.

"Chief Crisp," Sister Mary Margaret Marion said calmly, "And Mr. Baxter. Ordinances and trustees are marvelous things under ordinary circumstances, and they should be honored whenever possible. But, let me ask both of you; do you consider our current circumstances to be ordinary?"

There was silence for a few seconds, and then she spoke again softly. "Chick, Dana...there are twenty-three bodies in that hospital that, without benefit of embalming or refrigeration, pose an immediate health hazard to over a hundred patients that remain in the building. Without the availability of life support machinery, we may have a dozen more deaths by tomorrow morning. Perhaps we will have even more gunshot victims tonight than last night… perhaps *many* more. We must stay ahead of this issue or we will all pay a heavy price for our failure to act while we can."

As she considered the nun's words, Almost Police Chief Dana Crisp thought about what the mayor had said earlier in the day. He had said that, if necessary, ordinances must be set aside to allow businesses to function and to restore some degree of normalcy under such frightening circumstances. Surely this same principle would apply to the situation in the cemetery.

"Let's help them bury the bodies, Chick," Dana Crisp told the caretaker respectfully. "The city will accept responsibility for the situation. If the trustees give you trouble, tell them I was going to arrest you if you did not comply. If necessary, the city will move the bodies to another location later, when things get back to normal."

Everyone within earshot of the police chief responded to this last statement with an unspoken thought; "*If* things ever get back to normal." No one said it out loud, though.

"Sister, do you have permission from all of the families of the deceased to bury them in this fashion?" Crisp asked the nun.

"I do," Sister Mary Margaret Marion nodded, "with two exceptions. Two young gunshot victims are as yet identified. Both of them were dumped at the emergency room door and neither had identification on their person. Sister Immaculata, one of our novices, is an exceptionally talented artist. She has drawn remarkable portraits of the two young men in the hope that we can eventually connect them to their families." It had been a moving experience for Sister Mary Margaret Marion to watch as the young nun, a girl in her early twenties, painstakingly drew the peaceful faces of the two dead young men. It had truly been a labor of love. Their likenesses were captured perfectly, she thought.

By this time, the little crowd by the caretaker's shack had nearly doubled in size. The elderly nuns' efforts to recruit additional volunteers and shovels were obviously bearing fruit. "All right then, let's get this show on the road," said Dana Crisp. "Chick, please show these good people to the spots that you think are the least likely to disrupt things around here...plots that have not yet been sold, hopefully."

Baxter was still grumpy, even though he was relieved of all responsibility for what was happening. "We'll go over to the far end of the cemetery, Sister, by the chain link fence on the far side there. None of that area has been sold yet."

"Thank you, Mr. Baxter...Chick," Sister Mary Margaret Marion said warmly, cradling both his hands in hers. She looked into his eyes with great sincerity. "God bless you for your help, and for being so patient with me. You have been very kind."

Baxter had not been kind or patient; the crowd knew it, and so did Baxter. But her touch and her sincerity brought tears to the caretaker's eyes, and to the eyes of several who were watching the scene. "Well, Sister," he gulped the words past the lump in his throat. "Just glad to be of help." He grabbed a couple of shovels from the shed, tossed one to a teenager in the crowd, and started toward the spot he had indicated a moment before. Providing leadership was something Chick Baxter rarely experienced, and he was relished the moment. "C'mon, folks," he said with unaccustomed authority, "Let's get started!" A number of people from the small crowd called out words of thanks and encouragement to the caretaker as he started across the grass.

Sister Mary Margaret Marion turned and placed her hand on Dana Crisp's forearm, squeezing gently. As Dana looked at the nun's face, Sister Mary Margaret Marion gave her a pleasant smile and a wink. "The woman always seems to find a way to get what she needs to get the job done," Dana Crisp thought to herself.

The small crowd chatted and laughed as they walked through the grass toward the far side of the cemetery.

• • •

When Buck Schneider and his friends arrived at the Hanson Funeral Home, they found many other folks had used various means to transport the bodies of loved ones to the mortuary as well. Ed Hanson gathered them all together, and explained the situation. Embalming and customary funeral arrangements were beyond his capacity to deliver, so they were all going to have to work together quickly to get the corpses in the ground before they began to decay and overwhelm the area with their odor. Those who had previously purchased burial plots and had family members capable of digging graves were encouraged to proceed directly to the cemetery and get their loved ones' remains into the ground. Ed Hanson offered his storage facility as a temporary haven for those without a clear game plan, but cautioned them that they would need to retrieve the corpses soon, within a matter of hours.

Some of the families of the deceased weighed the possibility of burying their loved ones in their own yards, at least for the time-being. The whole thing had a feel of unreality. The people gathered in the parking lot of Hanson's Funeral Home simply could not believe this was happening was actually happening. But it was.

Ellie Pence knew that Robert had purchased cemetery plots in the Almost City Cemetery, which was on the other side of town. Buck, on the other hand, did not know what arrangements Bud and Julie might have made for his brother's remains. He did not think Bud had yet purchased cemetery plots, but he was far from certain. Buck elected to store the wheelchair and his brother in Ed Hanson's garage until he could get to his sister-in-law and discuss the alternatives with her.

Pillsbury and Debbie Franklin agreed to help Ellie get Robert's body to the cemetery, and, once there, to get him buried. They selected a route that would swing them by Ellie's house to collect a couple of shovels for the grim task. Buck decided to accompany them for the first mile or so, and then he would split off from the group and move toward Julie's house. Buck and Pillsbury agreed to meet at Buck's store in the early evening to compare notes and contemplate future moves.

One by one, the little groups that had assembled on the parking lot of Hanson's Funeral Home began to trickle away in various directions. As he watched them go, Ed Hanson felt empty and helpless. He wondered to himself if death would ever again become business as usual. If not, he wondered what the future would hold for the Hanson family, for whom, over several generations, death had been a way of life.

• • •

It was about sunset when Rod "Blackie" Blackmon pulled on a small backpack that was loaded with ammunition and a pair of extra handguns. He manually closed his garage door, then picked up his rifle and headed into the house. He was excited to get to the Schneider Brothers Corner Grocery Store soon and begin the night's adventure. As he passed through the living room, he saw himself in the large mirror above the fireplace. He looked good in his black t-shirt, black jeans and black ball cap. As he stared at his reflection, he drew his .38 revolver from the shoulder holster and held the barrel up to his lips. He blew some imaginary gun smoke from the pistol, and then gave the mirror a steely glare.

"Case closed, Toots!" Blackie said.

CHAPTER ELEVEN

isten:

It was another season.

I saw my second ghost the day after the thing went thump in the sky.

It was an early morning, and a mist was rising lazily from the spring grass. I was walking down Martin Luther King Drive when I saw a dark, distinguished figure up ahead. He was leaning against a telephone pole, thoughtfully smoking a cigarette. As I drew closer, I thought the man strongly resembled Martin Luther King himself. When I was within ten feet of him, I realized he *was* Martin Luther King, though he was kind of a shimmery, similar to what you might see on an old black and white TV with poor reception. (This was the only way I ever saw Martin Luther King when he was alive, come to think of it.)

"Nice morning," I said to the ghost.

Dr. Martin Luther King turned and smiled. "Yes, it is," he said quietly.

"So, what brings you to Almost, sir? Have you ever been here before?"

"No," replied the ghost. "But the man who shot me lived here for a time."

"Mmmmm," I said. "Is that why you're here?"

"No," he took a deep drag from his supernatural cigarette and blew smoke very casually through his intangible nose. "I get curious about streets which bear my name." He lit a new cigarette with the butt of the old one.

"I didn't know you smoked, sir," I said.

"Most people didn't know about that," Martin Luther King replied. "I was smoking at the moment I died, in fact. It's a very tough habit to break."

I nodded. After a moment, I asked, "So when you visit, do you just hang out near the street?"

"No," King replied. "Generally, I will visit a nearby church. I plan to go to that one up the hill there on Sunday morning. No one will be able to see me, of course. You're the first person who has seen me in years."

"Is that an African-American church?" I asked.

His hand was moving his cigarette toward his mouth when he stopped mid-motion and gave me a sideways glance through narrowed eyes. "I look forward to the day," said King, "when churches are just churches, and don't feel the need to add a label to identify what color the people inside happen to be."

"I haven't been inside a church since I was a kid," I replied. "I don't know who's inside any of them. Most of the people that go to them don't seem to practice what they preach."

King paused for a moment and said, "Most churches have a strange division between the sacred and the secular. People lead one life inside the church and a different one outside. In daily life, they trust scientific power more than spiritual power. Since science is now largely useless; many men feel useless as well. For twenty years or more, American life has been a quest for easy answers and half-baked solutions. There will be no easy answers in the coming days."

"Wow," I said quietly. "So is this the end of everything?"

"Not necessarily. Unarmed truth and unconditional love will have the final word in reality," King replied. "If this world is to survive the current crisis, its people must go back and rediscover those precious values - that all reality hinges on moral foundations. God measures men and women not by where they stand in moments of comfort and convenience, but by where they stand in times of challenge."

King tossed his cigarette on the sidewalk and ground it under the toe of his highly polished shoe. "Perhaps this is why these strange things have come about."

"So is God testing us? Did God turn off the electricity?" I asked.

King smiled enigmatically. "Everything we see is a shadow cast by that which we do not see," he said quietly.

I was not sure exactly what he meant by that, but I sensed at that moment that the interview was over. "Thanks so much for spending this time with me," I told Martin Luther King, Jr. "It's getting scary around here."

"Don't lose heart, son. There are good men and women in every town, every church," King replied as his image got snowy and started to break up. "But keeping chaos at bay will require a great deal of sacrifice, suffering, and struggle...and the passionate concern of dedicated individuals."

His figure became a solid black silhouette with a small circle of white light near its heart. After a moment, the shadow faded and disappeared, leaving only the dot of bright light. Then it winked out, and he was completely gone.

I stood on the street for a time, pondering this remarkable encounter. I started walking again, trying to process the information I had just absorbed.

I was two blocks away when a thought came to me. I doubled back to the telephone pole in the hopes of snagging a souvenir of my encounter with history. But when I reached the spot where Martin Luther King, Jr. had been standing, I did not find the cigarette butt I had hoped to collect and to save. In the tall grass around the telephone pole, I found only one object. It was a Mickey Mouse wristwatch. The index fingers on both overstuffed white gloves were pointing to the right side of the watch's face. Mickey Mouse had died at 2:17. The latest version of the American Dream did not survive him.

And so it goes.

CHAPTER TWELVE

Vivian Harrison awoke with a start, her feet splashing cold Epsom salt water onto her living room rug. It was nearly dark outside; she had been exhausted, and had slept most of the day away there on her couch. Her back and neck sent her a painful message that slumping on the couch for ten hours was not a very good idea.

She rose and walked to the wall switch, clicking it up and down. Still no electricity. This was not good, not good at all. How long, she wondered, before people in the city of Almost began to panic and do stupid things? Probably not long, she decided.

The fog in her brain slowly cleared as she wrapped her sore feet in elastic bandages. She decided that she would stop by the Almost Hope Center on her way to the hospital. She wanted to make sure that everything there was okay. That way, when she arrived at Bobby Anthony's bedside, she could assure him that the charity he loved was safe and sound.

Vivian Harrison took a moment to make sure there was food and water for *Aretha*, the cat she loved for no discernable reason. She made sure that, when the cranky cat decided to reappear, she would have what she needed. As she stepped out into the twilight and locked her door, she mentally added another brief stop to the itinerary for her trek toward the hospital.

• • •

Joe Kelly's Famous Grill and Bar had closed shortly after the sky had thumped, and bartender/waitress Kayla Ellis had been at her apartment ever since. She arrived home to find Darius, her eight-year-old son, safe but bored out of his mind. Without his X-Box, he was a completely lost soul. Her younger son, Micah, was only two; he had been gone for over a week and was staying with his daddy's new family in Indianapolis. Kayla had slept little that night; she wondered if the strange things happening in Almost were also happening in Indiana (they were) and she worried about her tiny son's safety. She was thrilled when, the following morning, her BFF (best friend forever), Christy Farmer had shown up at the apartment to crash with her for a few days. Gossiping and laughing with Christy would help keep her mind off the emotional chaos of her situation.

It was late in the afternoon when Kayla sat in a lawn chair in front of her apartment, smoking a cigarette. Christy was asleep; she had arrived on the brink of exhaustion. Darius was inside, actually *reading a book* by the light of the window. Kayla's aunt had given Darius a *Hardy Boys* mystery for Christmas last year. At the time, Darius could barely conceal his disgust for such a worthless gift. Now, he was totally engrossed in *The Tower Treasure*. Well, at least that was one thing she could be thankful for in her current circumstances.

As she smoked her cigarette, Kayla thought, as she occasionally did, about her unusual friendship with Christy Franklin. They had come from totally different worlds; Kayla had never met her father, and her mother had consoled herself with a vast assortment of damaged men and crummy places to live. A couple of her mom's men were half-decent father-figures, at least briefly. Others had elected to share their own damage by abusing her, sexually and emotionally.

Kayla began numbing the pain at an early age with pot, alcohol and sex. She had grown up envying girls like Christy Farmer, who had two parents and lived in one house the whole time they were growing up. She despised her mother's lifestyle, yet found herself paying it homage by adopting it as her own. Kayla desperately longed for her own house and a husband who would be a decent father to her sons, but she had no idea how to get there from her current location. Life was not in the habit of providing a GPS for women like Kayla Ellis.

Christy Farmer had been journeying in the opposite direction. She gradually left behind the world that Kayla Ellis longed for, but their paths intersected as waitresses at Joe Kelly's Famous Grill and Bar. They were both very attractive, and they loved going out together because they got a lot of attention from guys in various bars.

In the early days of their friendship, they had spent many nights, drunk and/or high, complaining about their lives and families. When Kayla had finally met Christy's parents, she was shocked. They were a little odd and old-fashioned, to be sure, but Kayla thought Christy's home looked a lot like the normal life that she had always dreamed of.

As time went on, Kayla watched in grim fascination as Christy self-inflicted the same sorts of damage that had been central to Kayla's life. Christy seemed drawn to dysfunction like a moth to a bug-zapper. Kayla, on the other hand, was more aware of her danger, and was struggling against the zapper's terrible magnetism, staring out into the darkness in a desperate search for an alternative source of light.

As she lit another cigarette, Kayla began thinking about what they would eat for dinner. The stuff in the refrigerator was almost warm, so she decided to barbecue all the meat she had on hand. How long would the power be gone? Forever? She had enough food in the pantry to eat poorly for a week, maybe two. She thought about all the food they routinely threw away each night at Joe Kelly's Famous Grill and Bar. What a waste. All that food, just thrown away.... and soon, she and her son may not have enough food to stay alive.

After finishing her cigarette, Kayla dumped some charcoal into her BBQ kettle. As she was getting the fire going, Darius came out and asked if he could go to a friend's house for a while. Kayla was apprehensive about letting him out of her sight, but Darius' friend Shane Drake lived only a block away, and his mother, Jamie, was a good woman and she was home. She decided that letting him go would make things seem a little more normal, so she reluctantly agreed.

She watched her son as he made his way down the street. He walked and moved just like his father, even though the creep was long gone by the time he was born. How is that possible? How is that even fair? The man had nothing invested in this boy beyond a tiny amount of body fluid. And here was her son looking and moving just *like* the deadbeat.

In an ideal world, his father's DNA would have faded away when it was not accompanied by his love and commitment. If life were fair, there would not be a trace of the man visible in the boy he had abandoned. By all rights, Kayla thought to herself, Darius should look like me…or at least like a mixture of the people in his life who truly care about him. That's not how it is, though.

Her son would always be a painful reminder of the cruel betrayal she had experienced, but she knew she loved the boy more than was good for her, and she always would. She would not trade Darius for anything in the world…not even a shot at true romance.

As the evening shadows grew, Kayla Ellis stood alone on the sidewalk, barbecuing hamburgers and waiting for Christy Farmer to wake up. She hoped she had enough charcoal to cook all the meat she had in the freezer.

● ● ●

It was around dusk when Pillsbury Franklin coasted his wife's bicycle into the parking lot of Schneider Brothers Corner Grocery Store. He knew there was trouble afoot the instant he set eyes on the two men sitting on the retaining wall near the rear of the building.

"Hey, Franklin, nice bike!" Blackie Blackmon called out, holding his beer bottle high in a salute. It was readily apparent that the beer in his hand was far from his first.

Of far more concern was that Buck Schneider also had a bottle of beer in hand. And his laughter was punctuated by funny little snorts; he always laughed that way when he had had too much to drink. Trouble with Buck was that, once he started drinking, he had a lot of trouble stopping. Once he started drinking, he usually could not stop for years.

Before his bicycle coasted to a stop, Pillsbury Franklin had already reflected on the past damage Buck had inflicted when he was drinking… and he was now dreading the new danger his old friend presented to himself and others. Pillsbury hated to be put in this position; how could he express his valid concerns for his friend without coming off as a self-righteous stick-in-the-mud?

Franklin pulled the bike to a stop just below the dangling feet of the two men. "Well, it beats walking!" Pillsbury replied with as much good humor as he could muster. "And the basket comes in handy. And what are you two knuckleheads up to?"

"We are doing what's right by America…by drinking these fine American beers while they are still kinda cold," Buck said. He was doing his John Wayne imitation, which was above-average. "It's a tough job, pilgrim, but somebody's gotta do it."

"Mmmmm," Franklin nodded. "Not so sure Officer Everwood is going to appreciate the shape you two are in when he gets here."

"Ha!" Blackie exclaimed. "He's been here and gone! Said we had to choose between having our beer and having him help us guard the store."

"We chose the beer!" Buck said, and the two men burst into another round of laughter.

Despite the weight of his concerns, Pillsbury Franklin could not help but laugh with them; until tears were rolling down his cheeks, in fact. He laughed not so much because the men were funny, but more because it felt so good to do so…and because he did not know when he might have the opportunity to laugh so hard again.

• • •

It had been the kind of time she always wished for, but never seemed to get. Ellie Pence had spent the afternoon puttering around her garden and the yard, without annoyance or distraction. The only sounds she heard during daylight were the children playing up the street and the sound of chirping birds; the only sounds in the evening were crickets and tree frogs. She sat for a while on the front porch, sipping herbal tea, and noticed the first lightning bug of the year. It was only the second week of May, so this firefly had made its debut a few weeks earlier than usual. She finally went inside when the mosquitoes became unbearable.

When she went inside, she realized that, though the last few hours had been pleasant, she had been carrying a lingering emptiness deep within that she had not quite managed to deny. Inside the house, denial of any kind was not possible. The emptiness exploded from her heart and head as quiet desperation. The dim light shining through the large windows revealed a large, old-fashioned living room that could seat ten people in antique splendor. Rarely, she realized, had there been more than four people in the room. Most of the time it had been just her and Robert. And now, Robert was gone.

Ellie suddenly realized that the perfect day she had always wished for, the day without his interruptions and annoying habits, carried a terrible price tag when the sun was gone. Ellie Pence was alone in the room. She was also alone in the vast, silent world that lay outside the room.

The furniture was all pointed at the TV, of course. *Joey*, a character on *Friends* (her favorite TV show) had pointed out that every home must have a TV, because without it, there would be nothing to point the furniture at. As

Ellie Pence stood in her moonlit living room, she realized that her best *Friends* were not just *on* TV…they included the TV itself. Ellie's TV, her best friend in the whole wide world, had died.

And so it goes.

The death of this device was a deep and personal loss, and it felt like it was hers alone…if felt that way for millions of other people at this moment in time.

Ellie wondered if TV, and the simulated companionship that came with it, would ever return. She decided that, even if the power never came back on, her TV would always remain right where it was, as the focal point of her living room. Though dark and lifeless, in her subconscious the TV represented her best future hope for a meaningful relationship.

● ● ●

It was just after dark, and Robert Anthony III sat in a folding chair on the front porch of the converted house that was the Almost Hope Center. Within easy reach was a baseball bat. His grandfather had been the best of men, who had taught him many things of great value, and he would always be grateful for that. At the moment, however, Robert wished that "avoiding guns at all costs" was not one of his grandfather's guiding principles.

Robert, known as *Three* to most friends and family, was determined that no harm should come to the Almost Hope Center, the charity to which his grandfather had been so dedicated. When he was five-years-old, his father, Robert Anthony, Jr., left home. Three never saw him again. Shortly after that, his mother was killed in a car accident. The day she died was the worst day of his life, but being raised by his grandparents was probably the best thing that ever happened to him.

And so it goes.

His grandfather had died in the hospital yesterday because the machine that was keeping him alive had died. Had he been able to make it just another day or two, there was a strong chance he would have recovered completely. Now he was gone. What a waste of a great man. The man had died, but Three would make sure his legacy, the Almost Hope Center, would survive the current chaos, even if its founding father did not. The Center had experienced a number of break-ins in the past, and with the alarm system useless, its storehouse of food and emergency supplies would be an attractive target if things got crazy in Almost. And if things weren't back to normal soon, Three knew that crazy was coming soon.

Three moved forward in his chair. To his right, he heard a strange sound, a sort of rumbling in the distance that seemed to be drawing closer. Then, from the corner of his eye, he saw movement to his left. A solitary figure was visible in the moonlight, and it was walking toward him rapidly. The fingers of Three's left hand wrapped around his baseball bat and he waited to see what would happen next.

• • •

Plenty of volunteers came to the Cemetery of St. Benedict of Reluctant to help dig the graves that were needed for the bodies that lay in the hospital across the street. Once the digging was underway, Sister Mary Margaret Marion and the other nuns returned to the hospital. Some resumed caring for the patients; the rest assisted the families in preparing the bodies of their loved ones for burial. They lovingly washed the bodies, styled their hair, and in many cases, dressed them in an outfit brought from home for the occasion.

Around sunset, a strange parade left the hospital; gurneys and stretchers with the bodies of over two dozen dead. The nuns, each carrying a candle, began singing and moving in rhythm as they worked their way across the huge hospital parking lot. Relatives and friends of the deceased, as well as recently recruited volunteers, all joined in the singing when they knew the words. The parade wound across the street, weaving among stalled cars, and down the gravel drive that led into the graveyard.

One by one, the bodies were gently lowered on sheets into the ground. A few words were said over each grave, and then a nun, a priest or a minister said a prayer or read a Bible verse. As one or two people hung back to cover each body with dirt, the rest of the crowd proceeded to the next grave. Everyone present, including many of the volunteers, stayed for every burial, regardless of whether or not they knew the person. It was a strange and beautiful evening.

After the last grave was closed, the crowd gathered in a circle, held hands, and those who were comfortable doing so offered prayers for their city, the nation and the world. When they were done, people milled around and talked until well after dark, and then gradually began trickling toward their homes, guided by the light of the full moon.

Chick Baxter had not touched his bottle of Southern Comfort all day, and even as he walked home, he did not feel the urge to do so. He glanced up at the full moon and chuckled to himself. Only once did he see a shadow behind a tree that gave him brief cause for concern.

• • •

Three's visitor at the Almost Hope Center turned out to be Vivian Harrison, who wept at the news that Bobby Anthony had died. Three had known Vivian all of his life, and he had never seen this side of her. She was a woman who seemed to be chiseled out of granite, and was a rock that many people relied upon. Seeing her cry was sad and wonderful at the same time. Watching her grieve for his grandfather validated his own grief.

The rumbling noise, still at a distance in the darkness, continued to grow louder. Three saw some shadowy figures on the street at the top of the hill. There appeared to be four men, and they were each pulling something behind them. Whatever they were pulling was the source of the rumbling noise.

"Robert, what are those people doing?" Vivian asked him. (Vivian was one of the few people who knew him well who did not call him, "Three.")

"I don't know, Miss Vivian," Three replied. "But I think we will find out pretty soon."

• • •

Pillsbury Franklin had finally convinced his two plastered friends to agree to his plan. Buck was sleeping it off in an SUV parked near the door of the Schneider Brothers Corner Grocery Store. Blackie was snoring softly as he lay in a sleeping bag up the hill a ways. Franklin himself was sitting in a foxhole just downhill from Blackie's position. Franklin was keeping the first watch, and he was to alert the others if he sensed anything suspicious around the store. He was hoping that the night would be uneventful; he had no intention of waking his two companions unless it was absolutely necessary.

Pillsbury Franklin had a rifle in the foxhole with him. He had not wanted the rifle, but his friends would not agree to his plan unless he accepted the weapon. And his foxhole...well, it wasn't really a foxhole, not exactly. It was actually the beginning of the hole that was to become Bud Schneider's grave. Bud's wife, Julie had decided that he should be buried at the store, near the hydrangea bushes that he loved so much. Buck had wheeled Bud's body back from the funeral home to the store, and had started to dig the grave, but ran out of steam just about the time that Blackie arrived and convinced him that a cold beer was just what he needed after such hot and sweaty work.

The hydrangea blossoms were a mixture of pink and blue, mostly pink, and were especially full and colorful this year. Pillsbury read once that the color of the flower shifted according to the amount of aluminum in the soil. When aluminum was added to the soil, pink blooms turned blue. The average human body, Franklin knew, contained 50 to 150 mg of aluminum. He wondered if the aluminum in Bud Schneider's body would be enough to turn the nearby bushes completely blue, once the earth had digested him and his remains became plant food for the hydrangeas he loved so much.

These strange thoughts, along with other stray observations and plot ideas, circulated through the Pillsbury Franklin's off-beat mind as the night progressed.

Around midnight, he was thinking about a novel he had recently completed called, *Love Your Neighbor.* He had been shopping it around for a publisher for several months without success. The basic idea was that God planted angels (disguised as humans) in communities around the world to see how ordinary people would react to someone who obeyed God completely and without question.

The plot centered on an angel named *Burt* who posed as a minister in a small Midwestern town called "Lovely." His congregation and people in his subdivision reacted violently to Burt's generous and ethical behavior, and eventually formed themselves into a lynch mob. When they dragged Burt to the edge of town and tried to string him up, Burt turned them all into pillars of salt and then disappeared.

Most of the remaining citizens of Lovely wanted to turn the scene of the lynching into a tourist attraction called, *Morton's Garden of the Gone.* (They hoped to line up the makers of Morton Salt as a major sponsor of the project.) Plans included an amusement park with various barf-inducing rides based on biblical plagues. However, after a couple of good rains, the salty, former humans were less recognizable as such, and the townspeople were concerned they would melt away completely before a profit could be turned.

The people of Lovely briefly considered equipping each of the saline statues with its own umbrella, an idea which would dovetail nicely with the plan for corporate sponsorship. This notion was discarded because it would not be sufficient to prevent the eventual erosion of the main attraction. So the town of Lovely invited some Chinese import/export executives to town, and through them arranged for the remains of the petrified crowd to be shipped back to China so they could be sold for outrageous prices as an aphrodisiac.

The people of Lovely took a portion of the profits and erected a monument to Burt, whose outlandishly authentic Christian lifestyle had set the whole chain of events into motion in the first place.

Pillsbury was certain that, once things got back to normal, he was sure he would find a publisher for *Love Your Neighbor* in no time.

• • •

Rick Gage (aka "Mr. Impossible") sat on the balcony outside his second-story bachelor pad. He lived in an apartment complex called *Rivers Edge*. It was on top of a big hill and had a nice view. He was not sure why they called it Rivers Edge, since it was about three miles away from the river.

Gage had not shaved or showered (he had an electric shaver, of course) and his hair was all sticking up, pointing in a variety of directions. He was wearing an old pair of gym shorts and a t-shirt, and had watched as darkness slowly descended on the city, and as the flicker of candles appeared here and there in the cityscape below him. As he enjoyed the evening breeze, he took inventory of the people in his life.

His Mom was living in Florida with...that guy. He last spoke to her on Christmas. Last he had heard, his Dad was in Montana somewhere. His Dad's sister had lived somewhere around Almost at some point...but he had never met her. His Dad always said she was a real witch. Speaking of witches, his ex had remarried and was living in Texas, and had a young daughter with her new guy. He had no other family as far as he knew.

In his world, people at work were just there to provide competition. He flirted with a few of the women. Slept with a couple of them from time to time. Had a beer with the gang sometimes. Chipped in five or ten bucks for the occasional birthday or wedding gift.

Probably he felt the closest to people he ate with at Joe Kelly's Famous Grill and Bar. As he sat in his lawn chair on the balcony, he realized he had no idea where any of them lived or whether they had any family. Except for Kayla Ellis. Gage knew she lived in the same apartment building that he did. She was single, but she had two little kids, which was the primary reason why he had never made moves on her.

He went into his apartment and got his last bag of pita chips, and returned to his lawn chair, eating the chips slowly and deliberately. He had no idea what he was going to do after that. Starting a little before midnight, the sound of a shouting voice or what might be a gunshot would occasionally punctuate the stillness of the night.

• • •

The four men came to the front of the Almost Hope Center, and turned up the driveway toward the converted house. Each of the men was towing a large, plastic trash can on wheels; the large variety that garbage trucks could empty with mechanical arms.

Three walked down the first couple of steps from the front porch of the Center, baseball bat dangling from his left hand. "Hello, gentlemen. What do you need? What are the trash cans for?" Three asked, with as much of a courteous tone as he could muster.

The guy that seemed to be their leader stepped forward in the moonlight. He was a white guy, unshaven but not bearded, with an occasional tooth. Scraggly hair spilled from under a dirty bandana. Three recognized the man as a frequent client of the Center. He was a difficult case who always seemed disrespectful to the volunteers and dissatisfied with the items he received there. Three thought for a moment. *Carter* was the man's name, he recalled.

"You mean these?" Carter grinned broadly, which was not a pretty sight. "These ain't garbage cans, boy! They's *shopping carts!*" Carter and his friends laughed a little. He gestured toward the front door as he spoke. "How bout you hold the door for us while we make a little withdrawal?"

"The Center is closed," said Three, managing to control his anger. "If you come back tomorrow between nine and five, we will see what we can do to help you."

Carter chuckled. "Well, now that just won't do, boy. We is here to stock up on canned goods tonight. We think they might come in handy on a rainy day, you know what I'm sayin'?" The three men in the shadows mumbled and laughed in support of their leader.

"I'm afraid that's not going to happen," Three responded firmly.

"Just you and that bat, you think you'll stop the four of us?" Carter and his friends laughed again. "You might just die trying….boy."

Three grasped the bat with both hands and began to move forward. Vivian's voice came from behind him. "Robert, stop! There's no need for you to take them on." Three stepped back and looked at Vivian while keeping an eye on Carter.

"Well, who do we have here? Whoever it is seems to have a lot more sense than you do, boy!" Carter sneered. "Thank you, ma'am, we are grateful that you are blessed with common sense enough to let us be about our business." Carter and his friends moved forward toward the porch. Three shifted nervously, wondering what Vivian was thinking. He knew she frequently carried a gun in her purse. Was she seriously considering using it in this situation? If so, things could get very wild in short order.

Vivian Harrison moved down from the porch and spoke with confidence. "Gentlemen, there's no need for Robert to take you on, because you are going to leave now, without causing more trouble than you already have."

Carter and his friends laughed again, hard this time. "Zat, right, fat lady? And why, might I ask, would we do that?"

"You'll leave because my son, who just returned from Afghanistan last week, was just a few minutes behind me coming down here. I would guess that he is watching you from cover right now, and probably has you in the sights of his rifle," Vivian replied.

Momentarily taken aback, Carter glanced back at his friends for support, and then recovered his bravado. "Heh. Nice try, fat lady. But I don't think he's anywhere around here. Do you guys?" Carter's three friends grunted their agreement.

Vivian Harrison cleared her throat, and spoke loudly into the darkness. "Albert, if you have this situation under control, would you please make yourself known?"

All six figures in front of the Almost Hope Center froze, and listened intently. There was only silence. Carter smiled broadly and began to move forward. And then stopped short. Out of the darkness came a distinct metallic sound. The sound that the bolt of a rifle makes when it is being thrown into place.

Everyone in front of the Almost Hope Center stood frozen like a statue in the moonlight.

About ten seconds later, visibly shaken even in the dim light, Carter turned and spoke to his men. "Y'know guys, maybe this boy is right. Maybe we should come back tomorrow, when they's open."

"Thanks for your understanding," Three said quietly.

The four rednecks grunted and shuffled quickly back in the direction they had come, leaving the trash cans behind on the driveway of the Center. As he departed, Carter looked back over his shoulder at Three. Three could not see the expression on his face, but he was certain it was not a friendly one.

• • •

It was well after midnight when Pillsbury Franklin caught himself nodding off. He took a drink of bottled water, and then turned his gaze toward the store, to see if everything was still as it should be. There was a full moon that night, though it frequently moved behind the clouds. Still, there was quite a bit of moonlight to see by. Was he mistaken, or did he detect movement near the entrance to the store? As he looked more closely, he became certain of it; there were two shadowy figures near the door; they appeared to be jimmying the lock.

"Hey, there! What do you think you're doing?!!" Franklin yelled at the top of his lungs. The two figures scattered, one darting behind a car on the parking lot, the other running full speed in the opposite direction, down the block and away from the store. To his dismay, Franklin saw that the remaining burglar was hiding behind the car where Buck Schneider lay in drunken slumber. He called out again, "You better get out of here! You're surrounded! We don't want to hurt you, so leave now while you can!"

The shadowy figure rose from behind the car and fired a gun up the hill in Franklin's general direction. Almost immediately there came the sound of a powerful gun from behind Pillsbury. Something slammed him head-first into the soft earth at the front of the fox-hole. He gave a loud grunt of surprise as his face hit the dirt.

"OhGodohGodohGodohGod," Franklin heard a voice from behind him, further up the hill.

• • •

Blackie Blackmon awoke from a deep fog to hear the voice of Pillsbury Franklin yelling something. "Showtime!" he thought excitedly. He stood up from behind the bushes where he had been sleeping and squinted down at the store, trying to see what was going on, raising his rifle as he stood. He heard a gunshot from down near the store, and a bullet whizzed by his left ear, so close he could hear it buzz through the air. His right arm reflexively jerked on the trigger of his rifle, and it went off. He heard a thud, and then the sound of a grunt. The grunt sounded a lot like Pillsbury Franklin. Shaking violently, Blackie Blackmon fell flat on the ground behind the bushes once again.

"OhGodohGodohGodohGod," he said.

• • •

In the back of a Ford Escape near the entrance of the Schneider Brothers Corner Grocery Store, Buck Schneider was awakened by Pillsbury Franklin's yelling. Then something slammed into the side of the car he was in, and he heard a couple of gunshots, one right in front of him. Slowly and silently, he raised himself up and peeked over the front seat through the open window toward the front of the car. A slim figure in a hoodie was squatting down near the front tire on the passenger side. He had a gun in his hand, and his attention was completely focused up toward the hill where Buck knew Pillsbury and Blackie were hidden. The guy in the hoodie was completely unaware of Buck's presence inside the car.

A furious debate raged in Buck Schneider's foggy brain. Stay hidden? Just shoot the guy? Or tell him to freeze and drop his weapon? His life depended on what he did next…his life, and perhaps the lives of his friends as well. He had no idea what the situation was beyond the drama unfolding in and around the Ford Escape itself…but he did not have the time to find out before he made his crucial decision.

Maybe just shooting the guy was the smart thing to do, but Buck couldn't do it. He slid his arm, holding the .45 automatic, to the top of the front seat and pointed it out the window. "Freeze!" Buck growled in the most menacing voice he could muster. "Move and you're dead." Buck breathed a silent prayer of thanks when the guy in the hoodie complied. "Toss the gun on the other side of the car and turn around." The guy in the hoodie slid his revolver across the hood of the Escape, and it clattered to the ground on the other side of the car. He turned slowly and stared straight down the barrel of Buck's .45.

Buck, in return, stared straight into the freckled face of the young man he had thrown down a huge hill the night before. It was the guy who had tried to steal his bike. Apparently, the young redhead recognized him, as well. It was at this point that the front of the kid's faded jeans grew dark with sudden moisture.

Pillsbury Franklin lay on his back at the bottom of what was to be another man's grave, staring up at the moon and the stars. He wondered if this was how his story would end. He had to admit, he admired the sense of irony; Pillsbury Franklin could end up dying in what was supposed to be the resting place of an old friend. As he lay there, he thought again about his latest novel. He wondered why it had not sold yet, and if any changes could be made to make it more marketable. Even now, shot and laying in a grave, the chemicals in his brain just could not stop creating offbeat ideas.

Perhaps, he thought, he should change the name of the angel, the one that the mob had tried to lynch before he turned them into pillars of salt. If he changed the angel's name from "Burt" to "Chad", he could update the title of the book to something a little more contemporary.

Hanging Chad would be a great title for the book that might well stir the curiosity of a publisher or two, Franklin thought to himself.

This was the last strange little thought he had before he lost consciousness.

● ● ●

At the Almost Hope Center, it had been about two hours since the four rednecks had attempted to steal a large amount of food. Three and Albert Harrison were shooting the breeze on the front porch while Vivian Harrison went inside the Center to attempt to make coffee.

Vivian was delighted to find the gas stove was still operational. She also found an old metal coffee pot that was designed to heat up on a stove. For once she was glad that most of the equipment in the Hope Center was almost as old as she was. Just as she came out to the porch with the hot pot and cups, two older gentlemen arrived. They were members of the *100 Black Men of Almost*, a civic organization that Three and his grandfather were heavily involved in.

As everyone enjoyed their coffee on the front porch, one of the men, Samuel Edwards, a retired cop, told Three about the plan they had for seeing that the Almost Hope Center was kept under a close and watchful eye. The Center would remain open, and would do what it could to help those in genuine need as long as supplies held out.

Robert Anthony leaned back in his chair and stretched. And smiled.

• • •

Dana Crisp, chief of the Almost Police Department, walked down the steps from the mayor's home at about two in the morning. She had been riding her bike all over town, checking in on groups of police that were standing watch at various major businesses.

Things were not looking good. The police had held off a mob at a local supermarket by utilizing tear gas and rubber bullets. They had not been so successful at the local K-Mart; two officers died and one was critically wounded as a well-organized group of about a dozen shooters stormed the store in a quest for food, bottled water and camping equipment, especially Coleman lanterns and stoves. The front doors of the store were broken down now, and dozens of scavengers showed up after the fact and carried off much of the store's merchandise, including tools and clothing.

Dana Crisp had strolled through the store when it was all over. Usually, TVs, computers and cell phones were the most targeted items when stores were looted. Tonight, all of those items remained completely undisturbed. Strange days, indeed.

"Word about the success of the group that stormed K-Mart is going to get around on the street, Sam," she had told the mayor. "We're not going to be able to maintain any kind of order, or protect the grocery stores, for much longer. "We are no more than a day, maybe two, from total chaos." Candlelight flickered across the solemn face of the mayor as he rocked slowly in his chair by the fireplace.

"I know, I know," Cavanaugh replied gravely. "I've got some ideas. They are way outside the box, they are risky, but I don't see any alternative at the moment. We just can't sit here and let things unravel right before our eyes."

Cavanaugh refused to share his thoughts with her, but told her to gather her most trusted personnel for a meeting at City Hall in the morning.

Almost four more hours until daylight, Dana thought to herself. She wondered what the city would look like in the morning.

CHAPTER THIRTEEN

*L*isten:

    Coco Coleman was the leader of a new gang in town. If the FDA was in charge of displaying the ingredients of people in a fashion similar to the way they labeled food products, Coco Coleman's label would have looked like this:

Personality Facts
Serving size: any is more than enough

African-American DNA	69%	
White DNA	31%	
Father's presence	0%	
Teachers who tried to help	6	
Intelligence	27% when stoned or drunk .	02%
Belligerence/Anger	100% of minimum daily requirements	
Respect for Women	35% for his mother; all others	0%
Arrests	10	
Stints in Jail	2	
Life Expectancy	35	

    Subject contains crack cocaine to preserve freshness. Also may contain a variety of other recreational chemicals that give the subject its distinctive, unpleasant flavor.

Unfortunately, Coco Coleman did not wear any such warning label on his leather jacket. Instead, he had a picture on the back of his jacket that featured three stripes of ice cream (strawberry, chocolate and vanilla). These were the colors of Coco Coleman's newly-formed gang, *The Neopolitans*.

Coco Coleman was the leader of the gang, of course. He was a tall, well-muscled African American, and he looked bad. And, in truth, he *was* pretty bad. There were two other guys in the gang: one of the guys was white, and the other Native American. This is why Coco decided to call their gang *The Neopolitans*, like his favorite kind of ice cream; one part brown, one white, one red. Coco smiled when he thought about the nice diversity of his new gang. He very much wanted to be an equal opportunity employer.

There was another reason why Coco Coleman liked the name, *The Neopolitans*. He had learned in school that Neopolitan was a famous French king who conquered a bunch of other countries, even though he was short. Coco was not sure if Neopolitan had invented ice cream, but he figured he probably had. That was another plus.

The leader of the Neopolitans had decided he was going to be an important person in the new world with no electricity. His conquests would begin tonight by taking valuable stuff from other people. Food, water and other things needed for survival. The rest of the Neopolitans thought that was a great idea. They *always* liked Coco's ideas.

That was primarily because the other two Neopolitans knew that if they did *not* like Coco's ideas, he would beat the snot out of them.

• • •

It dawned on Buck Schneider that he was caught in what seemed to be an endless series of incredibly stupid mistakes. Allowing Blackie to join him at the store was the first in the series of dominoes. When he twisted the cap off that first bottle of beer, the dominoes started falling, and now it seemed they would never stop. His closest friend was shot as a result, and the craziness was still not over.

The brief shoot-out in the parking lot of Schneider Brothers Corner Grocery Store had ended when Buck got the drop on his freckle-faced nemesis. The big question then became; what do we *do* with this guy? Buck had the kid empty his pockets. His driver's license identified him as *Jacob Snow*, and listed an address that was less than a half-mile from the store. Turns out that Buck knew some members of the young thug's extended family, including his uncle, who was a recently-retired cop.

Buck didn't have much time to decide what to do with Snow since Pillsbury Franklin was out-cold and bleeding on the hillside a few yards away. Buck had already decided that he was going to be taking his friend to the hospital. That left Blackie, still half-drunk and fully distraught after accidentally shooting Pillsbury, to deal with the situation at the store. The idea of leaving Blackie alone to keep an eye on things was scary enough in itself; to leave him alone and attempting to hold Jacob Snow prisoner at the same time was such an outrageous idea that he could not even briefly consider it. Even in his muddled transition between drunkenness and hangover, Buck knew that was the dumbest option at his disposal.

So, Buck had waved his gun under Jacob Snow's freckled nose and had talked tough about the consequences Snow would face if he ever messed with Buck again. The kid was scared to death of him, Buck knew. The wet stain on the front of Snow's jeans was strong evidence of that! Buck had to count on the kid's fear being strong enough to keep him away from Buck and the store, at least for a while.

The sound of Jacob Snow's rapid footsteps as he ran away from the store could still be heard when Buck had turned his gaze back to his shirt-tail relative. Blackie was still rattled, big-time. He hated to leave him alone under these circumstances, but he had no choice. Buck had to leave for the hospital, and he had to leave *now*. He told Blackie just to take care of himself and not to get killed defending the store. Blackie assured Buck that he was fine, and that he would keep things under control until Buck's return. Blackie was essentially begging Buck for a chance to make up for his blunders. Having been in that same position so many times before, Buck agreed to let Blackie have his shot at redemption. Besides, Buck thought, what choice do I have?

Buck did not really believe the words of encouragement that he then gave to Blackie, but it seemed like the thing to do at the time. He delivered his brief pep talk with as much simulated sincerity as he could muster. For his part, Blackie was equally adept at artificial belief in Buck's words.

Buck went into the darkened store and emerged a moment later with a wheelchair, the very one that he had used to transport his brother's body to the funeral home hours before. He and Blackie trudged up the hillside and hoisted the limp form of Pillsbury Franklin out of his foxhole and into the wheelchair. In effect, they raised Franklin from Bud Schneider's grave and plopped him into the canvas seat of Bud's hearse. Events were starting to transition from stupid decisions to very bad omens. Both of the chair's prior occupants were dead men.

Buck wheeled the chair onto the sidewalk and began the long trek to Our Lady of Perpetual Sorrows Hospital, which was over a mile away. After he had gone a few yards, he looked back at the store. Blackie Blackmon was standing on the parking lot. In the bright light of the full moon, Buck could see Blackie was again holding his rifle. It hung loose in his hands, and he looked at it as if it was an alien thing. Blackie stared at his rifle as if it were something he had never seen before, and he had no idea what to do with it.

Pillsbury Franklin moaned softly, reminding Buck of the urgency of his mission. Franklin was crumpled in the wheelchair like a limp dishrag. Buck looked down at the pitiful sight of his old friend and strangled his own cry of anguish. As he started to jog, Buck hoped desperately that he was not about to lose another key person in his life. Especially not like this.

Not like this.

• • •

Coco Coleman quietly walked up the stairs to the second floor of the River's Edge apartment building. The building had a long exterior walkway across the front of the second floor that led to the doors of the upstairs apartments. The Neopolitans noticed that some guy was sitting in a lawn chair in front of the open door of his apartment. They decided the pillaging would start with him. Rape would have to wait its turn.

Nilla and Ruby were right behind him. Coco had given the other two men new nicknames to reflect their role in the Neopolitans. Nilla was short for vanilla, and he was the white guy, of course. His real name was Terry Walker, and he liked the name Nilla. He was glad that he had joined the Neopolitans last week, because since the power went out, he had nothing to do. Following Coco Coleman was going to present him a real-life opportunity to do the sorts of things he had done for years playing video games. Things like raping and pillaging. Nilla did not sport a warning label, either, but he should have. If the FDA labeled Nilla, it would have looked like this:

Personality Facts

Serving size: if complete avoidance is not possible, limited doses highly recommended

White DNA	100%
Entitlement mentality	100%
Life lived in mother's basement	95%
Waking hours spent playing video games	87%
Laziness	100% of minimum daily requirements
Respect for Women	amount equivalent to "Grand Theft Auto"
Blame accepted for his problem	0%
Arrests	10
Stints in Jail	0
Life Expectancy	as long as mom's basement is available

Subject is loaded with polyunsaturated fats, and is guaranteed to be free of individual initiative and personal responsibility.

Ruby was the third member of the gang. He was called *Ruby* because it was the only word Coco could think of that was a synonym for *red*. Ruby did not know what a synonym is. Coco Coleman thought synonym was a flavor of Cheerios. Ruby's real name was Jonah Pitzer, and he did not like the name *Ruby*. *Ruby* was a girl's name from a country western song. Also, Ruby's DNA was 94% white, and he was sorry that he had ever told Coco Coleman that he had a great-grandmother who was part Shawnee Indian.

Ruby was a perfect symphony of dark green hair, black fingernails, tattoos, piercings, a wide variety of abuse and anger. If he had a warning label, it would have been much simpler than those of his fellow-Neopolitans:

WARNING: THE SURGEON GENERAL HAS DETERMINED THAT THIS PRODUCT IS SCREWED UP, PERHAPS BEYOND REPAIR, AND WILL GENUINELY HURT YOU IF GIVEN THE SLIGHTEST OPPORTUNITY.

Ruby was not screwed up because of the nature of his appearance, but because of the content of his character. He was screwed up because of the nature of his soul. It smoldered within him like lava, waiting for the chance to erupt.

These three model citizens approached Rick Gage as he dozed in his lawn chair in front of his apartment.

"Hey, man, we takin' your stuff," Coco Coleman said to Rick Gage.

Gage blinked a few times and focused on the three figures standing above him in the moonlight. "Okay," he shrugged.

Ruby stepped forward and snarled, "I don't think you heard the man, you dip-wad. The man said we are takin' your stuff! You get me?!"

Gage stared blankly at Ruby and blinked again. "Yeah, I hear you. Help yourself. Doesn't really matter much at this point." Gage turned away from the Neopolitans and stared out into the night.

The Neopolitans stood silently for a moment, puzzled by the strange reaction. Then Coco Coleman looked at his friends and shrugged. He nodded toward the open apartment door and the Neopolitans went into Rick Gage's apartment to go shopping.

• • •

Buck Schneider approached the huge, dark buildings of Our Lady of Perpetual Sorrows Hospital, which were outlined by the silver light of the full moon. Large neon signs that should have been beacons in the darkness were instead hulking shadows, looming without purpose. Light flickered softly from only a few of the hospital windows. Candles. It was a strange scene, both peaceful and ominous at the same time.

Buck wheeled his friend through the open doors of the emergency entrance into the darkened hallway. The air was hot and stuffy and filled with the smells of humans in distress. Sweat, blood, even death were in the air.

A little bit of moonlight trickled into the waiting room, which was filled beyond capacity. A number of other people were strewn along the hallway itself. Some were sitting on the floor, others lying there. A candle flickered on the desk behind the receptionists' window.

The receptionist's desk was empty, but Buck could hear people speaking softly in the treatment rooms beyond the reception area, and he caught an occasional glimpse of a nun or someone in scrubs moving in the hallway beyond. Buck jumped a bit as a voice spoke from the darkness behind him. "Sir, what is your situation?" It was a woman's voice, soft and concerned. He turned and squinted into the darkness, his eyes groping for a face to which he could connect the voice.

"It's my friend," Buck replied. "He's been shot. I'm afraid he may be dying."

"Let me take a look, Mister Schneider." Buck heard the sound of a match being struck. The sudden light of its flame blinded him, and the shadowy figure lit a candle. When his eyes adjusted to the light, the familiar face of Sister Mary Margaret Marion smiled up at him kindly. "We're trying to use the candles as little as possible. This one came from the altar in our chapel." Sister Mary Margaret Marion was a regular customer at the Schneider Brothers Corner Grocery Store. She was a good woman, Buck thought; he liked her a lot.

The nun quietly examined Pillsbury Franklin and his wound. "His pulse is weak and he's lost a lot of blood. The bullet seems to have missed his vital organs. But he's going to need surgery right away or he may bleed to death."

Buck stared at the nun, unable to think of a reply.

"Mr. Schneider, it may be some hours before a doctor can get around to him, and we don't have that kind of time," Sister Mary Margaret Marion said. "We have a volunteer who served as a medic in Vietnam and worked as an EMT for a few years. I think we should ask him to help your friend right away, to do what he can do." The nun's eyes glistened slightly in the light of the candle she was holding.

"Okay," Buck nodded, "Okay, Sister. I trust your judgment."

As Sister Mary Margaret Marion and her candle led Buck and the wheelchair down the hallway, she called to another nun, to whom she softly gave instructions. Then they continued down the hall and went into what had once been an office. The furniture had been pushed to a corner or stacked to get it out of the way. After placing the candle on a nearby table, Sister Mary Margaret Marion helped Buck hoist the limp body of Pillsbury Franklin onto the gurney that stood in the center of the room.

● ● ●

Coco Coleman's arms were filled with canned goods from Rick Gage's apartment. The Neopolitans had not thought to bring anything in which to carry their loot. Coleman walked out and stood next to the guy in the lawn chair. "Hey, man," he said to Gage, "do you have any garbage bags?"

Without turning, Gage replied, "Under the sink."

"Thanks," Coco said, and went back into the apartment.

• • •

Buck suspected it was the strong, stale smell of alcohol on his breath that prompted Sister Mary Margaret Marion to escort him out of the makeshift operating room and direct him toward the chapel. He groped his way down the hall in almost complete darkness, but after he turned the corner in the hallway, he could see a small flicker of light from the frosted glass in the wooden double doors of the chapel itself. As he entered the room, he saw there was a single candle lit beneath the crucifix. The three stained glass windows glowed softly from the light of the full moon.

As he quietly walked down the short center aisle between the small pews, he noticed 6 or 7 people in various postures. Some were praying. Some were crying. A couple of them were sleeping.

Buck guessed that during the next couple of hours he would probably do all three.

• • •

The Neopolitans emerged from Rick Gage's apartment, each bearing a fairly full garbage bag. Even though the devices were currently useless, Nilla could not resist the temptation to cop some of the man's awesome electronic stuff. He secretly hoped that before long electricity would return and he could disappear once again into his basement and his games.

155

Coco had decided that they would take a smoke break, and then hit one more apartment before carrying their stuff back to where they were staying. They knew now that they would need to get some wheel barrows or carts or something like that so they could haul stuff. If they were going to do a significant amount of looting, they were going to have to develop a better system for carrying off their swag. They were new at pillaging, but Coco was confident they would improve rapidly.

Nilla brought up the rear of the little parade out of Rick Gage's apartment. As he passed the guy in the lawn chair, he noticed he had something in his right hand, and he seemed to be squeezing it methodically.

"What is that?" Nilla asked the guy in the lawn chair.

"It's called a *stress ball*," Gage replied.

"Can I see it?" Nilla asked.

"Sure," Gage said, handing it to him.

Nilla took the stress ball and squeezed it a couple of times. It felt like a thick balloon, filled with sand. As he looked at the thing, he noticed it had writing on it. He held it up in the moonlight and squinted until he could make it out.

"Crap occurs," the writing on the stress ball said.

CHAPTER FOURTEEN

Debbie Franklin bolted upright in bed, panting and sweating, eyes bulging, chills running up and down her spine. She had an overwhelming feeling that something had happened, something was very wrong. She sat quietly in bed, gradually getting her breathing under control, and considering what to do next. As she sat in the silence, for a brief moment, she thought she heard the distant sounds of shouting and gunshots. Then, everything was quiet. So quiet she could hear the lace curtains flapping softly in the gentle night breeze.

She climbed out of bed and pulled on her jeans and the blouse she had worn the day before. She put on her tennis shoes and made her way down the stairs, holding a roll of toilet paper. She went into the moonlit back yard and squatted among a cluster of bushes a few yards from the back door. As she did what had to be done, she wondered what could be done with this waste if this situation went on for an extended period of time. They couldn't just keep trotting out into the yard like a family dog, could they? It was chilly out here at night, even in the spring. What would they do in the winter? She dismissed the uncomfortable thoughts with a grimace.

Debbie went back into the kitchen and grabbed a bottle of water. They had less than a case left, she noticed. Then she grabbed a hoodie and headed out the front door. She knew that Pillsbury had gone to the Schneider Brothers Corner Grocery Store to help Buck stand guard. She knew it was silly, but she just wanted to go there and make sure everything was all right. She had gone to bed peacefully, but the sudden awakening had rattled her soul and she needed to know that her husband was okay.

As Debbie walked up the hill, she noticed movement on Ellie Pence's front porch. The porch swing was swaying softly in the moonlight.

"Ellie, is that you?" she asked softly. Ellie Pence, unable to sleep, had come back to the front porch well after dark, when the mosquitoes were no longer so thick. The two women spoke briefly on Ellie's front porch for a few moments before striking out together for the Schneider Brothers Corner Grocery Store.

• • •

Buck Schneider knelt in the second pew from the front in the chapel of Our Lady of Perpetual Sorrows Hospital. He looked up at the wounded figure of the man on the cross. In the dim light of a single candle, the statue looked very realistic. If he spoke to the man hanging there, would he reply? Would his voice be a hoarse whisper, filled with pain, or a still, calm voice to reassure him?

Buck was never Catholic, but he had gone to Catholic School for a time. Buck's mother thought Catholic school was a better than public school, as far as discipline was concerned. She liked the grim authoritarian appearance of the full habits that the nuns used to wear, the ones with the big, swooping white breastplates and full headpieces. The only way Buck's mom would have liked those outfits more, he thought, was if they had swastikas on the long black sleeves.

To be sure, if a kid got too far out of line, it could mean a trip to the principal's office. Mother Magna Martyr was known for her huge wooden paddle, and her ability to apply it effectively. When Buck was in the sixth grade, the nuns had gone to a kinder and gentler appearance. Veils replaced headpieces, and they actually sat back on the head and showed the nun's hair! The breastplates were gone, and the nuns showed a little leg below the knee. With such significant lowering of the intimidation factor, Buck's mom felt it was no longer worth the money to send him to Catholic school. The following autumn, Buck was in the public school system.

As he knelt in the candlelight, Buck prayed an *Our Father*. The Catholics, he had remembered, asked that God would "forgive us our trespasses as we forgive those who trespass against us." This contrasted with the Protestants, who called Jesus' prayer *The Lord's Prayer*, in which they prayed about the forgiveness of *debts*. When people from different backgrounds prayed together, like at funeral homes, there was always a little verbal tussle between factions when it got to that part of the prayer.

"I've got debts," Buck whispered quietly, hoping it was loud enough for the suffering man on the cross to hear. "I have trespassed against Pillsbury Franklin. And my wife. And my kids." He paused. "Please deliver Pillsbury Franklin," Buck prayed. "Please deliver him from the evil I've brought him. Please forgive my debt." It was not much of a prayer, but he never was very good at that sort of thing. He wept softly for a time, kneeling in the pew with his butt wedged against the seat, and his head resting atop his clenched hands. After a while, he fell asleep there.

• • •

Listen:

While Coco Coleman and the Neopolitans were on the parking lot of the Rivers Edge apartment complex taking their smoke break, two very nice-looking young women came out of an apartment on the first floor to grab smokes of their own. Kayla and Christy did not notice the men at first. They were in the shadows at the corner of the building. The Neopolitans had already done a little pillaging to kick off the evening's activities. Ruby was now selling the others on the idea that perhaps a little raping was in order as well. This was an easy sell, as it was the part of the evening that Nilla had most looked forward to.

The next several minutes were a jagged mixture of yelling, screaming, chaos and confusion. When the Neopolitans decided to act on Ruby's suggestion, Rick Gage had suddenly appeared in the apartment and managed to hold the three men at bay long enough for the two women to run screaming out the door. They were able to reach the safety of the neighbor's house where Kayla's son had ended up spending the night.

The Neopolitans, deprived of their intended recreation activity, compensated for the loss by beating Rick Gage to a pulp. When they were done, Rick Gage lay in the darkness among the broken furniture in Kayla Ellis' apartment. Upon a brief return to consciousness, he felt a mildly annoying lump of some kind underneath him, near the small of his back. Slowly, he reached under himself and brought out the offending object.

It was his stress ball. He smiled to himself, and began squeezing it gently, in an erratic rhythm in tune with his breathing. He lay in the darkness, taking inventory of the room and his pain, and vaguely wondering if meaningful movement of any kind was ever going to be possible for him again. "Crap occurs", indeed. Yes, it sure does.

As he drifted in and out of consciousness, he could not remember for the life of him how or why he had managed to pry himself out of his lawn chair and actually get involved in something noble. Whatever it was, Rick Gage hoped it would not become habit-forming. Involvement, he had discovered, was very, very painful.

● ● ●

"Mr. Schneider?" A soft hand and a soft voice had come upon Buck as he slept in the chapel.

Groggy, Buck looked up at Sister Mary Margaret Marion. "Hello, Sister," he said. "How is he?"

"Our volunteer has stopped the bleeding. However, Mr. Franklin needs a transfusion. Unfortunately, we don't have access to his medical records at present, and we have no means for testing his blood type, either. If we were to give him blood, and it was the wrong type, it would be fatal, of course. Is there any chance that you might know his blood type? If he doesn't receive blood, he may not live through the night."

Buck fought through the fog in his brain. "I don't know his blood type," he replied. "Hell, sister, I don't even know my own!" A look of distress crossed the nun's features, and Buck's heart sank like a stone. Then, out of the fog, it came to him. His breath burst from him, half-joy and half-tears. "But I remember that he and I both have the same type! We found that out when we sold our blood for beer money when we were in college!"

For a brief instant, Sister Mary Margaret Marion's brow showed her disapproval. She locked her eyes with Buck's, and Buck found himself unable to turn away. He had a sense her eyes were actually peering into his skull, perhaps carefully counting the number of wrinkles on his brain, analyzing the quality of the information squirreled away there.

"Mr. Schneider," she said softly, "we must be absolutely certain that this information is correct. A transfusion of the wrong blood type would almost certainly prove fatal to your friend. In view of your current condition, I must ask if you're absolutely certain that your recollection is correct." She waited for his response. It was a pregnant pause. In fact, the pause seemed to Buck to be as long as the gestation period of the average elephant.

When it was over, Buck mustered as much confidence as he could, and sprinkled in a hint of indignation. "I'm certain, Sister. I know what's at stake. I remember distinctly that we have the same blood type."

The nun's eyes continued to pierce into Buck, weighing the depth of his conviction. (Buck considered this experience to be the religious equivalent of a Vulcan mind-meld. Spock would be proud of this woman!) Then Sister Margaret Marion's eyes relaxed and twinkled and she simply could not repress a slight giggle. "Well," the nun said with a warm smile. "God does bring all things together for the good of those who love Him. Come with me, Mr. Schneider. Your friend needs you."

As they walked down the hallway toward Pillsbury Franklin's room, Buck considered the irony of it all. Pillsbury Franklin had not had a beer in over 20 years. But at this moment of crisis, the dumb things of his life with Buck had come out of his past and were being used to save his life. Within the next few minutes, Buck and Pillsbury would be sharing a beer for the first time in decades (sort of). Only this one would be shared intravenously, as there was still some of last night's alcohol in Buck's veins.

"Pillsbury Franklin," Buck chuckled to himself. "This blood's for you!"

• • •

Kayla Ellis fingers pulled back the curtains slightly, and she peered into the darkness, toward her apartment house. "We've got to go back," she said solemnly.

"Kayla, are you *nuts*?!" Jamie Drake asked incredulously. Christy Franklin stood near them, in the dim light of a can of Sterno, stunned into silence. "You guys were lucky to get out of there alive!"

Kayla continued to stare out the window, seeing nothing, but trying to will her eyes to pierce the darkness and distance to her home. "I know that! But what about Gage? He risked his life for us, and there was no way he could handle those three guys in a fight. He's got to be hurt *bad*, maybe dying. We can't just leave him there."

"He's probably already dead," Jamie Drake shot back, "and if you go back there, you'll probably end up dead, too! You've got your kids to think about."

Kayla turned from the window and faced her friends. "You've got a gun, Jamie. You know how to use it. You can go with us."

"Yes, I've got a gun. And you can bet your three boyfriends have them, too! I bought that gun to defend my house, not to play cop. You came here to be safe. Stay here, Kayla," Jamie Drake implored, "stay here and be safe with us. Think of your kids. They need you now more than ever. This is no time to go off and play hero." The three women stood in the gloomy living room, looking at each other.

Finally, Christy Franklin spoke. "We need to go back," she said softly, "but we need to wait. It will be light in an hour, maybe two. Our chances are much better if we go when it's light. And it's doubtful those creeps will stick around when it's light outside."

There was a pause as the other women considered her words, and then each slowly nodded in agreement. "That's the thing to do," Jamie said, "so why don't we lie down for a while and get some rest while we wait for morning?"

"We can try, at least," Kayla replied. The women moved about the living room, using couch pillows and throw blankets to make themselves reasonably comfortable on the carpeted floor of the living room. When they were settled, Jamie blew out the Sterno. As she settled onto the floor, she double-checked to make sure her handgun was under the couch, within easy reach.

• • •

She knew! Debbie Franklin knew absolutely every detail of the circus at the grocery store. Buck did not know *how* she knew, but he was certain that she knew. Buck had been surprised when he returned to the room where Pillsbury Franklin was recovering. Sitting next to the gurney, holding his hand and stroking his face gently, was his wife, Debbie. When Buck entered the room, Debbie turned and looked at him. Her eyes hardened and angry tears sprang half-way into them, but stopped short of spilling free.

She said nothing (with her mouth). Her eyes, however, spoke clearly. "How could you?" they asked Buck. He gulped. None of his body parts had an answer. He closed his mouth and his eyes avoided hers. His feet moved in a small, guilty shuffle.

The uncomfortable silence was like a tangible thing to the others in the room. There was a burly, middle-aged guy, wearing khaki scrubs and busying himself around the room. The ex-medic, Buck concluded. There was another woman in the room, a small woman, sitting quietly in the corner. Squinting in the candlelight, Buck recognized Ellie Pence. She sat quietly, with a vacant look on her face, taking in what was happening in the small room.

"Zeke, this is Buck Schneider," Sister Mary Margaret Marion said, "Mr. Schneider indicates that he and Mr. Franklin have the same blood type."

Zeke stopped short and looked at Buck. "What type is that?"

Buck replied sheepishly. "I don't know. I just remember that we have the same blood type."

"And how do you know that?" Debbie could not keep her voice free of anxiety and anger. "How do you know you have the same blood type? This is no game, Buck! We need to be sure! And you're not even sober!" Buck hesitated and choked, hoping that Sister Mary Margaret Marion would share what Buck had told her. He looked over at the nun imploringly. She returned his gaze with some kind of stern sympathy. She cocked her eyebrow slightly and gave the faintest half-shake of her head. He was on his own.

"We used to sell our blood in college, Debbie. I remember clearly that we had the same blood type," Buck finally answered. "You have every reason to be upset with me. I have no excuses. But I know we have the same blood type. There's no doubt in my mind."

Zeke's voice was deep, with a slight Southern twang. "You understand, partner, that if you're wrong about this, it could be all she wrote for your friend here...."

"I understand," Buck said with as much conviction as he could muster. "And I'm not wrong."

The tension in the room eased a bit. A look of relief came to every face, except for that of Ellie Pence, who remained in the corner, smiling her vacant smile, quietly observing the small drama unfolding before her.

Buck studied Debbie's face in an attempt to find out just how much trouble he was in. She seemed to feel his gaze, and glanced up at him. Debbie's eyes told Buck that disembowelment was no longer a front-burner option, but he was far from being out of the woods. People's eyes were sure talking to him a lot tonight, Buck thought to himself. He wished everybody's eyes would just be quiet and go back to looking at stuff instead of sending him out on guilt trips. The series of silent scoldings had aggravated his hangover headache nearly as much as virtual shouting would have.

● ● ●

It was near dawn, and Blackie sat on the edge of the foxhole overlooking the Schneider Brothers Corner Grocery Store, smoking a cigar that smelled cherry-sweet and stale at the same time. He was still trying to figure out why he had spilled his guts to Debbie Franklin...why he had felt compelled to give her every stupid detail of how her husband got shot. For a moment, he thought she was going to actually demolish him, kick his butt up around his ears so hard he'd have two huge, pink earmuffs. But she hadn't. Blackie wished she had. The look of disgust she had laid on him was even worse.

He was now concerned about what Buck would do when he found out that Blackie had ratted out both of them. Regret was an unfamiliar sensation for

Blackie Blackmon, as he was not generally insightful enough to recognize his own faults. He was experiencing regret now, and did not like its taste one bit. He planned to get over it within fifteen minutes or so.

Blackie stubbed out his cigar and decided to take a short walk around the perimeter of the store. Other than the visit from the two ladies, the rest of the night had been uneventful. Which was fine with him. The earlier part of the night had more than eventful enough. Blackie was humiliated. He had blown his chance to perform as a studly hero should. As the early morning light began to paint the sky, he felt his fear from the night before gradually recede. Recede, but not disappear. Not by a long shot.

A few moments later, Blackie was rounding the corner, returning to the side of the store with the entrance. As he did so, he heard a slight noise coming from the back of the store, near the dumpster and the pallets that were piled up by the back door. He saw something move quickly near the dumpster. A cat? A raccoon, maybe, doing some dumpster-diving? He quickly moved behind the nearest parked car. Blackie had to be sure. He still had his rifle with him. It still felt strange and uncomfortable in his hands, which had suddenly gone cold and clammy. He cautiously worked his way down the parking lot, using cars as cover, constantly keeping an eye on the back of the store. There was another sound, and he caught a glimpse of a figure, definitely human, trying to press itself further behind the stacks of pallets next to the dumpster.

"I know you're in there," Blackie said with authority. He was pleased that his voice had more confidence in it than his body did. "Come on out with your hands up!" Even to Blackie, these words sounded corny, but what else are you supposed to say in a situation like this?

There was no movement behind the pallets, no reply. Had Blackie been mistaken? He didn't think so. He moved behind another parked car, closer to the pallets. When he did so, the slightly different angle gave him a better view. There was definitely somebody in there, among the pallets, with his back pressed hard against the concrete retaining wall.

Blackie felt cold and empty inside. He vividly remembered the terrifying sensation of having a bullet buzz past his ear, less than a foot away from his head. He did not want to die. The best way to prevent his own death was to shoot first, while he had the chance. If this guy got out of this spot, he might gain the upper hand. Blackie did not want to take that chance.

No flimsy wooden pallet would deflect a bullet from his rifle, Blackie was certain of that. He slowly took aim, and had the rifle steadied on the hood of the car in front of him. He had a clear shot. All he had to do was pull the trigger, and it would be all over. He and the store would be safe.

It was at this particular moment that Blackie had an epiphany. An *epiphany* is a watershed moment in a person's life where they come to grips with great truth. In his epiphany, Blackie received an unexpected gift, experiencing something he had never before had. Common sense made its debut in his hoosier brain.

Blackie winced a bit, and blinked repeatedly as the gentle breeze of common sense wafted through his redneck brain cells, renewing sense and sensibility. All at once, old Ray Stevens songs did not seem quite so funny, and he no longer had an uncontrollable urge to order weird items from late-night TV infomercials. Also, for the first time in his life, he thought it might be a good idea to put some money into a 401k and perhaps even change his underwear more regularly. And maybe…just *maybe*…he *should* put the toilet seat back down when he was finished.

Blackie also found he was unable to pull the trigger on his rifle. Sound reasoning had begun to stalk his mind like a stranger in a strange land. There had already been one senseless shooting that evening, and he had pulled the trigger then, too. To his surprise, Blackie realized that he did not want to make another mistake like that.

He aimed his rifle three feet to the right of the figure behind the pallets. He pulled the trigger, and his shot pinged off of the retaining wall, sending little concrete chips flying into the air.

"Okayokayokayokay!" came a voice from behind the pallets. Sounded like a kid, Blackie thought. Confirmation that maybe he had done the right thing this time?

"Come on out, I won't hurt you as long as you don't give me a reason to," Blackie called out.

Slowly, a tall, lean figure in a hoodie unentangled itself from the pallets. "Don't shoot, man! Don't shoot! I wasn't doing anything wrong, I was just looking for Mr. Schneider and I got scared when I saw your rifle!" The figure stepped out of the shadows and into the early morning light. Blackie thought he recognized the kid. He was pretty sure he had worked at the Schneider Brothers Corner Grocery Store from time to time.

"Turn around and put your hands high on the wall, kid. I just want to make sure you're not armed," Blackie said. The young man quickly complied.

Demarcus Johnson put his hands on the wall because he possessed a healthy portion of good, common sense.

No epiphany required.

CHAPTER FIFTEEN

I t was about an hour after dawn when Kayla Ellis and her two friends walked out the front door of Jamie Drake's house. They had decided to let the two young boys sleep while they went on their rescue mission to Kayla's apartment. Jamie was carrying her small handgun, but she didn't know what to do with it. It did not rest comfortably in her pocket, and despite the circumstances she did not feel comfortable walking in public with a gun in her hand. But she did. Her right hand, holding the gun, fidgeted at her side as they made their way down the street.

There was a light rain falling. Something about the rainfall seemed to amplify the crunching sound of their footsteps as they made their way down the gravel road. The houses they passed on their way back to the apartment complex were still; all the windows were dark and lifeless. It made the homes look empty, but somehow they knew most of them weren't. The entire walk back to the apartment had an eerie feeling about it. When the three women spoke, which was rarely, they seemed obligated to do so in near-whispers. Though their destination was only slightly more than a block away, the walk seemed to take forever.

As they approached the apartment building, they could see that the door to Kayla's apartment was wide open, and a few of her belongings were strewn on the walk outside. The young women approached the apartment stealthily, and felt pretty silly about it. They felt like they were imitating policewomen from some cop show; however, their fear of encountering the men from the night before was strong enough to motivate them to be extremely cautious, despite their embarrassment.

Christy Franklin stumbled slightly on a broken table leg on the sidewalk, and let out a nervous giggle. Jamie Drake shot her a stern look, which stopped the giggle before it could become contagious. She raised the gun from her side and held it in both hands near her face. They were about to enter the apartment, and she wanted them all to remember that, despite its apparent absurdity, this little excursion of theirs was very serious business.

Jamie peeked around the corner of the door and squinted into the gloom of the apartment. It was difficult to see anything inside. She thought she heard movement, but resisted backing away. As her eyes adjusted to the light, she surveyed the small apartment. Broken furniture, stuff strewn about the room. Then, near the center of the room, next to the rest of the shattered coffee table, she saw a crumpled male figure in gym shorts. Rick Gage, the unexpected champion from the night before. He stirred slightly.

Slowly, the three women made their way into the apartment toward the fallen man. It appeared he was the only person in the place, and they relaxed a bit. Kayla knelt next to Gage and lifted his head slightly. His eyes opened a bit, and he smiled slightly, fighting to keep his eyeballs from rolling back into his head. Then, suddenly, his brow furrowed and his face had a look of alarm. His left arm pointed across his chest toward the darkened apartment behind him.

"Kitchen," Rick Gage whispered hoarsely. "Someone's in the kitchen!"

• • •

Amanda Farmer stirred sleepily. She "spooned" her husband, snuggling as close as she could. She smiled slightly as she lay there, listening to the sound of the rain just outside the open window. At that moment, a great, big realization grabbed Amanda Farmer by the brain.

"Rain!" she said out loud. "It's raining!" She bolted upright in her bed and started shaking her husband. "Matt, wake up! It's raining outside! We need to collect as much water as we can!"

• • •

Pillsbury Franklin's breathing became erratic. He was obviously in distress. Zeke, the EMT/medic, took Pillsbury Franklin's pulse and frowned.

"What's wrong? What is it?!" Debbie Franklin was obviously alarmed.

"Possible reaction to the transfusion," Zeke said quietly. He pumped the blood pressure cuff and used his stethoscope. Debbie and Buck held their breaths while the sleeve slowly deflated. "Blood pressure is dropping like a stone. Might be the wrong blood type." He quickly disconnected Pillsbury from the IV.

Debbie Franklin's soft jaw stiffened into granite. She turned and shot a steely glare at Buck. Her eyes were filled with rage and disgust. "Well, Buck, congratulations." she said solemnly. "Looks like you finally managed to kill him after all." Her eyes welled with tears and she turned her full attention to her husband's quiet struggle for life. Buck knew it was all Debbie could do to contain herself...and all he could do was watch her agony and feel responsible.

Once again, he felt like dog doo...it was a familiar sensation. It was a dog doo déjà vu. He'd played this sort of scene many times before.

• • •

"Someone's in the kitchen!" Kayla Ellis warned her two friends. She dropped to the floor next to Gage, lying beside him. Jamie took cover behind a nearby couch; Christy stood frozen for a moment, then dropped into a crouch in the shadows, her eyes frantically searching for something to hide behind.

The kitchen was separated from the living room by a breakfast bar, with cabinets above and below. As the three women stared at the counter, they heard a slight rustle from behind it and they stiffened. "Who's back there?!" Jamie said loudly in a commanding voice. "I've got a gun! Don't make me use it!!"

Jamie realized her command sounded like something out of an old cop show…but what else are you supposed to *say* in such a situation?

• • •

Matt and Amanda Farmer and their three children were virtually singing in the rain. Well, not all of them were singing out loud; just Amanda, actually. The young mother softly sang Gene Kelly's signature song as her family went about the business of gathering rain water. Her four-year-old daughter, Eowyn, was working happily at her side, trying to pick up the tune. Hannah, her uber-independent six-year old, was a few yards away, doing her own thing. Amanda had bulldozed her family out of bed; they threw on whatever clothes were handy and rushed outside to harvest the steady rainfall.

Amanda and the two girls were lining up pots, pans, bowls and cups on the driveway in neat rows….any container they could think of…to catch the rain as it fell. Her eight-year-old son, Shane, was helping his father. Shane had quickly scrubbed out a kitchen trash can with rags and rainwater while his father was removing the lower section of the downspout on the front of the house. The guys then positioned the kitchen can beneath the downspout. It was filling quickly, and Matt was in the garage trying to find something larger for water storage.

As a home-schooling mom, Amanda was used to organizing the children for various projects and learning experiences. All of the kids were having fun; the girls enjoyed their driveway efforts as they would a game; Shane enjoyed the manly work he was engaged in with his father. In the midst of great uncertainty, happiness was still possible. Amanda hoped they would be able to have this same spirit in the uncertain days ahead.

Matt stood studying the two plastic containers that their garbage collectors had provided them. They were huge, made from thick plastic, which allowed them to be picked up and dumped by the automated metal arms of a state-of-the-art garbage truck. There was no hope under the circumstances that the garbage can could be cleaned enough for gathering water...but the recycling can would do nicely.

Matt dumped a kitchen can of water into the recycling container, then lifted his laughing, barefoot son and put him in the can as well. Shane took the scrub brush his father had provided him and the two of them began cleaning the inside of the container as quickly and thoroughly as they could.

As the Farmers worked, Matt noticed that some neighbors appeared, and were gathering their own rainwater. Old man Adams smiled and waved from next door. "Good idea on the recycling bin, Matt! Think I'm going to follow your lead!" Matt returned the wave and smiled broadly. The strange moment had provided him with a sense of community that he had not felt in quite some time.

Worries about the future repeatedly wormed their way into Matt Farmer's thoughts as he worked. Momentarily lost in thought, Matt played a mental game of "Whack a Mole" to keep them at bay. Just enjoy the moment, he kept telling himself.

• • •

Buck remained paralyzed, viewing the quiet drama of Pillsbury Franklin's struggle for life. It was about six in the morning, he guessed. He turned away from watching the Franklins and stared out the window. A light rain was falling outside; the blossoms of the hydrangea bush just outside the window were gently bobbing up and down. Mother Nature offered more peace than human nature at the moment.

He wondered if his memory was deceiving him; had it been another drinking buddy, not Franklin, who had accompanied him to the blood bank back in college? Buck's roller coaster life had played hell with his mind, he knew. He knew there was every possibility his brain had failed him on this critical issue.

Zeke the medic had discontinued the transfusion, in view of the uncertainty of the situation. Debbie refused to look at Buck. Sister Mary Margaret Marion had left the room long ago; Ellie Pence sat silently in the corner, perched on top of a desk like a little khaki gargoyle. She had not seemed to move, or even breathe, for hours.

Buck had to fight off the urge to defend himself. The tension in the room was an accusation of guilt, and he was the target. His heart was racing, pounding in his chest. He hoped it would not become a full-blown panic attack. He had experienced those in the past, and had no desire to revisit the experience. It took every ounce of restraint he could muster to resist fleeing the room. He found himself thinking longingly about the supplies of liquor that still remained at the Schneider Brothers Corner Grocery Store. At least, the stuff was still there a few hours ago.

Blackie and the store…he wondered if both were still in one piece. Buck realized at that moment that he cared more about Blackie's well-being than that of the store. He smiled slightly as he acknowledged that, the night before, he had held the store at a higher level of importance than his distant relative.

Buck realized that he deeply resented the Schneider Brothers Corner Grocery Store; he had sensed that vaguely for some time. Yet, the thought of life without it absolutely terrified him. His position at the store had always been a source of stability and security for him, even during periods where his drinking habits made him clearly unworthy of continued employment. On the other hand, being at the store had thoroughly locked him into the role of "other". The "other" son, the "other" Schneider brother, the "other" guy at the store you talked to when Bud was not around.

Looking back toward his friend, it seemed to Buck that Pillsbury was beginning to breathe more regularly. Zeke's posture seemed to be growing more relaxed;

Buck hoped that this meant Pillsbury's condition was improving. At the moment, Pillsbury Franklin seemed to be resting peacefully, not preparing to rest in peace.

• • •

To the best of his knowledge, Rod "Blackie" Blackmon had never been to this part of town. If he had been, he was completely certain he had not been on foot. If he had driven through, it would have been as quickly as possible. Blackie had stashed his rifle inside the Schneider Brothers Corner Grocery Store, but he still had the reassurance of his .38; its comforting weight pressed against his chest.

At the moment, Blackie and Demarcus Johnson were pushing a shopping cart down a thinly blacktopped street that was heavily lined with trees. The trees hung over the top of the street, nearly obscuring the sky; it felt more like a trail through the woods than a city street. At the moment, the canopy of branches made a nice umbrella, shielding the two unlikely traveling companions from the majority of the rain. Every so often he would catch a glimpse of a small frame house, nearly hidden by the foliage. The houses were all worn and needed repair. Nearly every house was in rough shape; most had faded and flaking paint, curling shingles and torn screen doors. The front yards, if you could call them that, were either tangles of dense foliage or little bowls of light brown dirt or mud.

Blackie asked himself for the umpteenth time why he had left the store unattended in order to follow this young black kid God-knows-where. Under ordinary circumstances, Blackie knew that white people were less than welcome in this neighborhood. Under current circumstances, he knew he might well be taking his life in his hands. Strangely, Blackie found himself dismissing those anxious thoughts without regret. His decision was highly questionable, he knew, but he felt certain he was doing the right thing. He was savoring the unfamiliar taste of that experience.

Back at the store, Demarcus Johnson had breathlessly explained his situation; his mother and little sister were very sick, and his younger brothers were alone at the house. The urgency in the boy's eyes completely convinced Blackie he was telling the truth.

A few moments later, Blackie and Demarcus had loaded a grocery cart with milk, bottled water and the makings for sandwiches. Blackie also tossed in some Tylenol and Pepto-Bismol; they were pretty much all the store had by way of medicine. He added a can of Lysol spray for good measure. The further they walked down this isolated street, the worse the pavement got. The shopping cart, designed for smooth surfaces, rattled and bounced violently in protest. Potholes filled with dirty rain erupted slightly when the wheels of the shopping cart plopped into them.

"Hey, kid!" Blackie called to Demarcus, "Your shift again!" The teenager smiled and dutifully took his place behind the bouncing cart. "How much further?" Blackie asked.

"Almost there. Three houses to go." Demarcus pushed the cart as fast as it would allow him to go without tipping over. Without warning, a muddy brown dog came charging out of some bushes, barking and snarling at Blackie.

"Khaos! Shut up!" Demarcus yelled at the dog. The pit bull's response was a menacing, low growl and a slight retreat. "Go *on!*" the boy added, and the dog shuffled slowly away, tossing an occasional, threatening glance at Blackie over his muscular shoulder.

"Thanks," Blackie managed to say.

• • •

For what seemed like forever, Kayla Ellis and her two friends waited for the person hiding behind the breakfast bar to make a move. There was no doubt someone was back there; they could hear movement. Kayla was lying on the living room floor next to the injured Rick Gage. She motioned to Jamie, who had taken cover behind a couch. After she caught Jamie's eye, Kayla pointed down at Gage and then slowly mouthed the word, "hospital." Gage was very badly injured, by all appearances. The women could not afford to wait all day for the intruder behind the counter to make a move. The man who had taken a beating on her behalf needed medical attention immediately.

Jamie thought for a moment, and then spoke with a loud, firm voice. "Look, whoever's back there in the kitchen; we know you're there. We don't want a fight, we don't want to hurt you, but you need to come out, now. We have an injured man here who needs help. Just come out and go your way so we can see what we can do for him."

No reply beyond a slight rustling sound came from the kitchen. It seemed to Jamie that their opponent had just changed position slightly. Another minute or two passed uncomfortably.

Jamie spoke again. "Okay, whoever you are, I'm tired of this game. If you don't come out, I'm going to pump a couple of bullets into that breakfast bar. I'm thinking that particle board is not going to be much protection for you. What do *you* think?"

Still, amazingly, there was no reply. Jamie cocked her gun as loudly as she could. "Okay, here we go!" she announced.

"Don't shoot! Don't shoot!" came a worn and squeaky voice from behind the breakfast bar. "I'm a senior citizen!" A small cloud of silver-blue hair rose into the dim light above the counter. The old woman had her scrawny arms held high, hands above her head. Her eyes, behind Coke-bottle glasses, blinked and squinted to adjust to the light from the front door. "Please don't hurt me," the woman croaked. The fear in her voice was evident.

An incredulous look swept across Kayla's face. "Mrs. Zimmerman??!" she gulped. "Mrs. Zimmerman, what the hell are you *doing*?"

The three young women rose from their defensive positions and gathered in the kitchen. The old lady turned to face them, hands still held high. "Oh, put your hands down, lady," Jamie growled.

"You know, you scared the crap out of us." Kayla repeated her question. "What were you *doing* back here?"

The old woman shuffled nervously, and all eyes were drawn to the laundry basket at her feet. It was half-filled with canned goods and other food stuffs. "Why you old..." Kayla stopped short of saying something vile. "You were stealing our food!"

"Yeah, and she walked right past an injured man to get to it," Christy Farmer noted. "Just left him lying on the floor. That's cold. Real cold."

The old woman stood speechless for a moment, then straightened her posture and set her jaw in defiance. "I didn't know what happened to you, Kayla, or if you were coming back," she hissed. "And I have absolutely no idea who that man is. Probably a hoodlum. A person needs to look out for themselves in a situation like this."

"His name is Rick and his apartment is right above yours, Mrs. Zimmerman," Kayla replied. "If you weren't so determined to steal my stuff, maybe you would have recognized him."

The old woman snorted. "I was afraid. I have to take care of myself," she answered angrily. "I'm just a poor, defenseless woman on a fixed income."

Jamie grunted. "And you think that makes this okay." She was not asking a question... she was stating an apparent fact. Everyone in the kitchen knew that's exactly what the old woman thought.

"You're a thief," Kayla said quietly, choking back her outrage. "Get out of my house."

The old woman snorted again. "Well, I *never*! You should have some respect!" She began, lifting a finger toward Kayla's face.

"Get out!" Kayla yelled it the second time. The old woman sped from the apartment at surprising speed, nearly falling as she stumbled over the crumpled body of Rick Gage. Kayla swept the angry tears from her eyes with the back of her hand, then bolted across the room to the front door. She planted her feet on the sidewalk and gestured angrily at the retreating figure of the elderly thief. "You know what, old lady?!" Kayla yelled, "Don't you ever talk to other people again about the way I live my life, you hear me? And don't you ever…ever tell me again how hard it is to be on a fixed income! I wish to God someone would fix my income, because it's broken! And I've got kids! You hear me, you old bag! *Thief!*"

The old woman was long gone before the end of this speech, having retreated into her apartment and bolted all three locks on its door. Kayla stood on the sidewalk in the rain, her shoulders heaving up and down and she regained her breath and her composure. For the second time in the last 10 hours, she felt violated.

She began to cry, and Christy Franklin embraced her tightly as they stood in the rain. Jamie turned her attention to the injured man lying on the floor, and began to wonder how in the world they were going to get him to the hospital… and what the hospital would be like when they got there.

● ● ●

"His vital signs are normalizing," Zeke the medic told Debbie Franklin. "Sometimes there can be an initial reaction to a transfusion even if the donor is the correct blood type."

"Thank God," Debbie Franklin sighed heavily. As her adrenaline faded, she suddenly looked and felt exhausted.

"Hey," a weak voice came from the gurney. Pillsbury Franklin had regained consciousness. "Hey, wife, how ya doin?" he asked, smiling feebly.

"Oh, thank God," Debbie said again, burying her face gently on his chest. She grabbed his hands and kissed his face. After a few moments, Pillsbury turned his head and looked around the room.

"How'm I doin, doc?" he asked Zeke.

"Pretty well," Zeke responded. "You've lost a lot of blood, but I think you'll be okay. I'm not exactly a doctor, by the way."

"Well, whatever you are, thanks," Franklin replied. "Hey, if I need blood, get it from him!" He pointed at Buck. "We have the same blood type. O positive. And he owes me, big-time!"

Debbie glanced up at Buck. Her sideways smile was a pretty good sign that Buck was on the way to being forgiven.

"He already gave you some blood," Zeke replied, "And I think we just might give you a little more right now."

Ellie Pence had been continuing her silent vigil from the dimly lit corner of the room. She had been sitting so quietly, the other people in the room had classified her as a piece of furniture. Ellie stirred and then stood. She made her way toward the door; she paused and looked up briefly, locking eyes with Buck.

"You're still a loser," she said quietly. Then she opened the door and disappeared into the hallway.

CHAPTER SIXTEEN

isten:

It was the off-season.

It was cool and overcast, and the wind was sweeping dry leaves down the sidewalk in front of the old hotel. The hotel had been many things; it had not been a hotel for decades, but people still called it that. It was an exciting resort in its day, around the turn of the twentieth century. It was built on top of a spring that dispensed mineral water in a gentle stream. A special pool was built to capture the water, which was thought to have healing properties. Guests of the hotel would leisurely soak the hours away, back in the days when entertainment did not require electricity.

The hotel had a ballroom, which for many years had held wedding receptions and other special events. It was closed and in a state of disrepair at the moment; there was talk of someone remodeling and reopening it, but there was no sign that such work was underway. The ballroom had a terrific view of the river, if you could overlook the railroad cars in the foreground. I took dancing lessons there twice a month while I was in the 8th grade.

The instructor had a little sound system, and he and his wife would teach us classic and modern dances. The girls wore dresses and little white gloves. The boys were required to wear a sport coat and tie. I always wore a bow tie.

The boys would be lined up on one side of the room, the girls on the other. When it was time for us to actually dance, the boys had to walk across the room, bow at the waist, and ask politely for a dance. When it came time to walk this last mile, my heart would be pounding wildly in my chest as I tried to decide who to ask.

I would generally ask Susie Ottmeyer to dance, because I knew she liked me. I thought she was okay, but that was about it. Every week I promised myself that I would ask Linda Sinclair to dance. I had a crush on her since kindergarten. She was pretty, and she had long hair, and she was always nice to me. Then again, she was nice to everyone. That was part of why I liked her so much. Every week, it was the same ritual; I would vow to ask Linda to dance; but when the time came, I always found myself bowing before Susie Ottmeyer. I was concerned that people would think I liked Susie more than I actually did.

Every lesson the instructors held a contest of some kind, featuring a different dance. I won a free record from the instructor for dancing the *Funky Chicken*. Naturally clumsy, it was the only dance I did well.

Finally, it was April, and the last dance lesson of the school year. It was now or never for dancing with Linda Sinclair. The music played, my heart thumped, and once again I was whirling Susie Ottmeyer across the linoleum floor.

The instructor then announced the last dance of the year, and it was to be ladies' choice. The girls would make the long walk across the ballroom and ask a boy to dance. This was a very bad idea, I thought. I felt the same way when the best ballplayers chose up sides for a baseball game on the playground. I was always last to be picked, or close to it. In the dance situation, I was hoping Susie Ottmeyer would come through for me as I had for her, so I did not end up standing there like some loser who just got left out in a game of musical chairs.

A moment later, Linda Sinclair was standing in front of me, extending her white-gloved hand. In an instant, we were out on the floor, dancing the waltz, which I generally handled pretty well. Clumsier than usual, I apologized repeatedly to her. She just smiled and said, "Don't apologize. It's okay. Let's just dance." So we did. I will never forget how it felt to hold her soft, gloved hand in mine, to look in her eyes up close, and to feel the slick fabric of her party dress, as my other hand rested on her waist. The dance was over in a few short minutes, but in my mind it has lasted forever.

Memories of that night helped keep me sane when I was hiding in the jungle, wondering if a Viet Cong bullet would slam into me any second, ending the big dance for good. Now, I'm nearly an old man, and that dance still remains the best thing that ever happened to me. That's pretty pathetic, I think.

The chilly autumn wind sent a shiver down my spine as I peered through the large window into the darkness of a storefront at the front of the hotel. When I was a kid, there had been a barber shop here. The letters on the window read, *Brick Walz' Barber Shop*. Brick was a tall and lanky man, with a stylish, wavy pompadour of dark red hair. He always had a cigarette dangling out of the left side of his mouth, even while he cut hair. Everybody smoked back then, and a haze filled the barber shop. Men did not make appointments to get their haircut; they just appeared at the shop when they felt like it, and sat in the long row of seats until their turn came.

It was a rare occasion when a woman dared to set foot in Brick Walz' Barber Shop. Most of the time, it was Brick's wife, who had a tall stack of blonde hair and wore tight black pants that looked like leotards. She had a cigarette dangling out of her mouth all the time, too. When she would leave, she would always say, "See you tonight, lover!" Brick would turn back to the head he was shearing and grunt.

"So long, Toots!" Brick Walz would always say.

The guys sitting along the wall would always chuckle when he said that.

Newspapers and magazines were provided, of course, but the primary entertainment at Brick Walz' Barber Shop was shooting the breeze and solving world problems. Back in the early sixties, when I was 12 or so, they talked a lot about some place about Vietnam. Even the mayor got his hair cut by Brick Walz. In fact, so many of the men who came to Brick Walz' Barber Shop were experts on world affairs, I often wondered why they were not called upon by the president to solve the issues of the day.

Vietnam sounded kind of like a war, but they didn't call it that at first. My friends and I played war a lot. Few of the yards in our neighborhood had fences. Our battles would range up and down the back yards for a whole block. I carried a camouflaged machine gun that resembled the one Sgt. Saunders used on the *Combat* TV show. We always had two teams against each other. Each of us considered ourselves to be the Americans, of course, and the other guys were the Nazis. The Nazis were the enemy of choice for kids playing war in the sixties, no doubt about that.

Back then, lots of boys ran around their back yards with toy guns. We made the sound effects for the guns with our mouths. Nobody at that time thought toy guns were a bad idea. *Mattel* sold Barbies to the girls, and machine guns to the boys. That's just how it was.

A friend's Dad had fought in Korea, he said. We didn't know anything about Korea. For a while, we did not know much about Vietnam, either…until Walter Cronkite started showing behind the scenes stuff on TV. Then it was all anybody talked about.

I liked life a lot better when I did not know anything about Vietnam. I liked war better when I pretended to kill my friends. I did not care for the real thing. Not at all.

My favorite part of the haircut experience at Brick Walz's Barber Shop was to sit in the chair and look at the mirrors. Both the wall in front of you and the wall in back of you were lined with mirrors. When mirrors face each other like that, they keep reflecting back and forth like ping pong balls of light, with a series of smaller and smaller images that seemed to go on forever. It felt like you could lose yourself in those mirrors.

I lost myself, but it didn't happen in Brick Walz's Barber Shop.

I wish the guys who sat in Brick Walz' chairs had solved the Vietnam thing early on, before I got there. But the president never called on them.

Now I stood in front of the old hotel in the crisp autumn air, peering through the big picture window that used to say *Brick Walz Barber Shop*. The electric, swirling barber pole used to be on one side, an American flag on the other. Both were gone. I stared into the dark and dusty room. There were no barber chairs. No chairs for waiting. No mirrors on the wall.

I had expected to see a ghost inside the hotel, but I didn't. For a few moments I stared through the glass, hoping against hope that Linda Sinclair might stand before me once again, extending her hand toward me. Sadly, she did not appear.

I guess that means she is still alive and well somewhere. Good for her.

I wish I was.

I walked around the side of the buildings, looking in the windows I could reach. This hotel has a nation-wide reputation for being haunted. Ghost hunters from all over the country come here all the time. Well, on this particular autumn evening, the hotel did not live up to its reputation. Not a single spirit manifested itself in any way.

Despite that, I knew the hotel was filled with ghosts, at least for me. They were just the kind that you can't see.

After one last peek through the window of what used to be Brick Walz's Barber shop, I turned away from the old hotel and pulled my flimsy flannel jacket up tight around my neck. As I walked away, I waved at the empty window, as if Linda Sinclair were on the other side, smiling her smile right at me, waving a white-gloved hand.

"So long, Toots," I said.

CHAPTER SEVENTEEN

Standing in the makeshift operating room, Buck heaved a heavy sigh of relief as he watched Zeke prepare Pillsbury Franklin for another transfusion. As his body relaxed, he discovered that he was feeling the call of nature. He eased out the doorway and headed down the hallway toward the restrooms, only to find the door was locked. Cursing under his breath with frustration, he noticed a large poster board on the wall between the men's and women's facilities. Someone with very nice handwriting had written some instructions in magic marker. A candle beneath the sign allowed just enough light to read it.

"We are sorry, but with no running water, we have closed the restrooms. We have set up some temporary facilities that you will find to your right as you exit the hospital's main entrance. On a table near the entrance, you will find toilet paper and feminine products, should you need them. The table also has hand sanitizer and paper towels; please utilize them upon your return to the building. Please accept our sincere apologies for this great inconvenience."

Buck stood in the hallway, staring at the sign for a moment. Then, he chuckled to himself as he headed for the main entrance of the hospital. Life just kept getting stranger and stranger around here.

• • •

Sister Mary Margaret Marion stood on the expansive, flat roof of Our Lady of Perpetual Sorrows Hospital. Initially, she had organized an effort to gather rainwater from the huge downspouts on the downhill side of the building. It quickly became apparent that the lack of sizable containers and manpower was going to allow them to collect only a small percentage of the water gushing from the downspouts.

While not abandoning this part of the operation completely, the resourceful nun led most of the volunteers up to the roof of the hospital, armed with bed sheets, pillows and curtains. Sister Mary Margaret Marion's plan was to turn the roof into a makeshift reservoir by plugging the drainage system on top of the building. If they could prevent the water from ever entering the downspouts, there was a chance that a lot of the rainfall could be retained on the roof and be utilized for a number of days…perhaps even a week or more, she hoped.

Standing in the rain, Sister Mary Margaret Marion could not help but smile as she watched several motley teams attempt to dam the roof. Rain-soaked nuns, firemen, policemen and even some elderly folks were working together to make the reservoir a reality. They were thoroughly soaked, and many were laughing as their early attempts to plug the drains failed. More than once, entire bed sheets were swept away, into the downspout.

The nun allowed herself the luxury of watching the unusual scene for a few moments. When it became apparent that the workers would succeed in damming the rooftop drains, her thoughts turned toward the next item on her list. It was time to start organizing breakfast for the patients once again. As she made her way down the stairs, she took mental inventory of what food the hospital still had on hand and how long it might be before some of it began spoiling.

• • •

Blackie followed Demarcus Johnson up onto the porch of the well-worn wooden home. The boards of the porch were weak, and bent dangerously as he walked toward the front door. Demarcus opened a screen door, if one could call it that. The screen was ripped almost completely across, and hung lazily against the lower wooden panel of the door.

As Blackie stepped into the living room, he felt he was entering another world. There were two couches, both of them worn and torn, one with stuffing hanging out of it. The living room had clothes strewn about, fast food and potato chip paperwork, and two very young sleeping boys. A large screen TV, dark and silent, kept a silent vigil over the strange scene of peaceful chaos.

"She's in here," Demarcus said softly, and moved through the living room to a dark hall. Blackie had been uncomfortable in the neighborhood, even more uncomfortable in the house, and now felt like he was about ready to jump out of his own skin as he followed the young man into his mother's bedroom.

Lamiqua Johnson was writhing on the bed, clutching her abdomen. She had a high fever, and seemed to be verging on delirium. The boy had not been exaggerating, Blackie thought to himself. One of Blackie's cousins had contracted the West Nile virus last summer. Looking at the sturdy dark woman on the bed, Blackie thought she looked like she was the same kind of sick. The woman was in serious trouble.

"Mama?" Demarcus said softly. The woman moaned as she turned over, and her eyes struggled to focus as she searched for the face of her son. Then she saw Blackie, and her face took on a look of complete bewilderment.

"Who...?" She leaned forward, rising up on one elbow, and squinted at Blackie. Her eyes widened, and then narrowed as her puzzlement became a scowl.

"You called me a nigger," she said quietly, but with conviction.

Blackie's heart jumped as he recognized Lamiqua Johnson. She worked at the nursing home where Blackie's grandfather had spent his final days. Grandpa Earl was a complete racist who considered black people little better than animals. He was constantly complaining about all the "coons" that worked at the nursing home, and how much he hated having them tend to his needs. In his final few days, he had even told many of the workers how he felt to their face. More than once, Blackie had chimed in on the discussions with enthusiasm; on one occasion, Lamiqua Johnson had been Grandpa Earl's target, and Blackie joined him in some twisted attempt to gain the dying old man's approval...and perhaps a little bigger share of the old man's meager estate.

Only now did he feel truly ashamed.

"I...I did," Blackie stammered. He babbled out some clumsy words of apology that hung in the air like stale cigarette smoke.

"Get out of my house," Lamiqua Johnson said. Blackie stretched out his hands helplessly, began to speak, and then turned to obey.

Lamiqua Johnson slumped back down on her bed with a deep sigh. Demarcus looked at his mother, and then watched as Blackie moved toward the front door. Just then, Demarcus heard his little sister cry from the next room. It was a weak and desperate cry that lasted just a few seconds.

• • •

Listen:

Almost Chief of Police Dana Crisp was in the police station in the basement of the old city hall, surrounded by marble and ceramic tile and the kind of wood trim you just don't see anymore. She stood by an open window, staring out at the rainy streets and quietly weeping. In other corners of the building, other women, and more than a few men, shed tears or fought them back, each in their own way. The chaos had begun. Six of her officers had died last night.

The evening had also resulted in forty-three dead civilians that she knew of.... and who knows how many others they did not know about yet.

And so it goes.

• • •

Kayla Ellis and Christy Farmer were rain-soaked and exhausted as they reached the edge of the parking lot at the Catholic hospital. With Jamie's help, they had managed to load Rick Gage's injured body into a little trailer that was designed for towing children behind a bicycle. The little trailer groaned under the man's weight, the wheels bowed out as if they would pop right off the flimsy plastic contraption. But the thing somehow held together. The two women pulled it like a rickshaw for over a mile. Fortunately for them, their route led them through a portion of the city of Almost that was relatively flat. Even so, getting Gage to the hospital required every ounce of strength the two women had.

As they stopped at the edge of the parking lot to rest, their attention was drawn to their passenger by the erratic, rattling sound of his breathing. They had done what they could to keep the man dry by tucking a tarp all around him. But the tarp shifted during the trip, and from all appearances, Rick Gage was just about as wet as they were. In unspoken agreement, they grabbed the tongue of the little trailer and pulled as fast as they could toward the entrance of the hospital.

• • •

Buck grabbed a roll of toilet paper as he headed out the front door of the hospital. He wondered what kind of restroom arrangement waited for him outside...in the rain, no less. A young nun, tall and slim, moved toward the table just after he did and snagged a roll of her own. As he held the front door open for her, their eyes met, and her face flushed with embarrassment. She was quite pretty, Buck observed. She was a novice, he guessed. He wondered if she would stay committed to her call all the way to her final vows.

It seemed that the prettiest women among the nuns never quite made it to that point.

He remembered a scene from a movie version of *Les Misérables,* where Liam Neeson, (as Jean Valjean), remarked that his daughter was too pretty to become a nun, that it would be a waste. When he heard the line, he thought it was a cruel and unfair remark to make. But deep within him, he shared some of that same sentiment. Despite the fact that he had known several nuns who were quite attractive.

Buck and the young nun walked toward the portion of the lawn where the temporary restroom facilities were set up. The rain was still falling steadily, but by now most people were un-showered and grungy, so adding rain-soaked clothing to the equation did not seem to matter much. Except for the young nun, of course. Despite the circumstances, she appeared clean and well-pressed until she had stepped into the rain. Now her habit began to take on water and droop over her slender frame.

Rather than being upset by it all, she flung her arms wide, tilted her head toward the sky and said, "Praise God for the rain!" Then she laughed, and Buck could not help but laugh with her. She had a slight accent of some kind, he thought, though he could not place it. South African, perhaps?

At that moment they arrived at the "restrooms." Aluminum frames with linen curtains, the kind you might find in an emergency room, separated the five "stalls." Within the stalls were portable hospital toilets; they looked like walkers with a toilet seat in the middle and a white plastic bucket beneath them. Three of the spots were occupied; you could tell by the moving shadows within. Buck chose the stall on the left end, because it had only a row of bushes to provide privacy on one side. This would allow the young nun to have the better spot in a far from perfect situation.

"Thank you, sir," the young nun said as she moved behind the aluminum and linen restroom wall.

It was a bit hard to concentrate on the business at hand during the next few moments. The steady rain, the feeling of exposure, and the muffled sights and sounds of those around made things difficult. When he finished, Buck grabbed the roll of toilet paper to return it to the building for others, but the rain had soaked it to the point that he was uncertain it was going to be of much use to anyone. As he moved out of his stall, the young nun was emerging from hers at the same moment. She smiled at Buck, and he walked alongside her back toward the hospital entrance.

"Quite the bonding experience, wouldn't you say?" the smiling young woman said as they walked.

"Absolutely. A unique experience, to be sure." Buck replied. "The last few days have done a lot to help me appreciate the simple things in life. Whoever would have thought that a working toilet would seem like a luxury item?"

They were laughing as they entered the hospital. The young nun took a bottle of hand sanitizer off the table and handed it to Buck. "Here you are, sir!" she said, and then she took a bottle for herself. After they had wiped the sanitizer off with paper towels, she extended her hand toward Buck, smiling broadly. "I'm Sister Immaculata."

He took her long and delicate hand in his and shook it warmly. "Buck Schneider, ma'am. Pleased to make your acquaintance! You know, we must do this again some time."

"No offense, Mr. Schneider, but I certainly hope not!" Sister Immaculata laughed. "I am praying with all my might that things get back to normal around here soon!"

"Well, if I were God, I would give you anything you asked for," Buck replied. Then he realized he might have said something too forward or inappropriate and it was his turn to turn beet red.

"It's all right, Mr. Schneider," Sister Immaculata assured him. "It would be simply wonderful if God shared your opinion." She patted his arm kindly. "And perhaps He does! Sister Mary Margaret Marion received some exciting news from the mayor about an hour ago. He believes that some limited water service may be restored within the next couple of days. Isn't that wonderful?!"

"Wonderful? It sounds downright miraculous. How is that even possible?" Buck asked.

"I don't know." Sister Immaculata said cheerfully over her shoulder as she moved briskly toward the hallway. "Something about a steam engine, she said. I have no idea! I'm an artist, not an engineer! Take care, Mr. Schneider, and keep praying!"

Buck stood in the foyer, watching her disappear, a dumb grin on his face. The light in the hallway was meager, so he could not be certain if she turned back to glance at him or not. (She hadn't.)

"Idiot," Buck said to himself as he moved back toward Pillsbury Franklin's room. "You're old enough to be her father. And she's a *nun*, for Christ's sake!"

Yet, he could not shake the feeling of enchantment that he felt as he walked away. It may be noted, however, that he did not make the slightest attempt to shake it away, but, as absurd as the notion was, he savored it like a favorite meal for which he had waited quite some time.

● ● ●

Listen:

When my older sister graduated from high school, she went to a nursing school 100 miles away that was a "teaching hospital." It was run by nuns of some kind. My sister was a little overweight, and had always looked older than she was. One time, on a lark, she used white bed sheets to dress herself up to look like one of the nuns. The finishing touch was a thick leather belt around her waist, from which hung a crucifix. She introduced herself as a nun from another area who wanted to visit the hospital. The authentic nuns who ran the hospital came and greeted her, and gave her a full tour of the hospital. Then, my sister thanked them and left.

Our family never really knew if the nuns were fooled, or if they simply had enough sense of humor to go along with the joke. All we knew is that my sister never got "caught" or received punishment for her charade. Personally, I'm guessing the nuns were in on the joke, and had a good laugh back at the convent that night.

Convents are like big dormitories where nuns live and do all sorts of secret nun stuff. Someday, no one may remember what actually happened in convents because nuns are an endangered species.

• • •

Blackie Blackmon was half a block away before Demarcus Johnson caught up with him.

"Hey, man, you can't leave now!" Demarcus said as he grabbed Blackie's arm.

Blackie stopped and turned, looking the young man in the eye. "You heard what your mother said. She told me to get out. And she has every right to do that."

Blackie was cold, wet, guilty and more than a little afraid. He was anxious to get back to a dry and comfortable place where he could pretend things were a little better than they really were.

"Look, what you did *sucked*, and I'm not happy about it. But my Mom and my sister are bad sick and I can't handle this alone. You need to help me."

"What about your Mom? She doesn't want me to help, and I don't blame her."

"Right now, my Mom, she ain't got no choice. I'm not going to ask her if you can help. I'm going to tell her you *are* helping me."

Blackie looked at the urgency in Demarcus Johnson's eyes and felt the young man's firm grip on his rain-soaked arm. In the last hour or so, a boy had completed his transition to becoming a man. Now Blackie knew he needed to face the consequences of his own actions so that this new man could do what he needed to do.

"Okay, bud. Let's do this, then." Blackie replied. The two men turned and strode purposefully back toward the house.

• • •

Ellie Pence had wandered the hospital hallways in search of a drink of water. She had arrived in the cafeteria area to find a maintenance worker opening the vending machines in order to empty them of their valuable contents. Ellie managed to talk him out of a bottle of water. It was lukewarm at best, but at the moment it seemed to be the best water she had ever tasted.

Ellie wandered the hallways some more, sipping her water. She meandered into the emergency room area, where there were a number of dramas unfolding. People with broken bones, cuts, gunshot wounds and people who were just plain sick. The air was heavy with the odor of blood, sweat and candle smoke. She decided to step outside the emergency room for some fresh air. It was still raining, but there was an overhang that was above the driveway that sheltered ambulances when they arrived in bad weather. She could stay dry and still get some air.

Under the canopy, Ellie stood breathing fresh air, sipping her water, and watching it rain. She glanced down the hill and caught a glimpse of some people doing something in the rain. She studied them for a while before she figured out they were filling trash cans, buckets and other containers with rainwater from the building's downspouts. Ellie realized that she was going to have to start thinking about her own plans for gathering water.

Some movement from the other side of the parking lot caught her eye. Two drenched people were struggling across the parking lot, pulling…something. Some kind of little cart or trailer. They look exhausted, she thought to herself, as she watched them travel the final fifty yards toward where she was standing.

"Here, let me get the door for you," Ellie said as the two…women, she could see that now…pulled the cart under the overhang. The women nodded and panted their thanks as Ellie held the emergency room door open wide enough for them to pass through. The cart got stuck on the lip of the entry way, and Ellie helped them push it through. At that moment, the flimsy bike trailer finally had enough, and the axle snapped, sending the man inside and one of the women to the floor.

"Well, at least it got us here!" Christy Farmer said as she picked herself up off the vinyl welcome mat. Ellie assisted the two women in removing a badly injured man from the ramshackle plastic ambulance. He had been badly beaten, Ellie could tell. But somehow, behind the terrible bruises, he looked familiar to her. At the moment, however, she was unable to recall where she had seen him before. One of the young women also looked familiar, Ellie thought. But she could not make that connection, either.

The three women dragged the man into the emergency room. He was unconscious, and his breathing was erratic. The waiting room was full, so they stretched him out on the hallway floor.

While Kayla Ellis went to the registration window to see about medical care for Gage, Ellie helped Christy Farmer tend to the man. A young nun brought a small stack of towels that the women used to dry him off a bit, and then the towels served as a makeshift pillow and blanket for the injured man. As Ellie gently patted his hair with a towel, she got a good look at his face. He bore strong resemblance to her brother, she realized. And then she remembered her brother had a son...by now, he would be right about this young man's age. Could it be...? No. She dismissed the thought.

Ellie turned and looked at Christy Farmer and she suddenly figured out who she was. "Say, aren't you Debbie Farmer's daughter?"

Christy looked up at Ellie. The look on her face made it obvious that Christy had no earthly idea who she was. "Yes, I am. Who are you?"

"I live up the street from your parents," Ellie replied. "Your Dad is here. He's been shot." Bedside manner of any kind was not Ellie's strong suit. In fact, the little package of elements named Ellie Pence contained no tact. She was tact-free. (One discovered this fact pretty quickly, even though she was not clearly labeled.)

The events of the last couple of days had eroded all of Christy Farmer's self-control. She exploded into tears and grabbed Ellie by the shoulders. "Oh, my God! Is he all right? Is he all right?!"

"Calm down!" Ellie gently swatted away her hands. "Yes, he's going to be okay. Your mom is with him now."

Kayla Ellis came back from the registration desk to see what was wrong with Christy. Her urgent question, "What's wrong? What's wrong?" was lost in the storm of Christy Farmer's meltdown.

"Can you take me to him?" She had grabbed Ellie's shoulders once again.

"Yes." Ellie growled, slowly swatting her hands away once again. "Settle down, and I'll take you there."

"You're *not* helping," Kayla shot Ellie a fierce look as she dropped to her knees to embrace her friend, who collapsed into her arms.

"Whatever," Ellie Pence said, rising to her feet and straightening her shirt. "Let me know when she's ready, and I'll take her to see her dad. I'll be just outside the door here. I need some air…and some space."

• • •

When the thing went thump in the sky, all forms of electricity no longer functioned, including batteries. Therefore the vast majority of clocks and watches in town stopped. Of course, people who kept track of the time by glancing at their cell phones were similarly out of luck. No LED bank signs, no radio stations, not even the occasional automated church bells to give anyone a clue.

As he stood in his office and looked out at the rain, Sam thought of a classic rock song related to the topic, *Does Anybody Really Know What Time It Is?* It was one of Chicago's early hits. At the moment, the answer to the musical question was, "for the most part, '*no*'."

In addition to missing time, Sam missed music. His strange new life of the past few days was one that had no soundtrack. No cars, no radios, no muzak and no elevators in which to hear it. The only music available was in his head. And he loved music. Almost as much as his wife did.

Sam was waiting. He had been doing that a lot lately. Yesterday, he met with his staff and as many police and fire officials he could gather and they had brainstormed together. They compiled a list of significant community leaders. Sam then instructed the police to gather every person on the list for a meeting at city hall. The officers fanned out, mostly on bicycle, all over the city to the homes of these leaders and asked them to attend. The meeting was set for "first thing in the morning." Since most people had no access to a working clock that was the best they could do.

Now it was the first thing in the morning. Sam could hear that some people were already gathering in the lobby at city hall. Their conversations bounced off the marble walls of the old building and echoed into his office. He would let them talk among themselves; he would wait a little longer before he made his way downstairs.

He thought about time, clocks and watches. In the coming days, if the electricity didn't return, watches that people had inherited as family heirlooms would become more valuable than ever. Travel alarms and wind-up Big Bens would go from being cheap drug store items to important commodities, worth more than their weight in gold, at least until someone figured out how to make some more without the benefit of electric power.

Sam had given thought to other things that would be crucial commodities in a world without electricity; paper, pens and books. Suddenly, the handwritten word would be on the cutting edge again, because the electronic word had gone dark. Schools would begin teaching cursive handwriting again. Books would become highly valuable, especially books of a technical sort that might assist in making practical items that would soon run out....like candles, for example. Or clocks and watches powered by springs instead of batteries. Sam's emergency plans for the city included dramatic steps to protect the town's two libraries, in addition to its pharmacies and grocery stores.

About fifty people had died in his town last night, and six of them were police officers. That was more murders in a single night than Almost would rack up in a decade. And those were just the ones they knew about. There might be dozens more that were unreported because there was no good way to report them. As bad as things were, Sam knew he was probably just looking at the tip of the iceberg.

Sam was nervous about meeting with the influential people downstairs. They were frightened, and would be short-tempered as a result. This was, without a doubt, the most crucial moment in his long and eventful life. He was glad he had one big piece of good news to share; it appeared that the water system was going to be semi-functional sometime within the next 48 hours. Fire Chief Gonzales' crazy idea about steam engines had actually borne fruit. The eccentric dentist and his Rube Goldberg machines were riding to the rescue of the whole city.

If the water problem were truly solved, it was probably the single most important thing that could prevent the city from disintegrating into total chaos. However, there was still the matter of food. While not quite as immediate a crisis, it ran a close second. People in this city were going to be hungry before long.

Sam had a plan for dealing with the food situation on both a short-term and long-term basis. But it involved invoking marshal law, an authority he did not truly possess. But he *had* to do something; the police were simply not able to maintain order alone. That was obvious.

His plan involved huge risk by giving control of current food over to the various spheres of influence in the city. Sam rationalized that he was not really dividing the town into factions. He was simply giving areas of control to the factions that already existed.

If the power came back on next week, he might end up going to prison. Assuming that he didn't up getting lynched by the very people he was trying to help long before that happened. But if the power did not return, Sam believed his bold plan was the best way to assure the survival of the largest number of people in the city of Almost…and perhaps the preservation of some semblance of civilized life for the survivors.

Scary thoughts. But the mayor of Almost decided he had no choice but to think this way. He looked at a photo poster of his favorite president, Theodore Roosevelt, that hung on his office wall. It contained snippets of one of his many awesome quotes:

"The credit belongs to the man who is actually in the arena, whose face is marred by dust and sweat and blood, who strives valiantly…who spends himself in a worthy cause, who at the best knows in the end the triumph of

high achievement and who at the worst, if he fails, at least he fails while daring greatly. ..His place shall never be with those cold and timid souls who know neither victory nor defeat."

Sam knew there was great appeal in the safety of timidity…but such safety always turned out to be temporary or an illusion. Life had taught him that repeatedly. He knew he had to act, and to act decisively. It was the only course of action he could live with. Or die with, for that matter.

The low rumble of conversation in the lobby had built a great deal in the last fifteen minutes. From the sound of things, the lobby was filling with Almost's movers and shakers of various colors and creeds.

It was almost time.

CHAPTER EIGHTEEN

Ellie Pence escorted the partially unraveled Christy Farmer down the hallway of Our Lady of Perpetual Sorrows Hospital. Ellie Pence did have a shred of pity for her, but that was overshadowed by her disdain. Of course, Ellie had no idea what Christy had been through in the last three days or so; the loss of her boyfriend, home and job; her near-suicide, followed by her near-rape; and now the news that her father had been shot. Had she known all that, perhaps Ellie Pence would have been a tad more understanding. Then again, perhaps not.

As they drew near the end of their journey, Ellie paused in the hallway and took Christy by the shoulders. "Say, let me ask you something. The guy you and your friend brought into the hospital. Who is he?" Ellie was interested in the man because he bore some resemblance to her estranged brother. She wondered if, in fact, he might be her nephew.

"I don't know who he is," Christy replied, using a tissue to her tears. "He lives in the apartment above my friend's. I think his name is Rick. You could ask Kayla, she would know. Why do you ask?"

"No reason," Ellie lied. "Just curious."

A couple of moments later, Ellie delivered Christy to her father's hospital room. Ellie quickly withdrew from the emotional explosion of the tearful reunion and headed back down the hall. She needed to know who this guy was.

Jordan Schneider Blackmon sat on the expansive front porch of the Schneider family's ancestral home. She was afraid, and as a result, she was angry. Her Mom and her sister were inside with Grandma Luella, fixing some lunch. The three grandsons were running around the huge yard, playing some form of hide and seek.

Megan's husband, Chase, was down at the Schneider Brothers Corner Grocery Store. He had already made three trips, bringing back shopping carts full of food to stash in the family home for safe-keeping. After his first trip, Chase had reported that there was no sign of Uncle Buck, or of Jordan's husband, Blackie, at the store. Despite this disturbing development, everything at the store had been peaceful when Chase arrived. No one understood why Buck and Blackie would simply leave the store unattended, without coming back to the house to inform the family.

Needless to say, Jordan was worried. She had already lost her father during these strange events of the last few days. She could not bear the thought of losing her husband as well. While she loved her Uncle Buck, at the moment he was not much more than an afterthought.

Jordan Schneider Blackmon was an intelligent woman. She knew what other people thought of her husband; that he showed himself, frequently, to be a bigot and a bore, and did not seem overly intelligent. (Grandma Luella simply referred to Blackie as "The Idiot." She did not confine the slur to speaking behind his back, either.) Unlike most people, Jordan felt there was more to Blackie than met the eye. Blackie loved her with a fierce dedication that won her hand and kept her feeling secure. And he loved their sons; he was an excellent father, and he spent time with his boys, teaching them to hunt, fish and play sports.

Despite the fact that he embarrassed her frequently, Jordan Blackmon had hope for her husband. He was like a big kid, still trying to figure things out. One day, she hoped, he would come into his own and would show her family that the sum of him was more than his quirky parts. Until that day, or even if that never happened, Jordan would continue to love Blackie just the way he was.

However, at this moment in time she wanted to kill him for being so inconsiderate…as usual!

• • •

Listen:

Like a cheap swing-set, love is frequently missing vital parts, such as healthy doses of logic and common sense. In many cases, the more stupid love is when it starts out, the more beautiful it becomes. Stupid love often results in crazy things like marriages that last 50 years and stuff like that.

Romeo and Juliet had very stupid love. In their case, it proved to be fatal. This is a rare side-effect.

• • •

Buck arrived at the Schneider Brothers Corner Grocery Store to find it intact, but under siege from a totally unexpected source. His niece's husband, Chase, was engaged in a vigorous conversation with three members of the Almost Police Department; a group which included Chief Dana Crisp herself. They had come to inform him that the mayor was invoking marshal law, and that vital resources (like his grocery store) were being appropriated for the public good.

"'Appropriated' is a big word," Buck had said to the police chief. "I'm not sure I know what that means. Does it mean the same thing as 'stolen'?"

Crisp had been extremely apologetic. She was not happy about the situation, either. Buck was glad of that, and did all he could during the conversation to make her squirm. It was the only form of resistance at his disposal.

The hardest part of the whole experience was turning over the keys. He had cursed about the store over many a beer. The store was his anchor of security in a turbulent life, but at the same time, it frequently felt like an anchor around his neck. He had longed for the day when he would be free of it, but to lose it this way, when it was not really his choice....well, it felt a whole lot more like another dismal failure than sweet release.

Now, he and Chase were headed up the hill toward the house on Schneider hill. This was going to be great fun, he thought sarcastically. In addition to delivering the news that they were losing the store, Buck was going to have to tell his niece, Jordan, that he had no idea where her husband was.

• • •

When Ellie Pence finally located Rick Gage, she found him lying on a gurney in another office that had been converted into a room for patients. He was alone.

Ellie slowly approached his bedside, staring at his face as she approached. The resemblance to her brother was unmistakable. She found herself thirsty for a connection of some kind to someone...perhaps anyone. If this man turned out to be her nephew, perhaps it would help fill the emptiness that Robert's death had left. Even if he was not her brother's son, it fell to her to be his friend in his time of need. According to Christy, the man had been a hero of sorts; had rescued her and her friend from danger at great expense to himself. He had been there for them; perhaps she could be there for him.

The young man's breathing was labored, and he seemed hot. Ellie took a cloth, dipped it in water, and began to gently stroke his face and neck. His eyes fluttered open and he looked at her with puzzled eyes. After a moment, his face subtly expressed simple gratitude, and then his eyes closed once again. Ellie settled in a chair next to the bed and held the man's hand, staring at his face all the while.

About ten minutes later, Kayla Ellis quietly entered the room. Her face registered some surprise at Ellie's interest in Rick Gage. "Do you know him?" she asked.

"I'm not sure," Ellie replied. "I think there is a possibility he's my nephew."

"That's a good thing," Kayla said. "I don't think he really has anyone."

"What's his name?" Ellie asked.

"Rick Gage," Kayla answered.

Not the right name, Ellie thought to herself. "Do you know if he grew up around here?" She knew her nephew had grown up in the general vicinity of Almost.

"He grew up near Columbus, Ohio. He's a huge Ohio State fan."

"No relation, then," Ellie sighed.

"Listen, I need to get home and check on my son. Do you think you could stay here for a while? You know, sort of be with him?" Kayla asked. "I will try to come back in a few hours."

"Were you two close?" Ellie asked

"No. I don't think Rick got very close to anyone, ever," Kayla replied. "I just feel like I owe him now. He saved us, you know."

"I can relate to not being close to anyone," Ellie thought to herself. Aloud she said, "Sure, I'll stay with him."

• • •

Lunch at Mom's house had been served with heaping portions of guilt and inadequacy, Buck thought to himself as he walked down the long set of concrete steps. Jordan was understandably upset that no one knew where her husband was. Luella Schneider had been typically condescending when he had given her the news about the store.

After an initial flash of outrage at the mayor, Buck's mother had patted his hand sympathetically. "It's all right, honey," she purred icily, "no one could expect that *you* could have done anything about the situation." The unspoken implication was, of course, that his father or his older brother would have fared far better in the situation because of their superior abilities. Her empty smile sealed the subtle stab with violently red lipstick.

A few moments later, he walked into his little house. No dog to greet him: Bilbo was still missing. Right now, he was just too exhausted to think about that, or anything else. He collapsed into his bed, and sleep claimed him within seconds.

● ● ●

For the first 45 minutes or so, Ellie Pence was a modern-day Florence Nightingale. She was attentive and comforting, an unfamiliar sensation that made her feel good about herself. During the second 45 minutes, she thought little about Rick Gage, but about all the things that she needed to do around her house. She looked out the window; the sun was shining now; the rain had given way to a beautiful spring day. It would be a wonderful day to be out in her garden.

It was not long after that that Ellie Pence viewed the sleeping Rick Gage as a burden that was not her responsibility, and besides, he didn't really need her anyway.

As she was slipping through the doorway, she thought she heard a gurgling sound. She stopped and poked her head back into the room. Nothing.

On her way down the hall, she stopped a nun and told her she was leaving, that Gage was alone. The nun looked exhausted and stressed. She opened her mouth as if to say something, and then simply nodded in resignation.

Ellie burst from the darkness of the hospital hallway into bright spring sunshine. The rain had finally stopped. The nice weather put a spring in her step that allowed her to practically jog all the way home.

• • •

Listen:

Sometimes when you are channel-surfing, you come across some disturbing images, like small children with large bellies swollen with hunger, clothed in rags, huge brown eyes looking mournfully at the camera. Or pictures of puppies and kittens that have experienced cruelty. Then a solemn voice asks for money. Upon occasion, such images may prompt calling an 800 number or writing a check. More often it results in the remote control being clicked in search of a more pleasant scene.

It is human nature to change the channel when faced with the reality that others need our help. Most of us are good at that. Ellie Pence was exceptionally good at it. That's why most of us human beings get so excited about people like Mother Theresa. We celebrate the fact that she did what she did, because somebody had to do it. We are very glad that it was her.

We are even *more* happy about the fact that we didn't have to do it.

• • •

Exhausted, Jordan Blackmon had dozed off on the couch after lunch at her grandmother's house. She awoke to find her sister and her husband asleep, curled up together on the plush living room rug. The three boys, two of hers and one of Megan's, lay on the floor near them. The events of the last few days had taken a lot out of everyone. Although the children did not fully comprehend what happening, they could sense the deep stress at work on the adults who cared for them. They did not need to understand the events in order to be affected by them.

Jordan stretched luxuriously, and then quietly slipped out the front door onto the front porch. She squinted as her eyes adjusted to the light; she was surprised to find the rainy morning had given way to an afternoon of bright sunshine.

Looking down the street, she saw three figures coming toward the house. The man walked like Blackie, but there were children with him. Jordan started trotting down the long stretch of concrete steps. Halfway down, she stopped dead in her tracks. She wondered if she was still on the couch dreaming. It was Blackie, all right....holding hands with two small African-American boys. Her face exploded in laughter and tears. She ran down the remaining stairs and flung her arms around her husband's neck.

The two young boys, hands released, stood frozen, watching the two adults embrace, this woman seemed pretty crazy, they thought.

After a moment, Jordan released her husband and recovered her breath. "Blackie...what...what's going on?"

"They needed a place to be," Blackie replied quietly. "Their mom is in the hospital. It's a long story."

Jordan Blackmon kissed her husband's cheek with a loud smack. "I want to hear every word of it!" Looking down at the boys, she added, "Are you guys hungry?"

The two young boys nodded vigorously, eyes wide, saying nothing. They took the crazy lady's hands and started walking up the stairs.

• • •

Listen:

Sometimes life puts us in a position where it is impossible to change the channel. Because of this, once in a great while, unlikely people do unlikely things. This is how a cold, cruel world tosses us the occasional curve ball to prevent us from becoming completely cynical. The world does this to keep us vulnerable until it creeps up behind us and kicks the daylights out of our simplest hopes and dreams.

The world is like that. Really sneaky and full of surprises.

Like Ashton Kutcher. Or Alan Funt.

• • •

Rick Gage's eyes fluttered open. He was alone in a strange room. It vaguely resembled a hospital room. Bright sunlight was shining through the open window. An institutional curtain was swaying in the breeze. He stirred a little bit. His body screamed in great pain. He had apparently soiled himself quite some time ago. Rick Gage was alone and terribly uncomfortable. He had a tremendous pain, deep in his chest, that was throbbing and building.

Back at Rick Gage's apartment, things were a mess. His big screen TV, his laptop, his phone and his tablet had gone dark.

Even though the sun was shining through the window in his hospital room, the edges of his vision had gone dark. There was a dark circle that was beginning to close out the light, despite his best efforts to fight it back.

The pain deep in Rick Gage's chest exploded upwards, into his throat. He couldn't breathe. He struggled alone, trying to make noise, to call out. All he could manage was a strangled, gurgling sound and the small crash of a metal tray that he pushed to the floor.

Within a few moments, Rick Gage went dark. There would not be a reboot anytime soon. In fact, it would be another day or so before someone even discovered his body.

And so it goes.

• • •

It was around sunset when Ellie Pence finally decided to call it quits in her garden.

She was going to have a great crop of tomatoes this year, she was sure of it…as long as the stupid deer didn't eat them first

CHAPTER NINETEEN

illsbury Franklin lay quietly on his gurney. They had moved him out of the office-turned-operating-room into the cafeteria. They were trying to keep the patients on the ground floor as much as possible, and so had turned the hospital cafeteria into an open ward. It reminded Franklin of the interior of the large tents where wounded soldiers were cared for on the battlefield. Providentially, he ended up by the sliding glass doors that led into a prayer courtyard. He stared out into the beautifully tended garden and a peaceful statue of St. Francis of Assisi. Though he was not Catholic, he held this champion of the poor and downtrodden in great esteem. St. Francis had lived one of the most inspirational lives in recorded history.

Early in the afternoon, Pillsbury Franklin finally convinced his exhausted wife and daughter to go home and get some rest. He had slept peacefully, off and on, throughout the entire day, and could feel that he was rapidly regaining his strength. While he floated in and out of sleep by the doorway to the garden, his mind had occupied itself by coming up with another idea for a new adventure for Idaho Jenkins, his Christian, time-travelling hero.

In his latest adventure, Idaho Jenkins would travel back in time to prevent the break-up of the Beatles. Thanks to his efforts, they stayed together long enough to record one more album after Abbey Road. It bore stylistic resemblance to *Sgt. Pepper's Lonely Hearts Club Band* in that it was the first Beatle album in several years that was truly collaborative, and actually combined the considerable talents of all four members in an amazing, synergistic piece of musical art. Entitled *Imagination*, it featured a slightly different version of John Lennon's *Imagine* and a killer take on George Harrison's *Beware of Darkness*. With Lennon still an influence on Paul, McCartney's *Uncle Albert/Admiral Halsey* had lost a bit of its pop whimsy and had been transformed into a collaborative, multi-song medley that resembled *Abbey Road*'s side two. Critics in the altered reality considered that last album to be the band's true magnum opus.

Despite the continuing efforts of Idaho Jenkins, who had disguised himself as a guru of deep philosophy, the Beatles still broke up, but not until 1972. They also re-united for a final, great concert at Shea stadium in September of 1980, just three months before John Lennon's death. The three hour jam-session included Eric Clapton, Bob Dylan and other friends and collaborators.

No matter how he tried to hash out the plot of the story, the science fiction author found himself in the middle of a great ethical dilemma. He could not, for the life of him, make the story work without having Idaho Jenkins act completely out of character. In order to make the whole thing work, one way or another, Idaho Jenkins would have to kidnap or cause the death of Yoko Ono.

• • •

Big Sam Cavanaugh was at the riverfront, watching as his police and community allies took control of the grain barges that were stranded along shore and pinned by the river's current against the bridge. Others were assuming command at the huge flour mill. Still others were combing all the stores in the area, gathering any tool that could possibly be utilized for farming. All available green space in Almost was going to be turned into fields for new crops. Empty lots, yards, parks, golf courses; basically any decent ground that was not covered in concrete would be turned into farm land. And every citizen would become a farmer...at least, if they wanted to eat, they would.

The engineers and volunteers had managed to utilize steam engines to provide limited water service to the city. Starting tomorrow, different segments of town would have service for an hour or two a day.

The next engineering task was to come up with a way to efficiently grind grain into flour without the benefit of electrical power. Whatever grain did not go into the ground as seed was going to have to feed a lot of people until harvest time.

If electricity never returned, then those dramatic moves would save many lives. If the power kicked back on in the next week or so, Sam knew he would be viewed as nutcase, a petty dictator. So be it. He knew that if he hesitated now, any semblance of control over the situation would disappear into chaos. The leaders of the city had to organize around a plan before mobs and gangs formed to take things into their own hands.

Though all the parks in town were designated to become makeshift farms, he was secretly hoping they would be able to spare nine good holes somehow.

● ● ●

The sun was setting when Buck Schneider appeared at Pillsbury Franklin's bedside. He looked worn out, unshaven and troubled, but sober. Franklin was glad of that. The only reason Buck was sober was that he no longer possessed keys to the Schneider Brothers Corner Grocery Store, and under current circumstances, he had no other access to alcohol. Buck told his old friend about the mayor declaring marshal law and how the police had come to take control of the grocery store.

"You know, what bothers me is that they *took* it from me," Buck said bitterly. "There were times I wanted to sell it, or just quit...hell, there were times when I wanted to burn it down! But if it was not going to be part of my life, I wanted it to be my choice."

"So you have an ending, but no closure," Pillsbury replied. "Like the ending of *Great Expectations*." Buck gave him a "what the heck are you talking about?!" look. Pillsbury continued, "By Charles Dickens. The hero is tormented by this cruel and beautiful girl his whole life, yet in the end, he doesn't end up with the girl. It's a frustrating ending. But despite that, it's my all-time favorite book. Maybe because it's a fairy tale with a real-life ending."

"I'm glad my screwed-up situation reminds you of your favorite book. That helps me a lot," Buck replied. "I feel better now, just knowing that."

Pillsbury stared at his friend, stunned by the harshness of the remark. They stared at each other a few seconds, and then simultaneously burst into laughter. After a moment, brushing a laugh-induced tear from his eye, Franklin said, "I love it when you talk so sweet to me!" They laughed again.

"So," Pillsbury Franklin said, "You don't really want the store, but you don't want it taken away from you. So give it away."

"What do you mean?" Buck replied. "It's not mine to give."

"Well, it still sorta is," Franklin said. "Look, you said earlier that there is a lot of food in the store that's going bad. Meat, dairy, bread and produce. That stuff needs to be eaten, not rotting away. Go to the mayor and tell him you want to have a big barbecue. A going-away party for the store. Make it a Mothers' Day party! Get some church groups and the VFW and the Lions Club to help you cook. Give away all the perishable stuff. Make it a going away party for the store, a funeral wake for your brother."

Buck considered the idea for a moment, and then said, "That's a great idea! The mayor won't want that food going to waste, either. And it might be a good way to ease the tension in this town. Dough, you are a genius!" Buck really did think that Pillsbury Franklin was a genius. He also thought Pillsbury was strange. Strangeness often shares the lease on brains where high intelligence resides.

● ● ●

A few moments later, Buck Schneider was on his bicycle, headed for the mayor's house. Pillsbury Franklin resumed looking out the window into the garden.

216

He was trying to think of ways that Idaho Jenkins might be able to lend St. Francis a hand, back in medieval Italy. There was a story in there, somewhere.

Maybe Idaho Jenkins could drop Yoko Ono off, somewhere in time, along the way? She might do a guy like Vincent Van Gogh a lot of good....and perhaps he could give her an ear for music.

• • •

Matt and Amanda Farmer tucked their children into bed by candlelight. It had been a long and tiring day. At first it was fueled by urgency, as they set about capturing rainwater and finding a way to store it. After the rain had stopped, they enjoyed a great family day, playing wiffle ball in the back yard, riding bikes and enjoying just being together as a family. In the back of their minds, the adults had their worries and concerns. They knew they had enough food to last a couple of weeks, but what happened after that?

As far as water was concerned, the seemingly endless supply of the Mississippi River was less than a mile from their home, but the thought of drinking that water without benefit of filtration was not a pleasant one. But it could come to that; they might not have much choice, before long.

Despite these reasonable fears, they had managed to pigeonhole their concerns and enjoy the day for itself. As they closed the door on the bedroom of their oldest child, they blew out the candle and embraced each other with gentle passion. At this moment in time, life was very good. It would be a waste, they decided, not to enjoy it to the fullest while they could.

Some time later, Matt Farmer rolled back over to his side of the bed and gave a heavy sigh. Amanda could not see his satisfied smile in the dark, but she knew it was there.

"Don't forget, your mother expects to see us at her church tomorrow," she told her husband.

"I think I just went to church," he smirked.

As she punched him, Amanda added, "And don't forget…it's Mothers' Day."

"Honey," he replied as he rolled over and draped his arm over her, "with everything that's going on, you've got to be the only person in town that remembers that."

"Hmmp! Shows what *you* know!" She tried to punch him again, but he caught her by the wrist. They wrestled for a moment before she let him win.

• • •

Sister Mary Margaret Marion awoke to find herself on the floor of her room, slumped against the side of her bed. She had fallen asleep while praying.

She had decided to take a break from the hospital early in the afternoon, even though things were in a state of chaos. She had been on the brink of total exhaustion, and she knew she would not be worth anything to anyone if she did not get some rest. Besides, it was during the night that things at the hospital were the most chaotic. Hopefully, she would be back in time to help when things got crazy.

The nun slipped all the way down to the floor, stretching her stiff back and neck. While she had been praying earlier, she could not stop thinking about food. When she was a girl in Bosnia, food had been scarce, and the menu very limited. When she first arrived in the United States, she had been impressed by the huge buildings, all the cars, and all the wealth. However, the most impressive thing of all had been the grocery stores. Aisle after aisle of incredible food. Her favorite thing was the produce aisle; so many fruits and vegetables she had never tasted. Many, in fact, that she had not even heard of. The first time she stood in a produce aisle, she wept for joy and bounced around the store like a child on Christmas morning. That night, she sat and ate oranges and other fruits until she nearly made herself sick.

Sister Mary Margaret Marion lay on the floor of her room, stretching her sore back, and again thinking about that very first produce aisle. She had grown up in desperate circumstances. The experience had made her tough without making her hard of heart. And now, after years of plenty, the years of famine were apparently returning. She was surprised to find herself weeping. Weeping not only for the loss of the produce aisle, but for the loss of the land of plenty....the beacon of hope that America had been for immigrants like her. The electricity was not coming back, she was convinced of that. She had no idea why it was gone, but it was not returning.

The people who had grown up in this land of plenty would not know what had hit them. Life was about to get very different for them, and many of them would not live through the change. She knew that when food and water get scarce, then the thin veneer of civilization peels away from a town. Some people you would least expect to become violent do just that. At the same time, noble gestures and self-sacrifice...genuine Christianity...show themselves as well. The most unexpected people are often the most noble.

She would survive. In her heart, in her spirit, she knew that. And she would do the best she could to help others learn how to survive. Not just survive, but live in dignity. In a way, the current state of affairs gave meaning to what had seemed to be a senselessly violent childhood.

As she lay on the floor, a passage of Scripture from the Old Testament book of *Esther* came to her mind. They were the words of Mordecai, a Jewish leader, to his niece, Esther. Mordecai was calling upon Esther to take her life into her hands and face the potential wrath of a cruel and murderous king.

"Do not think that because you are in the king's house you alone of all the Jews will escape. For if you remain silent at this time, relief and deliverance for the Jews will arise from another place, but you and your father's family will perish. And who knows but that you have come to your royal position for such a time as this?"

Sister Mary Margaret Marion had no illusions of grandeur, no aspirations for royalty. But she knew with certainty, in her heart, that God had placed her in this time and place to share what she had learned in the war-torn days of her youth. She had been brought to the city of Almost for such a time as this.

She picked herself up off the floor and brushed herself off, tugging her habit into some simulation of order. She brushed her teeth without water and headed out the door of her room toward the Emergency Room of the hospital.

She would do what she could, when she could, where she was.

• • •

Listen:

Once Vincent Van Gogh heard Yoko sing, he would probably cut off the other ear.

• • •

Luella Schneider walked quietly through the living room. "I never thought I'd see the day that black kids were sleeping in this house," she thought to herself. The two young black boys that *The Idiot* had brought home were curled up in the middle of the living room rug, surrounded by her three great-grandsons. "If my husband can see this, he's spinning in his grave like a top." Blackie's disdain for black people had been the one thing she had in common with Blackie, she realized. Now, even that was changing. What was the world coming to?

And what was up with her granddaughter? Ever since Blackie had returned home, Jordan had been giggling like a schoolgirl…especially when she looked at Blackie. She could hardly keep her hands off him. And when they had settled in for the night, the squeaking bed springs and accompanying sounds had seeped through the walls into her neighboring bedroom. Disgusting! Unable to sleep herself, she couldn't just lie there and listen to that. And so she was walking through the house. She would curl up in an afghan on the front porch and listen to the sounds of the night for a while.

Luella was a strange and twisted woman. She knew that about herself, but felt helpless to change it. She had been that way for so long…she knew that if she admitted her faults, she would have to go back and take responsibility for a good percentage of the unhappy events of her past. Events which she had always blamed on the shortcomings of others. And she was just too old to do that, she decided.

Luella sat on the front porch of the house and stewed. She stewed about the people who were inside it. She stewed about the people who were gone, who *should* be inside it. She sat there in the porch swing and loved them all, angrily. Paradoxically, even though she relentlessly persecuted those closest to her, the old woman would furiously defend the honor of the ones she loved if they were maligned by the outside world.

The love of Luella Schneider was a weird concoction of accusation and fierce pride, of possessiveness and control and the infinite depths of her own bitter insecurity.

It was a nasty drink, but the only one she had to offer.

● ● ●

Dana Crisp was coming out of Cavanaugh's front door when Buck arrived on his bike, and she looked at him apprehensively. Buck noticed there were two policemen stationed at the house. Both of them were watching him intently. One had his hand near his holster.

"Don't worry, I'm not going postal," Buck had assured her.

Buck visited with the mayor and the police chief for over an hour. They not only accepted his (well, Pillsbury's) idea for a big BBQ, they embraced it. They decided that they would have all grocery stores in town give away all food that was in danger of going bad. They would celebrate the day on a couple of counts; it was Mothers' Day, and they could also celebrate the return of (limited) water service.

Cavanaugh dispatched Chief Crisp with instructions to send a police messenger to every church in the morning, as all the city leaders were expecting them to be packed. Everyone would be invited to participate, and encouraged to spread the news of the party in their own neighborhoods.

Before she left, Dana Crisp pressed something into the palm of Buck's hand. "You can give this back to me later," she told him as she left. He looked down into his hand and saw his key to the Schneider Brothers Corner Grocery Store. He felt himself getting a little choked up as he slid the key back into its customary place on his key ring.

Later on, Buck rode back to his house to catch a good night's sleep. He decided he would rise early and gather his family to help set up the party in the store's parking lot. As he pedaled, he was especially aware of his surroundings. He avoided the deepest shadows and steered clear of other people as much as possible.

It was a good thing he did; two young men pursued him on foot at one point, and Buck had to pedal as fast as he could to avoid being caught. He was not about to lose his bike. Not now.

When he arrived at his house, he found his dog, Bilbo, waiting for him on the front porch. He looked fine, just dirty. Buck did not know where he had been, and he didn't care. He was just overjoyed to have him back. Buck parked his bike in the living room, locked the door, and sat on the couch by the open window, listening to the sound of dog food crunching. When Bilbo was done eating, he draped himself across Buck and they fell asleep together, there by the window.

● ● ●

Listen:

There was a dog in Argentina that disappeared after its master died. Three days later, the family discovered the dog lying on top of the man's grave, which was located in a large cemetery. They had never taken the dog there. He found it on his own. They tried to take the dog home, but he returned to the cemetery and to his master's graveside. The dog would take an occasional walk during the day. The staff of the cemetery fed him. And every night for six years, he would go to sleep on top of the grave of his best friend. He may still be there, for all I know.

Narrators have the power to reveal good and bad things that happen in the stories they tell. I can't imagine telling a story where a dog suffers. I could not have written *Old Yeller*. Whoever did must be a cat person.

A couple of years ago, there was this saying going around; "I wish I was the person my dog thinks I am." It's a good saying. Dogs think the very best of us. They love the way humans only dream of loving; with total devotion and without a single condition. They practice a form of forgiveness that is genuine and complete.

Perhaps if humans were more like dogs, we would actually be the people that our dogs think we are.

Enjoy this warm, fuzzy moment when Buck's dog comes home. Because soon, in the city of Almost, some bad things are going to happen.

CHAPTER TWENTY

By two in the afternoon, the party was in full swing. The mayor had been right; the churches of Almost had been packed on Sunday morning, and those who attended quickly spread the word about the Mothers' Day barbecues being held at every grocery store in town.

At the Schneider Brothers Corner Grocery Store, volunteers had pushed all the dead cars out of the parking lot, and had also cleared the street of them for over a block. Various groups had brought large barbecue grills and trailers and lined them up on the far side of the parking lot. (Getting them there had been no small task; the men had to push and pull them there without a motor of any kind.)

A haze of charcoal smoke hung deliciously over the whole block…one could smell the cooking meat for a quarter of a mile. The crew cooking the steaks, burgers, brats and hot dogs were mostly men. Many of them were drinking beer; it was warm, but nobody cared. Some ladies were frying ground meat on an open grill and making sloppy joes. Others were doing their best to whip up casseroles and other side dishes to go with the meat.

There was a big crowd at the Schneider Brothers Corner Grocery Store, which was known for the high quality of its meats. That was one of the things that had kept the store open for so many years, despite the proliferation of huge chain stores that swallowed most of the family businesses in town. The meat was not the only attraction; nostalgia was also a big draw. The store meant a lot to the folks who had grown up in the neighborhood around it.

There were people of all sorts milling around, ranging from Bible-thumpers to atheists, from black to white, from wealthy to homeless, and all were having a great time. Even the town's best-known alcoholics were represented, taking advantage of the free, warm beer. Chick Baxter, the caretaker for the Cemetery of St. Benedict of Reluctant, was making his way around the crowd, shaking hands like a politician. He was a "close-talker"; the kind of person who thrusts his face way too close during a conversation. Since his breath was a powerful blend of filterless cigarette smoke and cheap alcohol, a chat with Chick Baxter was an unforgettable experience…no matter how hard you tried.

Cherokee was there, waving his dirty handkerchief and calling out senseless sayings to the crowd. He waved at Buck. "Geronimo! Kiss 'em and feed 'em beans!" Cherokee stumbled up to Buck, throwing an arm around his shoulder. "Great party you're throwing here, kimosabe. If I were a mother, I would be especially honored to be here. Some people have called me a mother, but that's another story!" Cherokee laughed loud at his own dumb joke. Buck gave him a courtesy laugh, and quickly invented an important task that he needed to check on right away.

Buck was sorry that Pillsbury Franklin was not able to attend. He was recovering well, but was not yet strong enough to attempt a field trip like this. Pillsbury would have loved this kind of party, where the community was coming together. Debbie and Christy Franklin had said they would try to stop by on the way back from visiting Pillsbury at the hospital. He hoped they would make it.

Initially, Luella Schneider was pretty upset about the fact that a bunch of "freeloaders" were going to eat a substantial portion of the store's inventory without paying for it. But by the time lunch was being served, she was fully in tune with the spirit of things. She and her great-grandsons were busy bagging up perishables; fruits, vegetables, bakery goods and dairy products, and passing them out to the partiers. Demarcus Johnson's two little brothers were pitching in as well. Some of the food was already on the brink of spoiling, but everyone was glad to get it.

Every once in a while, as he was carrying meat out to the grills, Buck would steal a glance at his mother. She was smiling broadly, a genuine smile, obviously relishing her role as hostess and benefactor. She looked beautiful, Buck thought. It was the first time he had thought about her that way in decades.

He glanced up the hill at the grave of his brother, just below the hydrangea bushes. It was a shame Bud had not lived to see this.

There were several uniformed police on hand; they were there to make sure that the non-perishables in the store remained intact, and for crowd control, if needed. There was no need for crowd control. Everyone was having a great time, and they were especially grateful for the temporary feeling of normalcy. The cops were relaxed and having fun; they weren't drinking, but they were taking full advantage of the barbecue.

When the mayor arrived around 3:30, Buck gave a little speech that dedicated the party to his dearly departed brother and to his mother, for Mothers' Day. When Buck started choking up, Charles Whitmore, the pastor of the African-American church three blocks from the store, stepped up and prayed a beautiful prayer for Buck's family, for all the mothers, for the city of Almost, and for a world that perhaps had seen the last of electricity. On most days, many people in the city of Almost did not think it was okay to talk about God in public. This was not one of those days.

Then the mayor got up and made the announcement that some degree of water service had been restored throughout the city. This brought cheers from the crowd, and moods brightened even more. Maybe we will be okay, people dared to think.

Some local musicians had brought their acoustic musical instruments and were having a jam session in the middle of the street. The crowd applauded after every song, even when it was not particularly well-played. They were deeply appreciative of the first music they had heard in days. No one relished the music more than Big Sam Cavanaugh.

They were going to have to figure out a way to make more instruments, Sam thought to himself. In addition to improving the mood of the town, musical instruments would give idle hands that missed their video games something constructive to do.

Blackie was drinking beer and cooking meat, of course. Buck noticed Blackie was not drinking nearly as much as he usually did. Ordinarily, Blackie would be sloppy drunk by now. He was laughing and working side by side with young Demarcus Johnson, whose mom was resting comfortably at the hospital. Jordan was working a few feet away forming burgers out of ground beef and turkey. She was positively beaming. Buck didn't know what was going on with them, but he was very glad for whatever it was.

A bunch of nuns were there, including the ones who served at Our Lady of Sorrows Hospital. Monsignor Sloan, pastor of the largest Catholic church in town, had organized a large team of volunteers to relieve the weary women and give them a chance to get out of the hospital. The nuns were clearly enjoying themselves. Buck noticed Sister Mary Margaret Marion sitting in a lawn chair in the middle of the street, tapping her foot to the music. She had a big plate of fruit on her lap and she seemed to be savoring every bite.

Vivian Harrison momentarily stepped away from her cooking so that Matt Farmer could introduce his former teacher to his family. After chatting briefly, she returned to her post, where she mixed up another batch of her famous sloppy joes. Cherokee walked up to her, wiped his mouth with the sleeve of one arm, and extended his plate toward her with the other.

Vivian smiled broadly, "Back for more, Cherokee?"

"Mmmmmhmmmm," Cherokee grunted appreciatively. She handed back his plate with two buns on it, both overflowing with the spicy ground meat concoction.

"Thanks for the yip-yips, sister!" Cherokee said. He took out his filthy handkerchief, held it at eye level, and wiggled it at her. "Yippee I o kai yay, you sweet damsel of mercy!"

As she laughed and waved him off, she was quietly hoping that he would not dangle his famous handkerchief any closer to the food she was serving.

● ● ●

Listen:

In simpler times, the people of Almost had called sloppy joe sandwiches *yip-yips*. No one knew the origin of the term. But when *sloppy joes* began being advertised on television, folks gradually stopped calling them *yip-yips*. Everybody except Cherokee, apparently.

The people of Almost also called carbonated soft drinks, *soda*, despite the fact that most of the country called them *pop*. This had been a great controversy up until now. However, *whatever* you called them, soft drinks would not be around much longer. The factories that made soda had all died at 2:17 on the day the sky thumped.

And so it goes.

Another thing: were times really ever "simple"? Or did it just seem that way because it was so much easier to hide the complications in the old days?

● ● ●

Listen:

Sister Immaculata was at the barbecue. She was an artist and a sensitive soul. She was a free spirit and a very happy person who delighted everyone who knew her.

Sister Immaculata had been a wild teenager, and had an abortion when she was 15. She later considered suicide, but found God instead. Members of her family thought she became a nun in order to earn God's forgiveness. However, she knew she became a nun *because* she was forgiven, an important distinction. When she took her vows, she chose the name *Immaculata* to celebrate the clean slate that God had given her long before.

Once she had visited a small town in Wisconsin and had sensed something deeply menacing hovering over it. She did not find out until much later that the town was known for the large number of people there who practiced Satanism. A prayer vigil at a women's clinic in a small city not far from Almost had generated a similar, ominous pressure on her soul. To Sister Immaculata, spiritual things were nearly as tangible as physical ones.

The young nun had lived in Almost for five years. She was fully aware that the city had many problems. She saw plenty of evidence to that effect in the hospital ER every day. But in all the time she had lived in Almost, she had never felt that terrible pressure closing in on her soul.

Until today. She felt it today. And despite the music, the food, the laughter, and the fun all around her....she knew that darkness was looming right above the parking lot of the Schneider Brothers Corner Grocery Store. Something pretty bad would happen soon. It would be the first of many tragedies, she sensed.

The darkness was up there, lurking in the bright spring sunshine.

CHAPTER
TWENTY-ONE

Sometime later, Buck wrote a letter. He told everyone in his family where it was, just in case his son and daughter ever came back home to Almost. He wanted them to have the letter, especially if he was not around to greet them when they came. This is what the letter said:

Dear Chad and April;

Things have gotten really crazy around here. Wherever you are, they are probably crazy, too. I don't know if I will ever see you again. I don't know if I will ever have a way to send you this letter. But I need to write this down so you know what happened here. Your grandma is dead. I need you to know exactly how it happened.

It was Mothers' Day, the day we held the big party and gave away the store. The mayor busted up the party at six in the evening because he didn't want people getting too drunk. Everything had gone so well, he didn't want the day to end on a bad note. As you probably know, it ended on a very bad note, at least for me.

The parking lot had cleared out, except for a couple of cops who were smoking cigarettes and shooting the breeze over by the retaining wall. I was inside, gathering up some personal items and getting ready to go home. I heard something outside; it sounded like some kids shooting off firecrackers up the street; they did that a lot. While I was puttering around by the cash register, someone came into the store. I didn't look up at first.

When I finally looked up, I was staring into the barrel of a huge handgun. Clutching the huge handgun was Jacob Snow, a red-haired kid I had tussled with a couple of times. I realized I was standing in the very spot where your Uncle Bud had dropped dead a few days before. I thought for sure I was about to do the same.

I wondered where the hell the cops were. Jacob Snow answered the question that I didn't ask out loud. He told me he had just shot the two cops in the parking lot.

I realized the .45 automatic that I kept under the cash register for self-defense was only about three feet away from my right hand. It may as well have been a football field away. Jacob Snow had me cold. He smiled real big and said, "I've got you now.....*Buddy*."

I told him to take whatever he wanted from the store. He said he would, right after he shot me. I tried to tell him I could have killed him, but didn't. He told me that I was pretty dumb, that I should have killed him when I had the chance. He cocked his piece and aimed, slowly, right between my eyes. As his thumb pulled back the hammer, Snow said, "Goodbye, buddy."

Right then, somebody screamed, "NOOOOOO!" from behind the guy. He swung around fast, toward the voice, and fired two shots.

I dove beneath the counter and brought up the .45 as fast as I could. As he was turning back toward me, I shot him three times. He was dead before he hit the floor. All the time I had invested in training and practice saved my life.

I thought about what a waste it was for someone to die that way. I thought that before he even hit the floor. I didn't have time to throw up, but I couldn't help it. The gun dropped from my hand and I stumbled toward the door of the store, where your Grandma Luella lay in a heap, in a pool of her own blood.

I fell to the floor and swept her up in my arms. I told her I loved her. Her eyes opened for a minute. She looked at me and told me she was proud of me. And that she was sure that my Dad was proud of me, too. Her hand reached up and stroked my face, then fell limp. She died there, on the floor of the store.

My mom gave me life, and then made a lot of my life pretty miserable. Then, she died to save my life. She was proud of me. She said so. It never felt that way when she was alive, but I believed what she said when she died.

What do I do with all that? Still trying to figure it out. I don't think I ever will.

I don't know how long I lay there, my back against the wall, holding her. It must have been a long time, because I passed out from exhaustion. When I woke up the first time, I saw that mom's blood had spread across the floor, as if it were reaching for the blood of the guy that killed her. Blood does not belong outside of a person, I decided. Any person.

I couldn't move, my brain wouldn't let me. I just lay there, staring at it all. Strange stuff goes through a guy's head at a time like this. I thought about the words to a *Doors* song that your Uncle Pillsbury used to listen to all the time when we were in college.

> *Blood on the streets runs a river of sadness.*
> *Blood in the streets, it's up to my thigh.*
> *The river runs down the legs of the city;*
> *The women are crying red rivers of weeping.*
> *Indians scattered on dawn's highway.*
> *Bleeding ghosts crowd the young child's fragile eggshell mind*

I knew I had a fragile eggshell mind at that moment. I couldn't process what had happened. Somehow, after a time, I drifted off to sleep again. I don't know how that was possible, but I did.

The next time I woke up, the chief of police, Dana Crisp, was leaning over me. She was crying. She was tugging at my mom's body, trying to pull her away from me. She kept asking me if I was hurt. I think I told her I was dead. I'm not sure exactly what I told her. Mom's body was stiff and cold. I let Dana have her.

A little while later, Dana and several of her officers helped me bury Mom on the hillside above the store, next to Bud. Actually, they buried her. I just stood and watched. I didn't want the rest of the family to see her like this. I wanted them to remember how beautiful she was at the barbecue.

Things in the town got really ugly not long after that. Lots of people were killing other people.

Pillsbury comes to see me every day; he's fine now. He says that things are getting better, and there is great hope for the city of Almost; he thinks things will be better here than most places. The mayor is in charge of things, and Pillsbury says his plans are really working. But right now, things are still scary for us. If you ever come home again, I hope that things will be okay here.

Right now I'm not very okay. I spend a lot of time thinking about strange things. I hope I will be better soon. I still think about that *Doors* song a lot. Especially the part about bleeding ghosts.

I love you guys. Sorry I messed up your lives. If I ever see you again, I hope things will be better between us.

Dad

CHAPTER
TWENTY-TWO

isten:

I was well-seasoned. Shaken, but not stirred.

It was seven months after the sky thumped that I saw the third ghost. It was December, and the coldest winter I could remember. It was evening, and it was snowing as I walked slowly through downtown Almost. There was a full moon poking through the clouds, and the moonlight reflecting on the snow gave an amazing amount of light to the night. I stood across the brick street from the Majestic Theatre, which had not shown a movie in decades. The marquee was still there, as were most of its light bulbs. There had not been light in those bulbs for many years. They were like little glass Miss Havishams, standing mournfully by the altar, waiting for decades for a powerful bridegroom to electrify their nights.

The front display windows on the lower level were also intact, with red matting behind them; gold trim outlined the places where photos were supposed to be inserted in order to display what was *Coming Soon. Coming Soon* was still written in flowery, golden script above the empty photo slots. Nothing had been coming soon for well over 30 years. Every once in a while, talk would circulate that the theatre would be restored, but nothing ever came of it. With each passing year, the costs of restoration became all the more outrageous. And then the sky thumped and nobody even thought about it any more. And so, the Majestic Theatre just sat there.

At street level, the front of the theatre seemed to need only a few photos and some electricity to live once again. However, the windows above the marquee, where the manager's office used to be, were mostly broken out and deeply dark. This gave the observer on the outside a clue that, inside the brick walls, the theatre was in much more desperate condition than the marquee would lead you to believe.

When I was a boy, my friends and I would occasionally be dropped off at the Majestic for a Saturday matinee. Those were the last days of the Saturday matinee for kids, as television had just about abolished the practice. We would get into the theatre for a quarter, and another quarter or two would buy you enough theatre candy to make you violently ill. We would see a couple of cartoons, maybe a *Three Stooges* short, and then a movie or two.

Often, it would be a *Tarzan* movie starring Gordon Scott. We all knew that Johnny Weismuller was *really* Tarzan, and this guy was just filling in. Gordon Scott had too much bulky muscle to be Tarzan and his hair was too perfect. And he spoke English too well. But Gordon Scott did use Johnny Weismuller's Tarzan yell, so we at least had that to look forward to in every movie. Last I heard of Johnny Weismuller, he was a greeter at a Las Vegas casino. Then he died.

And so it goes.

I walked down the brick street in front of the Majestic and looked at the side of the old brick building. I had never noticed it before, but a tree was growing out of the wall on one side of theatre, with its roots apparently inside the building.

Another setback to the idea of restoring the place, I thought. If trees are growing inside a building, that's not a good sign.

I walked through the snow-covered grass to the spot where the tree emerged from the building. I theorized that the tree had originally peaked through a small opening in the bricks. The tree had enlarged the opening as it grew, and the wind and weather chimed in to make a pretty significant gash in the brick skin of the old theater.

I peaked into the building through the large hole in the bricks. The moonlight stabbed into the darkness within to reveal rows of broken and rotting seats, and tatters of what had once been a movie screen. Behind what was left of the screen, which was not much, was a shallow stage. A gust of wind from behind me blew into the theatre, and rustled some dry leaves and trash that were scattered inside the theatre. As I watched some leaves journey across the floor, they blew right through the feet of a ghost who was standing at the center of the stage.

The ghost was of the classic white variety, semi-translucent. He had scruffy, curly hair and a magnificent, bushy mustache. Was it Mark Twain? I decided to risk a journey into the old theatre to get a closer look.

As I stepped through the hole in the theatre wall, my foot dislodged a loose brick, which tumbled down over other fallen bricks and came to rest at the floor below the foot of the stage. This sound, or course, caught the attention of the ghost, who watched with some amusement as I carefully threaded my way through the debris in order to stand before the stage, where I could see him more clearly.

As I stood in the ray of moonlight in front of the crumbling stage of the Majestic theatre, saw a familiar face, one I had often seen on the dust jackets of some of my favorite books. The ghost was Kurt Vonnegut, Jr., one of the most talented American authors in the last 100 years. As I recall, he wrote his last novel in the late 1990s, and died slightly a few years after 2000.

And so it goes.

● ● ●

Listen:

I thought Vonnegut's best books were *Cat's Cradle* and *Slaughterhouse Five*. In those two books, Vonnegut perfected the narrative voice I admire so much. I use a cheap imitation of it to describe the events of my own life. When I told you this story, I used Vonnegut's voice, because I don't have one of my own.

I am a mockingbird. No need to kill me. War destroyed me long ago.

Vonnegut once said that being the narrator of your own story was like shaking hands with God. I never forgot that because he was right. All human beings are narrators who have almost infinite simulated control over the course of events when those events are contained within our own heads. We have the unfortunate ability to rationalize away any pesky facts that mess up our world-view. At least that works until reality becomes so doggoned annoying that we simply can't make it disappear any more.

● ● ●

"Kurt Vonnegut," I said at last. One side of his mouth curled in a slight grin underneath that magnificent, intangible mustache. He was pleased, I think, that I recognized him. "What are you doing here? You're a hoosier!"

This last statement was not intended as an insult, of course. Vonnegut grew up in Indiana.

One of the rotting seats in the front row seemed sturdy enough to support my weight. I settled into the seat for what I hoped would be a long conversation with one of the 20th century's most intriguing characters.

"I just love old theaters, don't you?" Vonnegut lit a phantom cigarette. Another smoker from the great beyond, I thought to myself. "Movies and books are the best things human beings ever had to offer," Vonnegut said. "Shakespeare said all the world is a stage. This stage is a good reflection of how the world shapes up right now. It's always been on the brink of total disaster. Now it has taken off its mask and shown us its real face."

"Yes," I agreed. "People are killing each other out there. Fighting over food, mostly. I never thought that could happen here."

Vonnegut looked up and said, "When all hell broke loose months ago, when the sky thumped, some unfortunate people pointed their guns at other people, but couldn't pull the trigger, which cost them their lives. Other unfortunate people somehow managed to squeeze the triggers, which cost them their souls. Some people, though, are born with the ability to pull a trigger without a second thought. They never have trouble pointing and shooting guns. After their great victory, they will write a history book that tidies things up, and puts a nice bow on top of the package." He blew out a puff of smoke. "It will be very inspiring."

"There are a lot of guns out there. Everybody seems to have one," I replied.

"For a long time, guns were like something you just have…something you collect, like coins or postage stamps. People never really thought through what they would do with them when the time came to use them," Vonnegut said as he strolled across the stage.

"Now, it's *go* time…Darwin time. Survival of the fittest. The thinning of the herd. The strong survive and the gentle perish. This new world is a hard one, short on creativity. I don't care for it much."

Holding his cigarette in the European fashion, (between his thumb and index finger) he cocked an eyebrow and continued, "Ten or fifteen years ago, a lot of people were asking the question, *What Would Jesus Do?* A lot of people even wore little bracelets on their wrists with 'WWJD' on them. After the sky thumped, not too many people gave a rip about *What Jesus Would Do*. They forgot what Jesus said about mercy and pity and picked up their guns. They shot anybody that tried to take the food and water they had stashed for an occasion like this."

"Not all of them," I replied. "Some of them have sacrificed a lot to help others. I've seen that. I've seen people die while trying to help others. Deaths like that must have some kind of meaning, right? Lots of my friends died in Viet Nam to help others. To protect the American Dream." I stopped and caught my breath. "Those deaths meant something, right?" The question was a plea.

"Good question," Vonnegut answered after a moment. "Dying for someone else frequently means something. Dying for the American Dream is far less certain. The big question is, whose version of the dream are you dying for?"

"'Whose version'? It was my dream. My father's dream. Back then, it was the dream of most people in a town like this. It was a good dream...." my voice trailed off and I paused before I whispered, to my surprise, "I miss it."

The ghost considered my reply and nodded slightly, smiling at me. "Believing that the world can be beautiful is a good thing. Don't let me, or anyone else, talk you out of that."

Vonnegut was clearly enjoying our conversation, and the opportunity to exchange opinions. He continued, "But in all practicality, we fought the last few wars to satisfy the whims of an over-indulgent government so it would take care of us in return. Government is not supposed to take care of people. Extended families do that. The thing went thump in the sky and it was lights out for our parental government. Desperate people formed new clans for mutual defense against everybody else. It's a form of extended family, yes. But it looks a lot more like the *Hatfields and McCoys* than it does *The Brady Bunch*."

"Is there no hope for people, then?!" I asked. "I want to have hope for people. Hope that somehow, something good will come of all this."

One of his eyebrows arched, and a smirk curled under the left side of his luxurious mustache.

I recovered my composure. My voice was firm now. "I *choose* to have hope for them."

"Suit yourself," Vonnegut replied as he took a long drag from his intangible cigarette. "During my lifetime, I found hope in places like this theatre. Places where the Creative Arts expanded the souls of men and women. At the moment, the Arts are nearly lost to us. They will be back. People will rediscover that they need them. But right now people are far more concerned with their survival than their souls."

"Really? The churches around here are crowded for the first time in years," I observed. "What about God?"

Vonnegut paused for a moment. His gaze moved back and forth between me and the cigarette he was smoking. After some deliberation, he spoke again. "God? Until recently, *science* was the god of Western civilization. Generosity and sacrifice were replaced with self-indulgence and electronic amusement. People were busy, but without knowing it, became lonelier than human beings had ever been before. Television started the destruction of what it means to be a community; the internet and smart phones finished things off. Now that electronics are gone, maybe we will form real communities again, once the shooting stops. I really don't know. God only knows."

"'God only knows?'" I inquired, curious. "I thought you were an atheist."

"I was," Vonnegut admitted, blowing twin streams of smoke from his nostrils. "Then I died."

And so it goes.

Just then, the rotten theatre seat I had been sitting in finally gave way, and I plopped to the floor with a crash. Vonnegut threw back his spectral head and laughed. I laughed with him. I laughed until breath was hard to come by, and tears were streaming down my face into the gray stubble of my five-day old beard.

I didn't talk much after that. I just sat on the floor and listened as he smoked ethereal cigarettes and made observations about human nature. It was getting colder, so I gathered some of the leaves and rubble and made a little nest of them. The colder it got, the sleepier I got. So I lay on the old theatre floor and decided I would go to sleep shortly, and I would sleep for a very, very long time.

As I lay there, I realized that the story I had been narrating for six decades or so was almost over. I was in the final chapter, and Kurt Vonnegut, Jr. was smoking a last cigarette for me, on my behalf. My story has been full of surprises, and was frequently disappointing. On the whole, though, even the worst of it could be funny if you viewed it through the lens of a slightly twisted sense of humor. A genuine appreciation for irony also came in handy. Vonnegut had taught me these things a long time ago.

As I lay there on the cold floor, growing sleepier, I wondered if my sister would ever find out what had become of me. To her, I would always be Jimmy, the little brother who came back from Vietnam not quite right in the head.

But in the grand narrative of my own mind, I am *Cherokee*. And now I am ready to jump forward and plunge into the deepest unknown of them all. Without a parachute.

"Geronimo!" I said quietly as I closed my eyes for the last time.

As I drifted into the deepest, most delicious sleep ever, I heard a distant voice from a few feet above me. It was Vonnegut, bidding me, "adieu."

"And so it goes," Kurt Vonnegut, Jr. said softly.

EPILOGUE

I t had been seven months since the thing went thump in the sky, and Big Sam Cavanaugh still had his hands full. Crops had been planted all over the city of Almost, and the harvest had been a good one. His biggest challenges now were making sure that people did not cheat on the system, and that everyone was being treated fairly. There were also problems with an increasing number of violent raids being carried out in the city. The raids were generally conducted by gangs from nearby urban areas. Sometimes trouble arose among people who had not participated in the city's farm/work program, but still wanted to receive its benefits. Even though the citizen militia became better-trained and more effective every day, defending the town from threats from the inside and the outside was never going to be easy.

A lot of people had died. Up until now, most deaths were the result of gun violence. Now, however, winter was taking its toll. Many people had died of exposure. Many others had died in house fires that resulted from risky attempts to heat their homes. Disposing of the dead was a continual problem, especially now that the ground was frozen.

Every day brought new rumors about what was happening on the east coast. It was impossible, of course, to determine what was true. A common theme ran through most of them; that the country was being invaded. Some said it was China or Russia. Others blamed Muslim extremists. Some even said it was beings from another planet.

Nearly all the rumors had one thing in common; whoever it was, their machines worked.

23693923R00134

Made in the USA
Charleston, SC
02 November 2013